Published by Inku
www.inkubatorl

Copyright © 2023 by J.M. O'Rourke

J.M. O'Rourke has asserted his right to be identified as the author of this work.

ISBN (eBook): 978-1-83756-073-8
ISBN (Paperback): 978-1-83756-074-5
ISBN (Hardback): 978-1-83756-075-2

TIME OF DEATH is a work of fiction. People, places, events, and situations are the product of the author's imagination. Any resemblance to actual persons, living or dead is entirely coincidental.

No part of this book may be reproduced, stored in any retrieval system, or transmitted by any means without the prior written permission of the publisher.

TIME OF DEATH

A DETECTIVE JACK BRODY NOVEL

J.M. O'ROURKE

INKUBATOR
BOOKS

PROLOGUE

Tamara always looked better as a woman than she ever did as a man. She was exotic, sexy, irrepressible and enigmatic. An illusion, a sensual powder keg, the star of her very own rollicking, X-rated extravaganza, and every man's wet dream. She was a comet across the sky, or in this case along the city streets, a ball of sparking effervescence, completely impossible to ignore. She loved it all, loved the eyes of every man that burned into her, making her come alive. And Tamara liked that, especially when the straight men hit on her.

But all this attention did have its drawbacks. Like now. Tamara was convinced that someone was following her. It happened occasionally. After all, even the most exotic of flowers drew maggots. But it was little more than a feeling, like a soft breath on the back of her neck. She stopped more than once, feigning looking in a shop window, her eyes scanning the reflections of those behind her. And when she thought she saw the person loitering there, a tall man in a belted raincoat and flat cap, she quickly turned. But he was nowhere to be seen. *Where are you hiding, my little chickadee? Afraid to show yourself to Tamara?*

That, she could understand. Of course, perhaps he hadn't been there at all.

She smiled, banishing it from her mind. It was early. The night was still young. She had options. Then again, Tamara always had options. She thought of those options, of what Dublin had to offer when darkness fell: the secret places, the hidden places, the dangerous places.

But still, she couldn't quite shake it, that feeling, looking over her shoulder now and then but seeing nothing there except the bobbing dark outlines of pedestrians, nondescript and featureless, like extras in a movie.

She continued, her knee-length red boots making a clicking noise on the pavement, like tinkling glass, and her short sequinned dress clinging to her like a coating of sparkly paint, her hair an explosion of blonde curls falling about her face and halfway down her back.

No, the night was not over yet.

She crossed the junction of South Great Georges and Dame Street, went into the warren of back streets that was Temple Bar. At this hour, being the middle of the week, Dublin's party quarter did not heave as it did on weekends. Still, they were always there, and a couple of wolf whistles followed her as she moved, radiating white heat into the cold, night-time air. She stepped off the pavement and crossed the cobblestone roadway, concentrating on maintaining her balance on those nail-thin stiletto heels. She entered a side street, the lights from along the river spilling through at the other end. A little way in she heard heavy footsteps coming from behind, echoing in the narrow space between the walls.

She glanced over her shoulder: so, the tall figure in the belted raincoat with the flat cap was real. Because he was standing there. And with a clear view now she recognised who it was.

Him.

Him!

Tamara stopped.

'What? You? What're you doing here? And why are you following me?'

He stepped closer... and laughed.

She saw something in his right hand catch the light and glint.

He laughed again, his face half in shadow.

'W-what?' Tamara suddenly felt afraid, very afraid. 'What've you got there?'

The laugh shrivelled into a twisted, malevolent smile. 'Can't you tell?' He held it up. 'This is what I have here.'

The knife was long and wide, with a serrated blade tapering to a fine point.

'Pleeease.' Tamara hated the pathetic pleading to her voice. 'W-why?'

'Why?'

His expression was one dredged from a pool of pure evil.

'Can't you guess?' Taking a final step towards her. 'Can't you fucking guess?'

1

Blue and white crime scene tape was strung high across the entrance to the alley, tucked in behind anchor plates in the old wall, pulled down and crossed to form an X, each end tied to a traffic cone at the bottom on either side. A uniformed sergeant with a clipboard in one hand stood on the pavement outside, while the other nudged aside the fragile tapestry to allow Detective Sergeant Jack Brody, Detective Garda Steven Voyle and Nicola Considine of the Major Crimes Investigation Unit to pass through. Brody recognised the sergeant, Con Murphy was his name, and if he remembered correctly, he played guitar in a rockabilly band at weekends. Which explained the '70s sideburns. Murphy checked his watch and wrote the time down on his crime scene log sheet fixed to the clipboard.

'Well, if it isn't. You know how long we've been waiting for you lads to show up?'

'What's the hurry?' Voyle said, nodding into the lane. 'It's not like he's going anywhere now, is it?'

Considine bristled. She was chalk; Voyle was cheese. 'Gobshite,' she muttered under her breath.

'What've we got?' Brody asked.

The sergeant used his pen as a pointer. 'Body of a deceased male, naked, appears to have a single deep laceration to the neck. The scene's relatively clean. Not as much blood as you'd expect. My guess is he was killed elsewhere... or maybe not, could have bled out into the drain, there is one. Who am I to say? Dr Mc Bain and the Technical Bureau are en route. Reported by an anonymous 999 call to Pearse Street. We kept our distance, didn't get too close... that's it, short and sweet, for now.'

'Good,' Brody said, and to Voyle, 'Stay here, and see what else the good sergeant has to say.'

He indicated for Considine to come with him, and they started into the alley. Sugar Lane it was called, and well known to every officer in the city's South Central Division. A row of four-wheeled green and blue bins were along one side against a wall, the favoured depositories for empty handbags, wallets and purses stolen in street muggings. Suspects also partially discarded their clothing in these too, usually T-shirts and hoodies, in an attempt to alter their appearance before re-emerging onto the street again. The bins often proved to be a treasure trove of DNA.

There was no breeze, and the air stank of stale grease and meat from the air ducts at the rear of the fast-food restaurants backing onto the alley. Brody could feel the stench wrap itself around him like cling film. He resisted the urge to pinch his nose. A vile, milky brown liquid leeched from one of the bins nearest the corpse, trickling its way between the cobblestones and mixing with congealing blood like a sandbank on a crimson tide. They stopped, leaving a good distance between themselves and the cadaver. Until the doc and the Technical Bureau got here and finished their work, this was not his crime scene. It was theirs.

Brody opened his suit jacket and clamped his hands on his waist, thumbs to the front, a rigid, studious posture rather than one of comfort. The body looked like it could have been dropped out of a clear blue sky – except for the gaping wound to its neck, that is. The sergeant was right, a relatively clean scene. Brody swung his eyes up and along the wall to his left, then to his right, over the back of the fast-food restaurants, three rows of windows over basements. He wondered whether the victim had had his throat slit *and* then been thrown from a window. None were open, and none looked like they had been opened in years. Next, his eyes wandered to the wheelie bins.

'I can't help but think...' Considine said, but her voice trailed off, and she didn't finish the sentence.

'Yes, you can't help but think what?'

'The victim. The skin, boss... look how smooth it is. I mean, it's smooth, isn't it?'

Brody peered at the body and thought the skin was nothing but grey and stiff and dead, with the exception of a couple of dark patches along the bottom where it touched the ground and where the blood had pooled. He did note something, however. The body was hairless. Completely Brazilian.

'See, smooth,' Considine said. 'See?'

'No, I don't.'

'Well, I do. I think it's really smooth.'

'Maybe. But I see something else.'

Considine craned her neck.

'It's got no hair,' Brody said.

'Oh, shite, so it doesn't. Not a smidgen anywhere, be God. He shaved it off?'

'Or someone else did.'

They turned at the sound of a commotion from behind. Brody saw Voyle gesture to a man beyond the crime scene tape, then shout at him, 'Stop. Don't come any further.' But the man paid him no heed and began to pass one long, spindly leg through the crime scene tape, attempting to follow with his head but becoming tangled up like a fly in a spider's web instead. Voyle pushed him back roughly. A little too roughly. But how was Voyle to know the man weighed less than a paper bag? That he would stumble back and fall onto his arse? All of which he did. Two pedestrians on the opposite pavement stopped for a gawk, one taking out her iPhone, ready to capture this unfolding scene of police brutality. Brody and Considine hurried over.

'Whaddya think you're up to?' Voyle shouted.

'A very good question if I say so myself, officer, oh yes.' The man had a surprisingly soft, cultured voice, containing a certain gravitas that stopped Voyle in his tracks. As the man struggled back to his feet, Voyle extended a hand over the tape that somehow had stayed in place, and helped him up. The man brushed himself down. Voyle could smell the alcohol fumes from him, pungent and hot like a desert wind.

'Yes, a very good question indeed,' the man said, without any hint of hurt or rancour. 'As Oscar Wilde once said–'

Voyle had already ceased to be impressed by this character's gravitas or anything else. 'I'm not interested in what Oscar Wilde had to, or had not to, say.'

'–he said,' the man continued, ignoring Voyle, 'we are all in the gutter, but some of us are looking at the stars. Oh yes, some of us are looking at the stars. That'd be me.'

The man narrowed his eyes as he looked to Brody and Considine.

'Hm, the firing squad, is it? I'd like to speak with the head bottle washer if I could. Or the head chef, whatever you want to call him, or her.'

'Why, have you something to tell him?' Voyle snapped. 'Because we're busy.'

'My good man, despite appearances and perceived misconceptions on your part, *I'm* a busy man too, yes indeed I am, and can assure you that if I didn't have something of great importance to say, then I certainly wouldn't be bringing myself to the attention of the forces of law and order in the first place, now would I? No, sir, I would not.'

'What's your name, fella?' Voyle asked.

The man's rheumy eyes looked from Voyle to Brody, as if sensing who the chief bottle washer was. His appearance wasn't as slovenly as first appeared, Brody thought. He wore chuffed but smart brown moccasins and green corduroy pants, a plaid beige and brown shirt with three buttons open at the neck, inside it a burgundy woollen scarf. Everything fitted together, even if in a jumbled way, but it did fit together when you looked closely, a matching mismatch ensemble. Stringy grey hair hung down from his head like cords on a damp mop, hair that looked like it hadn't been washed in a while. His cheeks and nose were red.

'My name?'

'Your name,' Voyle confirmed.

'Ernest Clarke, but my friends call me Ernie. You can call me Ernie, oh yes.'

'OK, Ernie,' Brody said, stepping through the crime scene tape with an economy of movement and physical deftness that befitted his prowess as a world-class boxer. The gawkers on the other side appeared bored now and had started to move off. 'What have you got for me?'

'What have I got for you? Well, I haven't got anything specifically for you. I mean, I have nothing to declare in this great big world of woe but my genius, to use another Oscar quote, sort of, or in practical terms, to use my own, only what I am standing up in. But in that is a great freedom, yes there is.'

'Tell him to piss off, boss,' Voyle advised.

The man looked at Voyle.

'Ignore him, Ernie,' Brody said. 'You were saying?'

'What I was going to say is that I saw a car. The car from which the body, which is now lying down there at the bottom of this lane, was removed from, dumped, whatever. Yes indeed, I did. And then I went to a public phone box, oh yes, one of those still exist, beside the taxi rank, and I rang the emergency services.'

That got everybody's attention.

'Wait,' Voyle said. 'That was you? You rang it in?'

'Certainly I did, oh yes.'

'Why don't you come with myself and my colleague,' Brody said. 'We can talk about this in the comfort of our car.'

The man's mouth turned down at the corners.

'I could insist,' Brody added.

ERNIE CLARKE WAS AN ALCOHOLIC. That much was obvious. And Brody realised his name was vaguely familiar to him, but he didn't know why. And Ernie was a skipper, a term not denoting a person who is a commander on the high seas, oh no, but in this case a denizen of the great outdoor spaces of the city, a poor unfortunate who lived on the streets. Not literally on the streets, usually he secured a bed at one of the city's homeless shelters. All he had to do was show up by a certain time each night and he was more or less guaranteed a bed. Except for when he didn't show up, that is, those times when he still had money for booze and didn't have to worry about a little inconvenience like where he was going to sleep for the night. Because alcohol was the great, if temporary, remover.

'I was in the lane,' Ernie said.

'What time?'

'I don't know. I don't own a watch, don't see the point in watches myself; watches are–'

'Where'd you sleep?' Voyle was sitting in the driver's seat and anxious to move things along.

'Why, in the lane. I just told you, oh yes.'

'I mean where exactly in the lane. Don't be a smart arse.'

Brody shot Voyle a look, *easy*.

'He doesn't have a very good attitude,' Ernie said, 'your colleague there. Does he?'

Brody ignored that particular, if accurate, observation.

'If you could answer, Ernie, please,' Brody said.

'In a bin, of course, where else, Detective? I would have thought that was obvious.'

'I would have thought the opposite, Ernie, to be honest. I would have thought it the last place you'd want to sleep down here. There are bins and there are bins.'

'Yes,' Ernie agreed, 'ordinarily that is, but once a week they put out the cardboard for recycling, fill a bin right up with it, all flattened down. It really is quite comfortable and cosy, all things considered. And last night was cardboard night, and I got here first, oh yes.'

'And,' Brody said, 'this car. Tell me about it. I know you don't have a watch, but was it late, early, could you tell?'

'I could tell, I could tell. It was late and early. Night and morning. If you get me? The restaurants were closed, so I knew it had to be after two in the morning. And it was quiet, like really quiet, and the colour of the sky, like a light glow from behind a curtain, turning purple, so I could tell it was early morning, real early morning, just before dawn.'

'What exactly did you see, Mr Clarke?'

'Please, Ernie.'

'Sorry,' Brody said, 'of course, Ernie.'

'I was already awake. Can't sleep in those bins. Even a comfortable one full of cardboard. Not really, all things considered. Those bins have to be emptied you know, oh yes, so anytime I hear an engine, I think it might be a dumper truck. It happens. I wouldn't be the first to be chewed up into the back of one of those. And the bin men don't check. They're supposed to, but they don't. So I sleep with one eye and ear open, oh yes, you have to. Also, I'd only taken enough to get me to sleep, not enough to stay asleep, if you understand what I mean. Do you?'

Brody understood. 'Drink, you mean? Alcohol?'

'Yes. The devil's milk.'

'And what then, Ernie?'

'I hear an engine, so I lift the lid a little and take a peek out. Last thing I expect to see is a car.'

'It's in the lane? Just to be clear.'

'It's in the lane, oh yes.'

'What then?'

'Detective Brody, that's your name, isn't it?'

'It is.'

'You don't happen to have a cigarette, do you? I could murder a smoke... no pun intended, I can assure you.'

'I don't smoke. But when this is done, I'll buy you a pack.'

'Oh, that's very kind.'

'Don't mention it. So it was in the lane. What then?'

'Well, there was one occupant, the driver. I could clearly see the silhouette of the person; they got out and went round to the boot, dragged a body from it. I couldn't believe it? Couldn't. It's not every day of the week you see that, now is it? Dragged it right over to where you see it lying now. Well, I thought maybe there was a movie being shot. But there wasn't.'

'Did you get a look, Mr Clarke? Sorry, Ernie. At the driver. What was he like?'

'Oh, I did. I got a look. I got a very good look, oh yes.'

'And...?'

'And... well, it wasn't.'

'It wasn't what?'

'It wasn't a *him*.'

'No?'

'No, it wasn't. It very definitely wasn't. It was a *her,* Detective. The person I saw was a woman, oh yes.'

2

Later, back at the ranch, Nicola Considine poured water from the dispenser into a cone-shaped paper cup and carried it to her desk. A divider wall between the public office and the reception area of the old station had been knocked to create an open-plan unit room. The old ceiling had been removed too, down to its bare wooden trusses.

She knew why Brody had assigned her to this laborious task, why he always assigned her to this laborious task. Because she had an eye for detail, she could sit in front of a computer for hours; she would never lose focus. Nicola Considine liked to think the differences between the sexes on the job existed only in the minds of men. She knew that wasn't strictly true, however. Her male colleagues didn't seem capable of trawling through hours of CCTV the way she could. It was a woman thing, that attention to detail – although she'd never admit it.

Two flights above her, the officer commanding the Major Crimes Investigative Unit sat at his desk. Across from him was the newest member of the unit, newly promoted Detective Garda Paul Quinn, on temporary detachment. His promotion was a moot point however, the rank of detective Garda being one that was purely discretionary, though it did carry extra pay. Paul Quinn had a kind, almost innocent face, but this was not a good attribute for any police officer except those involved in victim support and public relations, that is. A police officer needed a face that projected authority, sometimes fear, but always a face that, more than anything, demanded respect. The Old Man, Detective Chief Superintendent Tom Maguire, knew not to judge a book by its cover, however, as physically Paul Quinn cut an unimposing figure. He was a little over five feet in height, skinny, even puny, with a round face sitting on top of a fat neck that looked at odds with this slight frame, close-set blue eyes and short mousy brown hair. He was dressed casually in blue jeans, sneakers and a hoodie with the motif NYC across the front.

'Welcome to the unit,' the Old Man said.

'Thank you, sir.'

The Old Man stole a glance to Brody standing alongside his desk.

'You're based at Harcourt Terrace, that right?' It was Brody.

'Yes, sir, that's correct.'

'No need to call me sir. Jack will do.'

'Sorry, sir, Jack. Harcourt Terrace is a very formal place.'

'Your record is impressive,' the Old Man said. 'Very impressive indeed.'

'Thank you.'

'Fraud and criminal assets, yes, and traffic for a time.'

'Yes. But…'

'No need to explain. That's why you're here, after all, to gain some front-line experience.'

Paul Quinn twisted in his seat.

'That's right, isn't it?' the Old Man said.

'Yes, sir, it is.'

'And Trinity educated. On the Horgan Programme, the fast-track as we call it. Yes, very impressive. Ever met anybody who has a problem with that, by the way?'

'With what, sir? Trinity or the Horgan fast-track programme?'

The Old Man grinned. 'Just so you know, son, I don't have a problem with either. Even if I came up the hard way myself. Never went to college. But that's beside the point.'

Brody wasn't so sure that it was.

'Anyway, Jack will show you the ropes, won't you, Jack?'

'Of course.'

'Best of luck.'

In the unit room, Brody introduced Quinn to Nicola Considine hunched over her computer, staring at the screen. She barely acknowledged them.

'You can take that desk.' He pointed. 'It's got some old files on it. Just clear them off, put them on the floor for now.'

Quinn looked about the room. 'Quiet. Where's everybody? The body in the lane?'

'You heard?'

'Yes, I heard.'

'Correct, the body in the lane. We have no ID. Not yet.'

Quinn pursed his lips, like he wanted to say something but was holding back. Jack thought it likely he didn't want to come across as being too cocky, too soon.

'What is it? We value all opinions here, lad. Speak.'

'Nothing. Just wondering how you'll do that. Fingerprints?'

'Fingerprints. And DNA. Waiting on word back from the lab. Local units are canvassing the area for eyewitnesses, but I wouldn't hold my breath. And there.' Brody nodded. 'Nicola's going through CCTV.'

'The body was naked?' Quinn asked. 'That right?'

'That's right, it was.'

'And there was nothing in the vicinity. No wallet. Clothes. Nothing.'

'Nothing.'

Quinn pursed his lips a second time. 'Hm,' he said, and stared across the room towards his new desk, as if searching for inspiration. 'Now that is a conundrum?'

'Certainly is,' Brody agreed.

3

Daniel Willow emerged from the pedestrian exit of the Midlands Prison and stood outside in the crisp, night-time air, a free man for the first time in thirty-five years. He was tempted to turn when he heard the door shut behind him, a great big, hollow, clanging sound, to have one final look. But he didn't. After all, this was a moment he'd rehearsed so many times. Often, he could think of nothing else. So he did not turn; that was never part of the script. Instead, he did what he'd always planned on doing, he walked slowly away along the narrow pavement by the access road, the high gates at the end already open for him. Outside was the main Dublin road, and he could see his taxi pulled up onto the pavement, waiting for him. A screw was standing by the open gates, looking at him as he approached. But he said nothing as he passed through and did not avert his gaze. He didn't want to give the bastard any chance to have to talk to him.

He got into the back of the taxi, and the driver's eyes were on him instantly. Neither of them spoke. He closed the door, and the taxi immediately bounced from the pavement onto the road and pulled away. Again, he fought against an almost irresistible urge to turn around and look back, for one final look.

But he didn't.

He was free!

But thirty-five years inside had not dampened his enthusiasm for revenge. If anything, it had whetted it. Not a day had gone by that he hadn't thought of what he was going to do to the man who had put him inside, if ever he got the chance, that is. And he would now get his chance.

He smiled, caught the look of the driver in the rear-view mirror, a scared, wary look. No surprises. That's the way everyone on the outside would look at him once they knew of the crimes he'd been locked up for. And the law deemed the taxi man had to be informed. So that was the look.

He leaned forward in his seat, looking ahead into the night. They also deemed him a night-time release. But there was no need; no one was there to protest, no press camera lights flashing.

He'd been forgotten. He smiled as he looked ahead.

'Would you mind,' the taxi man said, 'sitting back, please, sir.'

Their eyes met in the rear-view mirror.

'Of course. I do apologise.'

He sat back. After all, it was important to maintain the façade, pretence, the same pretence that had fooled the parole board. Until he did what he needed to do, that is. After that, he wouldn't care.

4

The next morning, at eight o'clock, Nicola Considine had fifteen segments of CCTV ready for viewing, everything from traffic and shop footage to personal phones and dashcams. She pulled down the overhead projector screen and linked it to her computer. The rest of the Major Crimes Investigative Unit, including Paul Quinn, sat at their desks, looking on.

'I picked up the car travelling over Baggot Street Bridge,' she told them, freezing the image. The clock in the corner of the screen gave the time as 05:55 a.m. The car was a black Volvo estate, its reg number clearly visible, 05-D-75648, specifically a V70.

'And that's the first sighting?' It was Voyle.

'What did I just say? I just said I picked it up travelling over Baggot Street Bridge.'

'Yes. But that's not the same as a first sighting, is it?'

'It's a first sighting,' Brody said. 'That's what she means. Continue, Nicola.'

'Get this,' she said. 'It's registered to... drum roll, Jonathan J Harris.'

Marty Sheahan had been taking a sip from his Costa coffee. He nearly spat the contents from his mouth. 'What? That JJ?'

'Yes, that JJ. But don't get too excited. The car's been officially off the road for almost three years.'

'Well, it wasn't off the road last night.'

They watched the CCTV footage, different sections stitched together to give snapshots of the car's journey from Baggot Street Bridge, along Baggot Street, onto Pearse Street, then College Green, turning right onto Westmoreland Street, at the end crossing the Liffey onto the north side over the O'Connell Street Bridge. It went a little way along O'Connell Street before manoeuvring – with some difficulty for such a large vehicle – onto Sugar Lane. Another camera picked it up here, the headlights glaring as it turned in. It proceeded to travel halfway into the lane before it stopped. They watched as a female got out, just like Ernie had said, one wearing a long, tight – very tight – dress. In fact, the dress was so tight it forced her to waddle as she walked, and the outline of a pair of long, shapely legs was visible. It took a couple of attempts for her to get to grips with the naked torso inside the back of the car, but once she had, she dragged it out with little effort and brought it along the side of the Volvo and dumped it onto the ground in the full glow of the headlamps.

Considine froze the image as the female turned to go back to the vehicle, capturing her face.

'Well,' Voyle said, 'I can't be sure? Anyone know what JJ looks like in a cocktail dress?'

'Who's JJ?' It was Paul Quinn.

'You never heard of JJ?'

'Naw,' with a shake of the head.

'Let me educate you, then,' Voyle said. 'A bit of a sad case is old JJ. In his day, gunslinger for the Donoghues... you've heard of them, haven't you?'

Quinn shook his head again.

'No surprise really, I suppose, that you haven't. They weren't around for very long; they came and burnt bright for a time before' – he clenched his hand and uncurled it again – 'voomph, like a meteor shooting across the sky, they were gone. Voomph. Just like that. Anyway, he's an old man now, been in and out of prison for most of his life. Not a very good criminal, but God loves a trier. He appeared to be keeping his nose clean... until now, that is. Look, this all looks a bit weird to me, to tell the truth.'

'Nicola,' Brody said, 'take Paul here with you when we finish, and knock on JJ's door. Be careful, even an old dog can bite.'

'Will do.'

'I agree with Steve. Something's not right.'

He pointed to the overhead.

'This couldn't have been advertised better without taking a full-page ad out in a Sunday newspaper. Anyone else think that that woman there is built better than any pro wrestler? I mean, those shoulders.'

'And legs,' Voyle said.

'Yes, and legs,' Brody agreed.

'You mean she's not a woman?' Paul Quinn sounded truly baffled.

'What do you think?' It was Marty Sheahan.

Quinn said nothing. The truth was, he didn't know what to think.

5

As the members of the Major Crimes Investigative Unit and their temporary member, Paul Quinn, were wrapping up the review of the CCTV footage, a stone's throw away in Forensic Science Ireland at Garda HQ, Mercedes Camacho was wrapping up her analysis of the DNA and fingerprint samples sent to the lab by the Technical Bureau from the body found in the laneway.

Mercedes Camacho was Spanish. She'd come to Ireland as an intern and had never gone back. She loved Ireland. She loved the weather. Most Irish people didn't. In fact, they seemed to complain about nothing else. But Mercedes never complained about Irish weather. Never. Never ever. Where else could you get all four seasons in one day? Certainly not in her native Almera. That was for certain. No, in Almera it was practically summer all year round, except when it really was summer, July and August, hot, hot, hot, *dios mío*. She loved Ireland for the same reason Irish people loved Spain, only in reverse. Four seasons in one day, she loved it.

She walked across the lab now and sat at the desk in the corner by the door. On it was a landline telephone and a desktop computer. All the scientists and lab technicians in the lab used this one desk. It was enough. They used the computer to log their sample results and the telephone to convey the results to the relevant officers in the relevant departments.

She picked up the telephone and pressed the speed-dial button with a sticker on it that had the initials MCIU. She hoped it wasn't the one called Voyle who picked up, the *engreído*, the cocky one. He reminded her of some of the men in her home village. He would fit right in back there, she had no doubt. Mercedes didn't like Voyle.

She ran a hand through her thick, curly, jet-black hair. Even with a strong hairband and numerous clips, she had only barely, if temporarily, managed to tame it. Thankfully, most Irish men weren't like Voyle. They were polite, reserved, and shy, until they drank Guinness, that is; then they became entertainers.

The phone was answered on the fifth ring. Mercedes held her breath.

'Hello, Major Crime Investigation Unit, Paul Quinn speaking; how can I help you?'

She was surprised, and relieved. She'd never heard of this one.

'Who? Paul? Quinn?'

'Yes, Paul Quinn.'

'I don't know you. How's that possible? The unit is a small one.'

'I'm new... so to speak.'

'Whatever. Mercedes Camacho, FSI. I have results for you. The body in the lane.'

'Yes, the body in the lane. Great. Go ahead. I'll write it down.'

'There is nothing to write down. Because there is nothing.

Results are negative. All negative, DNA, fingerprints. Nothing.'

'Nothing. Completely negative. Like, nothing at all?'

'Negative is negative. You cannot be a bit, no?'

'Blood sample?'

'What about it?'

'Oh... that would be... sorry, if there's no DNA match, then there can be no blood match either.'

'Of course. It was O positive, by the way, the common one.'

'Yes, like my own. Yes, OK, that's fine, thank you... Mercedes Camacho you said. That's an unusual name.'

'I'm Spanish. You will tell Sergeant Brody I called?'

'Yes, of course. Thank you again. Mercedes... as in the car, right?'

'What?'

'Your name. Mercedes. As in the car?'

She laughed. 'Yes, as in the car. You're welcome, Paul. Thank you.'

'Goodbye.'

'Goodbye.'

He hung up.

'THAT WAS THE LAB,' he said, replacing the handset into the cradle. 'No match for DNA or fingerprints. Nothing.'

'Of course,' Marty Sheahan said.

'Because that would be too easy.' Considine pulled on her windbreaker with the letters GARDA emblazoned on the back. Brody told Marty to contact the press office and organise an appeal – Facebook, other social media and news sites, whatever.

'You'll have to use the crime scene photograph.'

'He's clearly dead in it,' Marty said.

'Of course. Because he is. But we don't have any other choice.'

Considine went and stood in the doorway. She looked across at Paul Quinn, who looked back at her.

'Well?'

'Oh, JJ.' Quinn got to his feet.

'Yes, JJ.'

He stood and walked over to her.

'You firearms trained?' she asked.

'No.'

'Just me, then. Come on, we need to stop by the armoury first.'

6

The address on the Garda computer system, Pulse, didn't match the vehicle owner details on the national register. Both were incorrect, and both had not been updated in years.

On the drive over, Paul Quinn casually mentioned he'd missed breakfast. Nicola Considine ignored the remark. She wasn't going to waste time stopping for him to get a bloody breakfast roll. Probably not a breakfast roll, he didn't seem the type. She guessed Paul Quinn might be vegetarian, vegan even.

Childers Road was officially in the well-to-do Dublin suburb of Rathgar. But 214, where JJ lived, was on the border with Rathmines, or flatland as most people referred to it. Like many of the houses along the row, 214 was a grotty three-storey red brick converted into flats. His was number six.

'Does he rent a flat, or does he actually own the building?' Quinn asked as Considine drove past the house, pulling in a little further down against the kerb.

'I don't know. But I doubt it. In fact, I'd be pretty certain he hasn't a pot to piss in. Why'd you ask?'

'Thought old gangsters usually had enough salted away, that's all. They kept us busy in Fraud anyway.'

'Really? Maybe some of them did. But not the JJs of this world. Definitely not.' She turned off the engine and got out of the car. When Quinn joined her, she said, 'And the reason for that is simple, they always get caught.'

Number 214 was set back from the street in a rectangle of gravel bordered by twisted iron railings. They moved quickly across the gravel, past a collection of overflowing refuse bins with the flat numbers scrawled in white paint along the sides. A car was parked by the door, a decrepit piece of shite with flat tyres and missing hubcaps. In fact, it looked like it had been laid up for months, if not years. Chained to a railing was the rusting wheel of a pushbike, the rest of the bike long since gone.

They mounted the steps, and Considine pushed the door. It was locked.

'What now?' Quinn said.

'We wait.'

'Why not ring the bell? Someone'll let us in, surely.'

'I'll pretend you didn't just say that. A surprise, remember. A *surprise*. No advance notice given. Believe me, and only for JJ's an old man now, I'd have a full raid team with me. He has a quick temper and a bad reputation.'

'Really?'

'Really. Take no chances with him, and we'll be fine.'

Considine opened her windbreaker and removed the big Sig Sauer from its hip holster. She transferred it into a pocket, kept her hand in there along with it.

They didn't have to wait long before the door did open, a woman emerging, struggling with a baby in a buggy and a toddler holding on to her hand. She paid the detectives no attention, didn't even seem to see them standing there, even as Paul Quinn reached in and held the door open for her.

When she'd passed, they entered the grimy hallway, the air cold and damp and smelling of mould. Considine silently counted off the doors, two to her left, one to her right, a staircase in the middle to the upper floors. None of the doors were numbered. She pointed to the stairs, and they crossed to it and started up. On the landing opposite them were two further doors, and to the right, along a short, narrow corridor, three more. Considine spent a moment counting off doors again and working out which was number six, then led the way to the first door along the corridor. She spent another moment looking at it, weighing it up, calculating what it would take to kick or shoulder it in if she had to. She could tell it was old and sat loosely in its frame. So not too much. She listened. No sound came from inside.

She glanced over her shoulder to Quinn. She wanted him on the other side of the door. He was standing in the middle of the corridor. She waited for him to make eye contact with her so she could nod to where she wanted him to be. But he didn't. Instead, he stepped past her and stopped, turned to face the door. She watched as he raised his right arm and clenched his hand. She blinked as he reached out. And couldn't believe what he did next. Quinn knocked on the door. Considine's mouth dropped open as he said the words, 'Gardai. Open up, Mr Harris.'

She waited. He waited. They waited. In a silence that seemed to stretch to eternity.

Before all hell broke loose.

An ear-splitting boom accompanied the disintegration of the centre of the door, chunks of wood flying through the air amid a cloud of tiny splinters, one, a long thin piece, sharp as a dagger, catching the edge of Quinn's arm, spinning him round. He screamed in pain. Another boom, a section of masonry this time exploding in the wall next to his head. Quinn dropped to his knees, a strange howling sound coming from him, a mixture of fear and pain. Nicola Considine was temporarily deafened, could hear nothing except a low hissing noise. Her back was still pressed against the wall. She became aware of someone rushing from the room and then past her. JJ, the old dog, had attacked.

She twisted round and brought up the pistol and took aim into the centre of his back, she wasn't fussy. Her finger began to press on the trigger. And then, her hearing came back in an explosion of sound. One in particular. That of a child crying. She eased her finger off the trigger, her eyes scanning for the source of the sound, as a tiny head appeared over the top of the last step of the stairs directly ahead of her. She lowered the gun and cursed as JJ flew down the steps with surprising speed and was gone. She looked back to Quinn, blood pouring from his arm. But he'd live.

'You stupid bollocks,' she shouted, 'you stupid, stupid bollocks, you almost got us killed.'

7

'He did what? The stupid bollocks.' The Old Man was standing by his window, through which he could see out over the back wall of Garda HQ and across the plains of the Phoenix Park – the largest urban park in the whole of Europe. Detective Chief Superintendent Maguire found it relaxing sometimes just to stand here and gaze. Especially at this time of year, at the approach of the rutting season, when the normally shy deer emerged into the open, and if he were lucky, he might witness a couple of big stags fighting for the honour of mating with the females. It was quite a spectacle when that happened, these big, majestic animals locking horns. From a hook on the wall dangled a pair of binoculars he kept for this very purpose. The Old Man had been about to reach for them when Brody had come in to tell him the news. 'The stupid bollocks,' he said again.

'He's not injured,' Jack added, 'didn't even need stitches.'

'Really?' Like the Old Man was disappointed to hear that news. 'And he really did that? He *knocked* on the door? While standing in *front* of it.'

'He did.'

'Jesus Christ. You know what this means? It means I'll be now asked to explain why two of my officers and not a full raid team were allowed to approach a property with a known dangerous criminal inside, who was armed with a shotgun.'

'But no one knew that, boss.'

'Well, they know it now. And that's the same thing.'

Brody didn't speak.

The desk phone rang. The Old Man snatched it up. 'Hello... hello...' He waited a moment, then slammed it down again. 'That's the third time today, and two times yesterday, some dickhead just breathing down the line into my ear.' He laughed. 'Or maybe I should be flattered, eh, Brody... anyway, where were we? Yes, they know it now, and that's the same thing. They could have got themselves killed. And now I have to explain it all. The stupid bollocks, that Quinn. Any word on Harris?'

'We're looking. We found street bags of cannabis in his flat.'

'He's dealing?'

'Looks like it. A small operation, probably nothing more than a little extra spending money for him.'

'Really? The pensioners I know looking for a little extra spending money do it by working in their local Tesco, not dealing drugs. Oh, they're going to love this.' He nodded vaguely toward the corner of the room, on the other side of which, through a wall and across a courtyard, was the annex to the offices of the deputy commissioner. 'Oh yes, they're going to love this... you know what he's like, Jack, don't you? Deputy Commissioner Irwin, with his clipped fingernails and starched shirts... his shoes, my God, his shoes, have you ever seen his shoes? They'd blind you from forty metres they're that shiny. Oh yes, he's going to love this. He'll write his report, all about the need for greater *oversight*. He loves that word, *oversight*. The commissioner will tell him he's doing a great job and pat him on the head, tickle him under the chin. Then they'll go to lunch. Then he'll come back and sit on his arse in that big office of his and spend the afternoon clipping his fingernails and shining his shoes. And then, in a couple of years' time, when the commissioner retires, he'll take his place in that even bigger office, clipping his fingernails and shining his shoes. Then *he'll* retire too with his lump sum and a weekly pension twice the salary of most uniforms and go live in Spain – he likes to go to Spain, you know, has a holiday house there somewhere, Fuengirola I think. There, he'll sit on his arse and clip his fingernails again. He won't have to worry about shining his shoes because he'll be barefoot in the sand. Or sandals. And he might even polish those too. Spare me, Brody, but it's like *Animal Farm* around here, it really is. And when that Quinn bollocks gets back here, you send him straight in to me.'

'Um,' Brody began, 'boss, we all make mistakes. I wouldn't; I'd give the lad a chance. He knows he fucked up. I'll have a word with him. He'll learn.'

'Learn? He needs more than to learn...' The Old Man rubbed his chest with the palm of a hand. 'This is giving me heartburn, this is. Right then, you have a word with him.'

'Will do. I'm collecting him from the hospital.'

'Oh no you're not,' the Old Man growled. 'You'll let him take the bus.'

8

The body in the lane wasn't the only case the Major Crimes Investigation Unit had to deal with. Steve Voyle was at his desk, taking details from a district commander in Wexford regarding the theft of a million euros' worth of plant equipment from a builder's yard. The investigation had met a brick wall, and the district commander was convinced the whole thing was an insurance scam. What he needed was an outsider to come down here and break through the wall of local silence. 'Because I can't. I have to live with these people, you know.'

Voyle turned from his desk when he'd finished his call and shook his head.

'The stupid bollocks did what?' He had listened to Considine in the background relaying the story. 'Really? He stood in front of the door *and* knocked on it?'

'He did,' Martin Sheahan answered.

Considine was reading the comments on the Garda Facebook page appealing for help in identifying the body in the lane. She was working hard on being civil with Voyle, so she was actually trying to ignore him. One of the comments on the page caught her eye.

How do we know, it said, *this isn't fake news, not just the coppers trying to find a rat squealer to work for them, yeah.*

'Bloody asshole,' she said.

'Whoo.' He sounded genuinely hurt. 'I don't deserve that. Come on now.' He looked at her.

'Not you, for God's sake. I didn't' – her desk phone rang – 'mean you.'

But Voyle didn't seem convinced.

Considine snatched up the receiver.

'Yes.'

'This is Ita Donoghue. May I speak to the person in charge?'

'Ita Donoghue. Who exactly are you, Ita Donoghue?'

'The principal officer at the Department of Urban Planning and Infrastructure. That's who. Ita Donoghue.'

'Great. How can I help you, Ms Donoghue?'

'It's Mrs.'

'Mrs.'

'But you can call me Ita. I don't stand on ceremony.'

'Fine. Ita. What is it?'

'Are you the person in charge?'

Considine took a breath and rubbed her front teeth back and forth over her bottom lip. 'He's just stepped out for a minute. But really, you can tell me. I'm a Garda. Have you information about something?'

'Information... well, no. Or maybe. I don't know what you'd call it. Yes, I suppose it is information. It's to do with the body found in that lane. I think I recognise the photograph. Someone brought it to my attention. On Facebook. Although I'm not on Facebook, you understand, but someone brought it to my attention. But I only want to speak to the person in charge. I have to be careful, you understand; in my position, I need to be discreet. I hope you understand. It's my position, my job. I have to be careful.'

Considine rubbed her front teeth over her lip again. 'Fine, Mrs Donoghue. If you won't speak to me, then I'll have the person in charge ring you just as soon as he comes in.'

'No. I'll have to ring him myself, I'm afraid. I can't give my number out, you understand. It's policy.'

'Fine, Mrs Donoghue. You can ring him, then.'

But what Mrs Donoghue didn't know, or didn't care to consider, was that her number was displayed on Considine's phone. And if she really was a principal officer at the Department of Urban Planning and Infrastructure, like she had just said she was, then she really should have known this. Which made Considine think that she probably wasn't.

'Goodbye, Mrs Donoghue,' she said, and hung up.

9

Newly promoted Detective Garda Paul Quinn was released from hospital later that evening. He did not get the bus back to the station. Because he did not go back to the station. The Horgan fast-track whizz-kid had never felt more humiliated in his entire life. He did not want to go back to the station; he did not want to face anybody at the MCIU. Not yet anyway. Maybe never again. What he wanted to do, what he really wanted to do, was go hide somewhere and stay hidden there forever. But he knew that that wasn't an option. There was only one option, and that was to make this right again. He had to find JJ Harris. Had to. No one else. Him. He was the only one because he was the one who'd fucked up. His unshakeable belief was he had to make this right. But Paul Quinn wasn't thinking straight. He was acting like somebody who'd lost all their money on a horse at Leopardstown, who was now maxing out his credit cards in gambling everything on the next race in a last desperate bid to win his money back.

He left the hospital and got into a taxi, and fifteen minutes later the taxi dropped him off at his flat. An hour later he was sitting in his car – a two-year-old Golf – parked on Childers Road, just down from 214, where he had a good view of the grotty red-brick house. He would sit here for as long as it took. There was nothing else he could do. JJ Harris had to come back at some stage, just had to, and when he did...

No, there was no other way.

He must have nodded off. When he awoke, he found a flesh-eating zombie staring in the driver's door window at him. He jerked back in fright.

'What the fuck?'

He watched the creature open its mouth and reveal a row of crooked, yellow stumps of teeth, like old headstones in a graveyard.

'What the fuck?' he said again.

A long finger tapped against the window, and Quinn blinked, rubbed both hands up and down briskly across his face a couple of times, wiping away the sleep, then looked again. It was real, she, it, whatever, was still there.

'What the fuck?' for a third time. But his mind had begun to process the situation, a pathetic junkie he knew, one he felt sorry for and reviled at the same time. He lowered his window.

Just like knocking on JJ Harris's flat door, he really should have known better. Because you never let a zombie in.

'You want to have sex with me?'

'No. Now go away and...'

'Listen so, we'll skip right to the end, just give me the fucking money, yeah.'

She shoved it up to his face. Quinn would have really, *really* much preferred anything else: a knife, a gun, a bazooka, *anything*. But not this. Not a blood-filled syringe. Or what looked like blood. He had no choice but to take it at face value. It was enough to make the toughest mule quiver at the knees.

'Are you deaf? Give it over, ya faggot, or I'll jab ya with a dose of the cooties.' She drew back her hand and made a stabbing motion through the air. 'Hand it over. The bread. Come on.'

'No.'

He'd said the word before he even realised it.

'No?' She turned her head to the side, genuinely puzzled.

There was only so much a person could take, after all, and Quinn had reached his limit. Even the fear of being jabbed by a syringe filled with HIV-infected blood wasn't enough. Then everything happened in a blur. Quinn, again without making any conscious decision on his part, silently pulled the door handle open, rammed his body against it. The door shot out and hit her; there was a squealing sound like a wild boar caught in a trap. But she was still standing. She was still bloody standing. Quinn pulled the door back and rammed it into her a second time. This time she went down in a dangle of writhing arms and legs. He jumped out and stomped his right foot hard onto her wrist. She squealed again, not as loud this time, and her hand opened and released the syringe. Quinn kicked it to the side, but kept his other foot pressing down.

'What,' he demanded, but he wasn't looking at her; instead he was looking to the sky, 'did I do to deserve all this? Have I upset some spirit of the universe and unleashed its wrath upon me? Is that it? Well, is it? Is *that* it?'

'*Pleeease*, you're breaking my hand. Let me go.'

His head snapped towards her.

'Will I fuck.' And he pressed down even harder as he fished out his phone from his pocket and rang it in.

They were in the area and arrived a couple of minutes later. Quinn explained to the two uniforms that he was on the job too, just not the specifics of why he was here, and they didn't ask. The zombie was known to them; they told Quinn she went by the street name of Paris. Quinn thought, *Paris?* That was like saying a nag and a thoroughbred were both the same just because they were horses. They told him she operated along the Canal by Baggot Street Bridge.

'But she's been drifting over here lately, and we know why.' The uniform nodded to the house, 214. 'But no one seems really interested in doing anything about it.'

That would also include you two, Quinn thought.

'Anyway,' the uniform said, 'what'll we do with her? You want to press charges?'

'No.'

'No?' The uniform shrugged. 'We'll be off, then.'

'You won't. I might do. Later. Lock her up while I think about it, can't leave her wandering about the place in the state she's in.'

But they looked like they'd have no problem in doing just that.

The uniform shrugged again. 'Okay, we'll bring her in. It's time for a tea break anyway.'

'What about the syringe?' Quinn pointed. 'It's somewhere around here.'

'What about it?'

'Find it and bag it.' Quinn thought of something. '*You* can charge her under the public order act. I'll make a statement. Search her, and I'm sure you'll get a possession too. What, you want me to do your job for you too?'

'He stomped on my wrist,' Paris whined. 'I think it's broken. Wha' they call that? Excessive force, yeah.'

The uniform snapped, 'I didn't see anything. Shut up.'

'I'm starving. Gis me up a burger and chips on the way to the station. And I want a breakfast roll *without* da hash brownies in the morning, if you're keeping me in, yeah. Now, can youse get goin'? I'm bleedin' freezin' standing here.'

They found the syringe at the edge of the road, perilously close to a drain cover. Quinn went home, writing off the day as a complete and utterly jinxed waste of time.

10

The Old Man was walking with Riley, one of his best friends, out for some fresh, night-time air. He liked this time, liked the feeling of cosiness, the lights of the houses glowing from behind curtained windows on the residential streets that now glistened following a recent shower. It was like he had stepped into a picture postcard. They'd been strolling for the best part of an hour. The Old Man loved spending time with the old girl any chance he could, she being the most perfect of companions.

As he and Riley neared the end of one street, she started to get excited. Riley being a dog, that meant barking and straining on her lead. Because she knew what lay ahead, just round the corner. The park. The Old Man laughed.

'Steady up, Riley; we'll get there.'

Just as they reached the corner, a man came round it from the opposite direction, walking quickly and just managing to sidestep at the last moment to avoid bumping into them.

'Ooops, pardon me.'

'That's alright,' the Old Man said. 'Nobody's fault.'

He was about to move on, but Riley had other ideas. The

five-year-old Yorkshire terrier-Pomeranian cross jumped up, planting her two little front paws on the man's trouser leg.

'Riley, naughty,' the Old Man said, pulling gently on the lead. But he wasn't really cross. He could never be cross with Riley.

The man smiled. The collar of his coat was up, but the Old Man could see he had a heavy beard with a prominent patch of white along one side.

'Oh, that's alright, he's only doing what doggies do. What a beautiful little fella.'

'Girl, actually.'

'Oh, pardon me once more. What's her name, did you say?'

'Riley.'

The man reached down and offered the back of his hand to her. 'Hello, Riley, aren't you the little beauty?' She sniffed it and gave it a lick, and he tickled her behind her ears. The Old Man was about to compliment the stranger on this textbook greeting of a dog that wasn't familiar to him: most people immediately tried to pet Riley, and that usually spooked her. But he hadn't. Anyway, the park was just around the corner, it would be closing soon, and he needed to get moving.

'Thank you. Now come on, Riley. And goodnight to you.'

'Goodnight to you too.'

The Old Man and Riley continued on. As they passed through the gates into the park, the stranger stepped back around the corner and stood by the railings, looking on as the Old Man unclipped Riley from her leash and she bounded away.

'You didn't recognise me,' Daniel Willow muttered. 'But soon you will. I'll make sure of it. Soon, when I kill you, that is.'

11

The next morning, Brody didn't bother to ring Mrs Ita Donoghue, principal officer at the Department of Urban Planning and Infrastructure. Instead, he drove to the department's offices in the trendy, newly redeveloped Dublin Docklands area, hoping he would meet her there. From what Considine had told him, the woman sounded like a typical career civil servant – if she was a civil servant at all, that is. If she was who she said she was, then she was a species better taken by surprise rather than one allowed to ruminate over answers to any questions she thought he might ask.

It was just after eleven o'clock when he pulled into the car park near the imposing, grey stone building that, despite being over two hundred years old, blended in with all the modern glass-walled office blocks around it. He walked from the car park, pausing to allow a bunch of skateboarders to pass by on the cycle lane outside, dressed in their uniforms of baggy pants and oversized T-shirts. They were older than your average skateboarder, Brody considered. He put them down as software engineers. He'd heard they liked to come out and skateboard around at times during the day, to clear their heads, or maybe to remind themselves that a real world existed, that they didn't completely dwell inside a computer-generated *Matrix*-type universe. But what struck him was that they all looked a little lost, like surfers in search of a beach. Off to his left was a funky vintage Citroen food van; other surfers gathered around it. He knew funky vintage Citroen food vans only ever sold overpriced gourmet coffees, croissants and crêpes, a choice of fillings or just plain. *Like some cheese with that?* That was an extra charge, although they never told you that when you ordered.

Brody walked across the road and passed beneath a stone arch onto the forecourt of the government building. In the centre of the forecourt was a bronze statue, two sailors, hands wrapped around a coil of copper hawser, staring off to a distant horizon.

He went through the revolving doorway into the building and was standing in an atrium. Far above, he could see a vaulted roof. The atrium was ringed by walls of glass, and he could see into the offices behind them. He glanced at his watch, 11:17.

The security man told him Mrs Ita Donoghue's office was on the third floor. So she did exist; this was not a waste of time. Then he pointed to a couple of elevators and told Brody to turn right when he got out on the floor; hers was the first door. Brody took the elevator. He waited after he'd knocked. And waited. He was just about to knock a second time when a voice said, 'Yes. Yes. Come in.'

She looked exactly like he thought she would, but at the same time, she reminded him of the software engineers. Like she was a little lost. Lost in this avant-garde building, this mixture of old and new, this icon to cool urban planning. Just lost, like she didn't belong.

'Mrs Ita Donoghue?' he asked, standing in the doorway.

She was pulling on her coat, a long dark coat, wrapping it round a long dark skirt and a long, loose-fitting dark blouse fastened to the neck.

'Yes. You must be Executive Officer Davies. That right? Well, I won't change my mind, just so's you know. No use coming down here trying to make me. Just like I told planning, those studs are dangerous, they really are, but no one will listen... And like I told them, I don't care how aesthetically pleasing they are, if we don't test them further, and test again and again, to be absolutely sure, then I won't give my approval, I simply won't... I mean, can you imagine? What if someone slips on one of *those* things? What then? They're supposed to stop people from slipping, not cause them to slip. No. I just won't. Now, I have a meeting to attend across town.'

'Mrs Donoghue, Detective Sergeant Jack Brody. You rang. The body in the lane. I'd like to talk to you about it.'

He watched as her mouth dropped open, and she stared back at him. Then Mrs Donoghue stretched herself to full height, and Brody realised she was taller than she'd first appeared. He thought of Popeye's girlfriend, Olive Oyl. Ita Donoghue reminded him of the cartoon character.

He stepped inside but left the door open.

'How did you find me? I didn't give out my phone number... or anything else for that matter.'

'Mrs Donoghue, your phone number showed up on the phone at our end. That's all. That's how I got your number.'

'Oh, it did, did it? I didn't know it showed up like that.'

Brody had the feeling she rarely, if ever, had to deal with anything outside pre-planned spreadsheets and action plans. His showing up here like this was the equivalent of having the boiler burst in her attic. Mrs Donoghue looked confused and a little anxious. Civil servants were institutionalised creatures, Brody knew, denizens of a behemoth organisation, a flag bearer to inefficiency, a furnace for the burning of public money.

'Can we sit down?'

Her eyes darted towards her desk. She looked even more anxious as she pointed vaguely in its direction. 'Well, I...' Like she was incapable of deciding on anything other than that which had already been passed and rubber-stamped in triplicate by a deciding committee.

Brody crossed the room and sat on the chair before her desk, and only then did Mrs Donoghue move and occupy the one behind it. She did not undo her coat.

'Tell me why you rang the guards?' he asked, getting straight down to it.

She fidgeted with the shiny black leather handbag on her lap. It had a bright red trim along its side pockets with gleaming buckles. Brody couldn't help but stare at it for a second, like she was revealing a dirty little secret.

'Oh...' she began, and fell silent, staring past him to a point on the wall.

'I'd rather you didn't think about it, Mrs Donoghue. Just tell me.'

'I thought I recognised the photo, that's all. Like I said.'

'And who is it?'

She looked at him curiously, as if the question was a trick one, too easy to be answered off the cuff. Like there had to be a catch. Like she had to think about it. She said nothing.

'Could you answer the question, Mrs Donoghue?' She was starting to irritate him. He took a breath, said slowly, 'You rang us, remember. You did ring us, didn't you, Mrs Donoghue?'

'Oh yes, I did ring you.'

'Then could you tell me why you rang us? Tell me who you think this person is. Tell me, Mrs Donoghue. I haven't got all day.'

'Well...' She looked at him, as if stung. 'William was always a little... odd. He's probably gone to Amsterdam or some such place. I'm probably completely wrong. I don't want to cause any trouble, that's all. He does, you know, go to Amsterdam... or Tangiers. That's in Morocco, by the way. Look, I'm wasting your time. I mean, that photograph could look like a lot of people, when you think about it. And I've been thinking about it, since I rang, that is... what did you say your name was again?'

'Jack Brody, detective sergeant. Tell me what you know, Mrs Donoghue.'

Their eyes met. Neither of them spoke. Mrs Donoghue smiled, seemingly reassured. 'Yes, of course. I will.'

She sat back.

'Well...'

And started to talk, telling him all about William Anderson, the man who looked like the man in the photo of the Facebook appeal. She was William's boss, had been for almost twenty years. But still, she couldn't be sure... *I mean, that nose, it doesn't look like his, and his forehead was higher... at least, I think it was.* Jack Brody had a feeling that it was – William Anderson, that is. Just a feeling. And he trusted his feelings. Unlike Mrs Donoghue, who was not used to dealing with dead bodies, dealing with the subtleties of a life extinguished, of a body that changes its colour, its shape, shrinks a little, stiffens, becomes waxen... different to how it looked when its heart was still beating. Jack was used to all that and made allowances.

And yet, even now, when William Anderson had not shown up to work for a couple of days, when a body had been found that looked just like him, as always, she doubted herself.

'William Anderson looked like the body in the exhibit?' Brody asked, 'By exhibit I mean photograph.'

'Oh, yes, he looked like it... but I had to think about it.'

'Do you have a recent photograph of Mr Anderson? And an address?'

'Yes. I insist that all personnel files be updated once a year with such details. People tell me every five years is sufficient. But I insist.'

And right now, Brody was glad that she did.

'I'd like to have a copy of that photograph, please.'

'Yes, of course. I'll arrange for you to get it before you leave.'

'Thank you.'

'Because it looks like him, but I just can't be certain, that's all. I hope I'm not making a fuss. But William has never not shown up to work without ringing in first. And the picture does look like him. I mean, it does. So what was I to think?' And, in what Brody took as a searingly honest display of self-analysis, she added, 'Even me.'

12

Considine was waiting for Brody outside the apartment building – the Elms it was called, in the heart of Ballsbridge, a part of Dublin favoured by wealthy solicitors and businessmen. She had a key, obtained from the management company. The agent she spoke with told her William Anderson was renting a one-bedroom apartment on the ground floor and had done so for five years, that he was a model tenant, paid his rent on time, and there had never been any issues with him. The building appeared new, a modern lattice of brickwork around a five-row stack of bay windows.

'Can't be cheap,' Brody said, walking to the front entrance, 'an apartment in a place like this.'

'It's not. I asked. Twelve hundred a month is what he pays for it.'

'That's half his wages gone already, and for what? A glorified bedsit?'

Considine had also obtained the code for the keypad by the door. She punched it in, and they entered, standing in a marble-floored foyer surrounded by an array of tall, mature, dangly potted plants. A hallway ran off to the side with number seven at the end. They went to it, pulled on latex gloves, and Considine placed the key in the lock and turned it.

What Brody first noticed was the smell. Not a smell, because a smell can indicate something rotten or gone off. No, this was a nice, pleasant smell, an *aroma*. He sniffed, a mixture of honey and cinnamon he thought, warm too, if that was possible for an aroma, and welcoming, like a soft embrace.

The curtains were drawn, and the place was in darkness. Considine found the light switch and flicked it on.

He forgot all about the aroma.

They both silently cast their eyes about the lavish collection of furniture, the drawn brocade curtains across the windows, the textured wallpaper, the lamps with their tasselled shades, the sculpted stone fireplace... and the carpet. Brody felt his feet sink into it. It was like he'd just stepped into an actual, life-sized doll's house.

'Get a look at this place,' Considine said, and whistled softly.

Along with this room, the living room Brody decided, there was also a small bedroom and an even smaller kitchen, the former taken up by a king-size with a red, velvet spread on it. Considine went through to the living room while Brody went through to the bedroom. He looked up, nodding at his reflection in the mirror above the bed. He wondered what *Mrs* Ita Donoghue would make of this. He squeezed past the bed and slid open one of the doors in the wardrobe that took up the length of the wall opposite. The smell, the *aroma*, jumped out at him. He located its source at once, a series of small potpourri bags hanging among the clothes.

Clothes. Female clothes: dresses, lots of dresses, all short dresses, lots of black, lots of lace. The wardrobe floor was taken up by a collection of stilettos and knee-length boots. A shelf in the wardrobe above held an array of mannequin heads sporting different-coloured wigs. Brody slid the door closed and opened the door to the other side. More clothes. Male clothes: shirts – lots of shirts – a couple of suits and lots of cardigans, each one assigned to its own hanger. On the wardrobe floor were a couple of pairs of brogues, one pair brown, the other black, also a pair of sneakers and a pair of walking boots. On the shelf above were a couple of suitcases. He bent down to the locker shoehorned between the bed and the wardrobe and opened the drawer. Scattered in there among the various receipts, a box of tissues, eye drops, a pair of foam earplugs, were some photographs. He picked one up. On the back was written *Tamara*. He studied the photograph; the woman in it reminded him of a US country star who'd once starred in a movie and sang a song about working from nine until five. He glanced to the wardrobe, went over and found the dress with the lace shoulders and the sequins down its front, the same one as in the photograph. The blonde wig on a mannequin head above was the same too. William Anderson was the woman in the photograph. William Anderson was Tamara. But was he the body in the lane?

Brody had to admit he made a very good woman, a woman who, especially if a drink or two was taken, and the lights maybe a little dim, could convince any man that *he* was a *she*. Some men mightn't need any convincing at all.

For the first time, Brody began to think of a motive for the killing; if William Anderson was the body in the lane, then maybe there was someone who had found that particular surprise too much to bear.

'Boss.'

'In here.'

Considine appeared in the doorway.

'What the...?' Taking in the Danny La Rue stagewear in the wardrobe. 'This place is starting to freak me out. Reminds me of that Hitchcock movie. What's it called? You know, where your man, Norman Bates, kept his dead mother's corpse in a locked room. Yes, reminds me of that.'

'*Psycho*.'

'Yes, that's the one. *Psycho*.'

'You think we'll find a body in here?'

She crinkled her nose. 'Doesn't smell like it... Based on a true story, by the way, that movie, not a lot of people know that. Ed Gein, the real psycho, liked to make chairs upholstered in human flesh.' She held something out to him in her hand. 'I found this.'

He squeezed past the bed and took it. It was an address book. 'People still use these?' he said, turning it over in his hands.

'Yes. Old ways are the best sometimes. No one can hack an address book, after all.'

Brody flicked through some pages. 'I'll take this with me. Can you request scenes of crime?'

'Of course. But I don't think they'll get here until this evening at the earliest, maybe tomorrow morning.'

He nodded. This wasn't a crime scene, after all. 'If it is tomorrow morning, make it first thing.'

'Yes. Will do. But his social security details should tell us something, yes?'

'Yes. It'll tell us lots. But what it won't tell us is if William Anderson is the body in the laneway. And John Doe needs a name.'

'You mean Jane Doe, boss.'

Brody glanced to the wardrobe.

'Whichever,' he said.

13

After watching 214 Childers Road for almost three hours the evening before, and becoming an unwitting extra in a scene from *Attack Of The Zombies*, Paul Quinn had observed a slow but steady trickle of people coming and going. And he was doing so again now. Only this time his car doors were locked, and his windows would not be coming down – for anyone. There was no sign of Harris. But Quinn wasn't giving up, no matter what. He'd keep coming back, day after day, night after night, until JJ did show up. Because he had to show up. For the first time, Quinn added a caveat – didn't he? He was beginning to think that maybe JJ never would. Brody had rung a couple of times, but he didn't answer. He didn't want to talk to Brody; he didn't want to talk to anyone.

Quinn had noted that those who entered 214 Childers Road through the front door generally didn't come out again, or a couple of hours passed before they did. But those who disappeared down a short flight of steps to the side of the house were invariably back out again within minutes, if not less, and scuttling away. Paul Quinn didn't care as to the reasons why. But he could guess. So what if the place was a fast-drug takeaway? So what if it attracted hordes of zombies just like Paris? He shook his head. *Paris?* Seriously, *Paris?* No, he didn't care. All he cared about was getting JJ Harris. That's all. Nothing else. He admitted, he was becoming a little obsessed.

He'd been sitting here for almost three hours again now. He badly needed a piss and got out of the car, not knowing exactly what he was going to do. His judgement was clouded by both that sense of humiliation and that gambler's sense of desperation, but also an edginess after last night's events. He wasn't a gambler, yet he had to win this; his horse was running, and he had to make things right again. He started walking back along the street towards the house.

But Quinn was nothing if not a little arrogant too, and he failed to see that this arrogance was what had got him into this mess in the first place. After he nipped into some bushes in a corner and relieved himself, he decided to cross the gravel in front of the house and go along the side to see what was at the bottom of those steps. Now he stood looking down them. There was an open door at the bottom. He went down and passed through into a large, dimly lit basement. Through an open door he could see across to the other side the steps leading up into the very hallway he and Considine had stood in yesterday afternoon. He found the light switch and pressed it, and when it flickered on, he saw there was a table in the centre of the room. He detected a smell on the air, a mixture of weed and something else, like burnt plastic. Methamphetamines, he guessed, because that was what he'd been told it smelt like. There'd be a lookout. Had to be. They would have seen him coming a mile off. If they knew he was on his own, they might kick the shite out of him. He'd take that chance. He kept walking.

Quinn crossed the room, went up the basement steps and

into the hall, then went over to the stairs and up. Still, no one jumped him. The door to Harris's flat had already been boarded up; the scenes of crime team been and gone.

He knocked on the door next to it. There was no reply. He knocked again. A door opened. But not that door. It was the one next to it. A girl stepped out into the corridor and looked at him.

'There's no one there. You going to keep knocking on that all day?'

She wore black leggings and a black polo-neck jumper. Her hair was black and tied back in a ponytail. But her skin was snow white. She folded her arms over her chest, ran her eyes over him, like she was trying to make her mind up about something. Quinn guessed she was older than she looked.

'He's gone.'

'You know where he's gone to?'

She made to step back into her flat.

'No. Wait. It's OK. I'm just asking. I'm a guard.'

'A guard. You don't look like a guard. They were here earlier, by the way. I heard one of them got hurt.' Her eyes took in his bandaged arm. 'That was you, was it?'

He nodded. 'It was.'

She gave him an uncertain smile. 'Look, I don't like standing here. You want to come in?'

The flat was one room with a couple of partitions in it, a bed behind one – the bedroom – a cooker and small table and couple of chairs behind the other – the kitchen. Light came in through a single, high, narrow window. The bare light bulb hanging from the ceiling was turned off. She looked at him. For the first time, Paul Quinn wondered about someone else's predicament rather than his own. He wondered about hers, about how she had ended up living in a place like this.

She seemed to read his mind.

'It's purely temporary. I was living with a guy, and it didn't work out. This was the only place I could find. You know what Dublin's like; flats at an affordable rent are like hen's teeth. My name's Susie, what's yours?'

'Paul. Did you know him?'

'Who, Harris?'

No, the tooth fairy. 'Yes, Harris.'

'I didn't know him. I didn't want to know him... hey, would you like something? A drink? I have bottles, took them with me when I left, Finnish vodka. I was just about to have one.' She laughed. 'I mean a drink, not the whole bottle.'

'No, thank you. But don't mind me; you go right ahead.'

'Don't want a drink? I don't think you're on duty, are you? Don't they give you leave until it heals?' She nodded to his arm.

She waited for Quinn to speak, but he said nothing. She shrugged.

'I was in my relationship ten years. I know all about healing. I want to do something, with my life, I mean. Maybe I left it too late. Are you sure you won't have a drink?'

'I'm sure, thank you. You didn't want to know him you said, JJ. Why?'

'Dirty old man. Creep. People coming to his flat at all hours, waking me up. His eyes. You ever see his eyes? He's got evil eyes. Go on, tell me, what's he supposed to have done?'

'It was on the news.'

'I don't listen, watch, or read any news, too depressing.'

'His car was involved in–'

'He doesn't have a car.'

'No?'

'Well, I never saw him with a car.'

'A car registered to his name anyway. A Volvo estate. A body was dumped from it in a laneway off O'Connell Street the night before last.'

'Oh, that. I *did* hear about it. They're calling it the body in the lane thing.'

'Yes, that's it, the body in the lane... thing.'

'Jesus, Mary and Joseph. Like... him. You think it's him? He had something to do with it. Really?'

'The car was registered to him. So... we need to find Harris. And we need to find him fast. Very fast.'

She looked at him oddly, like she knew something he didn't, and nodded to his arm once more. 'I don't think they'd let you come round here like that if you were working. Not on your lonesome, no, they wouldn't? Not if he's so dangerous like you say he might be. What's really up?'

'I told you. Did he ever mention any places that he liked to go to?'

'I'm going to have a drink. It's in the fridge. That's how the Russians drink it. Straight up and chilled. Are you sure?'

'Thought you said it was Finnish?'

'It is Finnish. They drink it like that too, I suppose. I don't really know. Will you have a drink with me or not?'

'Why d'you want me to have a drink with you so badly anyway? You don't even know me. A good-looking girl like you, you don't need to drink with strangers, with me.'

'If I want a psych report, I'll ask for it, OK? I just want to do something, that's all. Something I've never done before. Ten years, that's how long I lived with him. Ten years. You're a guard. Guards can be trusted... can't they?'

'Yes. We can be trusted. And I can be trusted, even if I have to die proving it.'

She looked at him oddly again. 'What's that supposed to mean?'

Quinn turned and strode towards the door.

'Goodbye.'

He had almost reached it when she spoke.

'The Cabin.'

'The what?' Turning round to face her.

'It's a drop-in centre. He mentioned it more than once... these walls are paper thin, you know? Said if he wasn't here, in this kip, that's where he'd be, at the Cabin. I know the Cabin. I've been to the Cabin myself. Have a drink, and I'll tell you all about it.'

But Quinn walked out the door. 'Thanks,' he said from the hall, 'but no thanks,' and walked away.

14

Brody was back in his office by four o'clock. He was still getting used to having an office. It had taken a team of sociologists and advisors to tell the government that isolating staff in private workspaces, or offices, was not good. It created a culture of us and them. Instead, it would be better if everyone worked together in open-plan offices – bitching and water-cooler gossip besides. It was called democratising the workspace and was government policy. But Brody could have told them this already, at absolutely no cost. Anyone could. So while the future lay in funky open-plan offices like Ita Donoghue's Department of Urban Planning and Infrastructure, here at Garda HQ, the architecture was still very much last century. Even so, Ita Donoghue had an office of her own. Brody imagined that the Ita Donoghues of this world would always have offices of their own, which defeated the whole purpose, he supposed. Such was the way of the civil service; only they could tackle a problem and claim to have solved it by leaving things exactly as they had been in the first place.

In any case, as Brody donned a pair of gloves and began

to go through William Anderson's address book, it suited him just fine to have an office of his own right now. No distraction.

The book was small and slim, wrapped in a thin, gold-coloured band. It had a green cover, with embossed gold lettering across the front that simply said *Address Book*.

Brody was a superb boxer, who, if he funnelled all his power up through his leg, into his shoulder, down his arm and into his fist, made it as powerful as a sledgehammer at full swing. Yet he handled the address book with great deftness and delicacy, like a rare museum exhibit. His fingers slid the band off and placed it to the side. He slowly opened it and spread his fingers across the pages, holding them open as he placed it onto the desk, taking care not to flatten it. Books like this, diaries, address books, memorandums, usually had their spines broken from being repeatedly laid down flat. It also caused the pages to detach and fall out. The spine on William Anderson's address book was not broken. And Brody guessed the book was old, but he had taken care of it. The least Brody could do was the same.

On the inside cover, the section headed *Owner Details* had been filled in with a neat, almost beautiful, cursive script. The page opposite, the first page, had five sections with, *Name, Address, Telephone Number*, all bordered by gold, squiggly lines. But these sections hadn't been filled in. Instead, the page was covered in a heavy, untidy scrawl. Brody tried to make out what had been written, but many of the words had been blotted out, and others were without spaces so it just looked like a string of random letters. It was impossible to make sense of them. He turned the page, and the next, and the next...

The whole address book was the same. William Anderson had used it as a diary, for a stream-of-conscious ramble maybe, and judging by some of the odd words that Brody could eventually make out... *bastard ... hate him ... hate* her ... fuckers ... the fuckers ... I don't care ... I smile ... hate them all ... *BASTARDS!*... there were some anger issues going on beneath that respectable, calm exterior he displayed to the world.

Except for the last page, that is, and the inside back cover. Both contained names, addresses, telephone numbers, also email addresses. On the left page, a different name with accompanying details filled in each section of *Name, Address, Telephone Number*. On the right, the inside back page, which was unlined, were four more, the entries not so neat, some of the words curling downward, but there was no mistaking it was the same, cursive, almost beautiful script as used to fill in his own details on the inside front cover. A total of eight entries. Eight names. A line had been drawn through half the entries. The remaining four were: Colm Preston, Senan Richardson, Shane Martin and Alan Callaghan. Next to each, in tiny writing, was a date, the oldest: 23/3/2001, and beneath, a set of initials inside heavy brackets. Brody quickly calculated that the entries scored out were all older ones. Some of the initials accompanying the entries were duplicates, (T/M) thrice, (S/W) twice, (C/B) twice, (V/N) once.

What was this all about? What secrets do you hide, Mr Anderson?

He used his phone to photograph both pages, then sat back, thinking. He leaned forward again and brought up Facebook on his computer, typed in William Anderson and pressed return. There were a lot of William Andersons in the world. He narrowed it down by work and address details, and just like that, out he popped. Brody clicked on the image, looked at the face staring blankly back at him, a face without expression. There were a couple of other photos. He seemed heavier in all of them – heavier than he did as a corpse, that is. And the hair, that was different too, darker, longer.

Something else came to mind, and Brody typed Tamara

in the search screen and pressed return. There were a lot of Tamaras in the world too, just not as many. But it didn't really matter, because by some mysterious Facebook algorithmic formula, by some computer wizardry voodoo, Facebook had recognised Brody's previous search and returned Tamara. That *Tamara*. The Tamara who was William Anderson's – or was it the other way round? – alter ego. Even from within the small, circular profile photograph from which Tamara stared back, it was unmistakeable; she was unmistakeable, her ebullience leaping from the screen, spiky black rock wig, pink eyeliner, cerise puckered lips. It was hard to imagine that the staid, morose person in William Anderson's profile photo was this person too. But he was.

Brody's desk phone rang.

'Brody.'

'Um, Brody, is that yourself...? Yes... now, let me see.'

Brody always got the impression Dr Mc Bain was reading a map when he was talking to him. Like he was wondering if he shouldn't have taken the turn off a half mile back and would the first left up ahead be best to take him back onto the route he wanted to be on. But it would be a mistake to think the assistant state pathologist was a bit doddery. He wasn't. Those that had – usually some young whippersnapper or other – were quickly brought to heel by a well-timed bark. He liked to bark, given the opportunity. Oh, and the good doctor didn't suffer fools gladly either.

'I missed you, Brody...' The doc had a refined, soft, Donegal brogue. 'Aye, well, I didn't miss you *miss* you, you understand, no, no... I mean to say you weren't there when I arrived... at the scene, that is, in the laneway.'

Brody had interrupted Doc Mc Bain only once in the twenty or so years he'd known him, when he'd been a young whippersnapper himself. 'Can't we just get there a little quicker,' he'd said, cutting off the meanderings. 'It's like you're rambling all over a map or something, taking every back road possible to get where you're going. Do you get me?'

That was when it had come to him, the map metaphor. And he still used it to this day, but kept it strictly to himself.

'Go fuck yourself, ye little runt. Do you get *me*?' the doc had snarled, his soft Donegal brogue gone, replaced by a verbal knuckleduster. 'Ye little prick ye, you uneducated piece of offal. Aye, that's what you are. Never interrupt me when I'm speaking to you. Do you get me? Do you?' Brody had wondered if the good doc had become possessed by an evil spirit. How could a Labrador become a frothing-at-the-mouth hyena in the blink of an eye like that? And then the doc had continued as if nothing had happened, his tone reverting to one of reserved, well-spoken politeness. And he had never spoken to Brody like that again. But Brody had never given him any reason to.

'I'd already left, Doc. It would have been nice to catch up.'

'I didn't mean that, Brody. I don't want to catch up with you, man. I just said you weren't there; aye, you weren't. Now, um… now… yes…' Brody could hear a keyboard being struck in the background. 'No surprises… um, no, none at all… well, I mean, aye, for him maybe, our victim, it must have been… yes… but no time to understand… what was… anyway, I do have a surprise… yes…'

Brody waited. Only when he was sure the doc had finished did he dare speak.

'And what is the surprise, if you don't mind my asking, Doc?'

'Oh, I don't mind you asking… indeed, you should ask, aye, you should ask… you're not afraid of me, Brody, are you? I sometimes get the impression that you are.'

'Yes, I am, Doc. I thought it was obvious.'

A gentle laugh came down the phone. 'That's funny, aye, that is… you're afraid of me, eh…'

Brody waited. 'And the surprise?'

'Oh yes, aye, the surprise. The thyroid cartilage, Brody.'

'The thyroid cartilage. What exactly is that?'

'Or better known as the Adam's apple, or the throat knuckle... that knobbly piece of tissue you find in a man's throat.'

'What about it?'

'Well, the victim didn't have one.'

'Didn't have one? How's that?'

'Because it'd been ripped out, Brody, that's why. Pay attention.'

BRODY THOUGHT about that for some moments after he'd finished speaking with the doc. It seemed more and more likely that someone had reacted badly – very badly indeed – to the discovery that Tamara was not all that she purported to be. But then again, if that were the case, why did the killer leave the greatest marker to Tamara's maleness in place? That curled-up rodent appendage. While the killer had ripped out his Adam's apple, he had left his dick in place. Or was that some kind of twisted joke?

Brody's phone rang, a sergeant in Wexford on a follow-up to a burglary some months before that the MCIU had been involved with. Two offenders were now charged, and the case was about to go to court. The sergeant wanted to thank Brody for his help. When he finished the call, it was almost eight o'clock. He yawned and stood, pulled on his jacket.

Tomorrow was another day.

15

The Old Man had been gifted a bottle of single malt and made the mistake of opening it for a quick snifter before walking Riley. Well, it was so good he'd had a second snifter, and then, well, his favourite armchair looked so inviting he just had to sit down and have one more, a good three fingers this time, no more of those little snifters, those were for wimps. When that was gone, well, his eyes grew so heavy that he just had to close them, just for a minute, mind, and a little later, alerted by the sound of his snoring, that was how Alice found him. Mrs Maguire then looked at Riley sitting forlornly in front of her sleeping husband like a crestfallen child. Then she looked at the open bottle of whiskey standing next to its fancy box.

Which explained why Alice Maguire was walking Riley now and not the Old Man, along the same streets he'd walked along the night before, heading for the park.

Willow had never met Alice, he didn't know who she was, but he recognised Riley and put two and two together. As he walked towards her, he felt like a puppeteer with a new puppet, and there was that rush of power, the ultimate power, the power over life and death. There was a poo bag tied to the handle of the dog lead, he noticed. The Old Man hadn't any that he could remember when he met him the night before. But then again, that didn't surprise him. Chief Superintendent Maguire didn't do picking up dog shit, he imagined. Little Riley could squat anywhere she wanted to – just not in his own back garden, he'd bet. That's the filth for you, a law unto themselves. But the day of final reckoning was coming for sure, and he was looking forward to it.

He smiled as the woman, who he guessed was Maguire's wife, drew level with him, but she was paying him no attention. Riley was, however, wagging her tail and straining on her lead to try to reach him. The man tugged on a puppet string. 'Hello there, Riley. Well, aren't you the cutest?'

That got her attention. She stopped, looked quizzically at him.

'You know Riley?'

'Yes.' He stepped closer and bent down, tickled Riley behind an ear, straightened again. The woman pulled back on the lead to stop Riley jumping up on him. 'I met her last night, with your husband, well, I presume it was your husband who was walking her.'

'Oh, yes... yes, it was.'

They stood looking at one another silently. He smiled.

'He walks the dog most evenings.' A statement, not a question. Give her something else to think about. 'Well, you tell Tom I said hello.'

He started to walk on.

'Wait.'

He turned back. 'Yes?'

'You know his name?'

'Of course.'

'So you really do know him. How? And how come I don't know about you?'

'I've been away for a long time; maybe that's it. Now, I must be off.'

'One more question. What is your name? I can tell him who's asking for him.'

'Yes, silly me. Of course. My name's Daniel Willow.'

'Willow?'

'As in the tree, two l's.'

'Your name doesn't ring a bell.'

'No, but it will with your husband. It will ring a bell with him alright, my dear. Goodnight.'

When she got home, Tom was watching TV, reclined in his armchair, the bottle of single malt sitting back on the dresser, cap in place, the same amount in it as when she'd left.

'You never mentioned,' she said, unclipping Riley, who ran across to him and jumped onto his lap.

The Old Man didn't care that she was wet. Alice, who normally did, didn't now either.

'Didn't mention what?'

'That you met anyone on your walk last night, that is.'

'What did you say?'

'Turn that bloody thing down, will you?'

He did.

'I said you never mentioned meeting anyone on your walk last night. I met a man who said he met you by the park last night.'

'I didn't meet anyone last... oh wait, yes, there was somebody alright, he said hello, he liked Riley, but it's a stretch to say I met him. We just exchanged pleasantries. He was a stranger. A bearded fella, that right?'

'Yes, it was white down one side.'

'That's him.'

'He said to give you his regards.'

'He did?'

'Yes.'

'Bit odd, don't know the fella from a hole in the wall.'

'He seems to think that you do. I asked his name.'

'You did? Well, what is it?'

'Um, Daniel Willow.'

The TV remote fell from the Old Man's hand.

'What did you say?'

'You've gone as white as a ghost. Daniel Willow.'

'Are you sure?'

'Yes, of course, Willow, two *l*'s, as in the tree.'

'That's what I thought.'

An uneasy silence settled between them, shattered by the sound of the telephone ringing in the hallway. Alice went to answer it. He listened. 'Hello... I said hello... Who's there... Hello... Look, I know you're there, I can hear you breathing... One last time, who is this?'

She hung up and came back into the room.

'I've been getting phone calls like that too,' he said softly. 'In work.'

'You never mentioned.'

'I thought nothing of it. Par for the course in my line... but this may be different.'

She gave him a searching look. 'What do you mean?'

He pointed to the settee. 'Sit, Alice. I need to tell you about Daniel Willow.'

16

On his way home, Brody picked up a takeout meal from the Imperial Dragon restaurant. He sat at his kitchen table and ate it straight out of the container, washed down with a bottle of Heineken. When he'd finished, he placed the empty packaging into the recycling bin and went into the living room. It was circa 1970s, little changed since the last occupant, Mrs Keane, had lived here. He sat on her old, floral-pattern cloth sofa, placed his laptop on his knees and opened it, went onto YouTube and brought up the 1974 fight between Muhammad Ali and George Foreman, the Rumble in the Jungle as it was better known, direct from Kinshasa, Zaire. This was how he sometimes relaxed, those times when he wanted to clear his mind, to see things a little clearer again.

The Rumble in the Jungle was arguably the greatest sporting event of the twentieth century. Ali, the underdog and former heavyweight champion, against Foreman, the reigning and undefeated champion. Brody was a boxer, winner of the International Police Brotherhood middleweight title belt. He could have gone professional.

Instead, after winning the title, he'd retired from competition. He knew he was unlikely to ever win such an accolade again – not as an amateur anyway. And he had no interest in turning professional. That was never on the cards for him. So he'd retired.

He was about to press play when his mobile rang. It was in the kitchen. He waited, hoping it would stop. It didn't. He sighed, got up, went in and snatched it up from the table, not bothering to check the screen. He pressed it to his ear.

'Hello, Brody.'

'Well, you took your time.' The voice was female, bright, friendly... playful even. 'A girl would think you didn't want to talk to her.' He pulled the phone from his ear, checked the number, put it back again. No, it wasn't one he recognised.

'Hands up. You've got me. Who is this? Maybe you've got a wrong number?'

'Jack Brody, detective sergeant. That you?'

'That's me.'

'No. I haven't got the wrong number... maybe you wish I had. Aw, Jack, I'm disappointed. You don't remember?' She laughed. 'It's OK, I'm not disappointed, not really... well, maybe just a little bit. It was a while ago after all, and we met only very briefly... nothing coming back to you yet?'

There wasn't. He said nothing.

She laughed again. It was a nice laugh.

'I'll give you a clue, Jack, will I? Dublin Castle.'

He thought about it, and from a fog of memory it emerged. A coffee morning a couple of months back, a public relations exercise between the City Council and An Gárda Síochána. Jack had said a few words on the links between low-level crime and the serious crime he dealt with every day. He finished with what he thought were a couple of good one-liners, that the career criminal of tomorrow is the youth on a mountain bike snatching phones today, and the eleven-year-old smashing windows because he thinks it's great craic and posting the videos on TikTok. That had got him a round of applause.

She worked in the youth affairs department of the City Council, had approached him afterwards, said she liked what he'd had to say, that he'd shown a sensitivity she found lacking in most senior police officers. Less of the senior, he'd laughed. No, seriously, those officers all say the right things, but half of them don't mean a word; they're all on career ladders, only saying what they think people want to hear. He'd taken a couple of cups from the stack on the cloth-covered trestle table and filled them with coffee from the urn. They'd chatted for maybe half an hour. He'd liked talking to her. Then when they were saying their goodbyes, he'd asked her for her telephone number. I'll give you mine if you give me yours, she'd laughed. That laugh. He loved that laugh. And that was what they did, exchanged numbers. That was the last time they'd spoken, until now, that is. In fact, he'd pushed her from his mind. Maybe because he wasn't ready; maybe because he felt guilty. Maybe, who knows. He didn't know. But he'd pushed her from his mind.

And now, for the life of him, he couldn't remember her name. But what he could remember was her long, straight, auburn hair; her open, smiling face; and her big, green, beautiful eyes.

'I remember it now,' he said. 'Dublin Castle…'

And then it came to him. Her name.

'Ashling Nolan, right?'

She laughed again, but softer this time, a lot softer, a laugh that petered out to silence.

'I'm glad,' she said, 'that you remembered my name, because if you hadn't, I would have been disappointed. And I think I would be hanging up right now.'

'I'm glad too,' he said, and he was.

'The truth is, Jack...'

'Yes, the truth is?'

'Well, the truth is I dropped my sister off at the airport earlier. I'm on my way home. I picked up a bottle of wine. I was going to have a glass later and unwind a little. But then I changed my mind. I took a detour. I didn't go home.'

'Where did you go?'

'I came here. You told me you lived on Bishop's Road. I worked it out. I'm parked right outside.'

ASHLING NOLAN WAS DRESSED in a navy-blue tie waist jumpsuit, with flared legs and chiffon sleeves, and low, chunky-heeled black shoes. Her perfume filled the room. Brody was acutely aware of it. He was also acutely aware of the photograph of Caoimhe on the mantelpiece above the empty fireplace, in front of which, on either side, he and his visitor sat in armchairs that, together with the sofa, formed a three-piece set. Ashling had hardly touched her wine. Understandable, she was driving, after all. She sat sideways in her seat, one long leg draped over the other, her foot swinging like a slow pendulum. She was speaking, but Brody barely heard a word she was saying. He tried to, but it was useless, his own voice drowned everything out, the voice inside his head, that is, chattering away with a thousand questions, but all, essentially, asking the same thing... *Why is this beautiful woman here?*

He suddenly realised her lips were no longer moving, and that her big, beautiful eyes were looking at him, still and deep. The ceaseless chatter in his head ceased.

'You haven't been listening to a word I said, have you?'

'That's not true,' he lied. 'I heard you just now.'

She smiled and pointed to the photo on the mantelpiece. 'Caoimhe?'

'Yes. How did you know?'

'You really think I didn't ask around and do my homework? That I'd ring you up, not knowing your' – she paused – '*status*? And I'm sorry, I truly am; that can't have been easy. I met Caoimhe once.'

'You did?'

'Yes, I did. Something or other. We were introduced very briefly. I was told she was engaged to a guard at Pearse Street. I remember how happy she seemed. Her eyes, they sparkled; she seemed, just... so happy.'

Brody said nothing for a moment. 'No,' he said then, 'it wasn't easy; it's not easy.'

Those big eyes stared at him; he felt like there was an ocean in there, the currents shifting and the swells rising and falling, on and on as if forever but meeting eventually, somewhere far over the horizon, on a distant shore.

They talked. They talked about a lot of things, world affairs, sports, work. She told him she was moving from youth affairs, taking up a new role in corporate governance, *sounds boring, but it's really not, it's very exciting*. Jack didn't talk so much about work. More than anything, he was just happy to listen, to watch. He was good at both. Jack liked her company, and she seemed to like his too. He thought how nice it was, this surprise, just how nice it was. Three-quarters of an hour had passed, and she was standing again, placing her glass – still half full – onto the mantelpiece.

'I'll be off, Jack. Like I said, I just thought I'd drop by. I hope it wasn't a mistake. Next time, I'll leave it to you. If you want to, that is.'

He got to his feet and stood awkwardly, looking into those endless oceans that were her eyes. He leaned forward slightly, and so did she. They kissed, soft and gentle. From the corner of his eye, he could see Caoimhe's photograph watching on. But Jack didn't feel the guilt he thought he might. Even as

Ashling's lips remained on his, even as they gently wrapped their arms around each other. He heard a voice, a voice that only he could hear, Caoimhe's, telling him, *It's alright; don't be afraid, Jack; it's alright.*

They kissed harder, pressing into each other. But then... Ashling pulled back.

'Whoo,' she said, 'this is...'

'Too much? I'm sorry.'

'No, Jack, in some ways, it's not enough. In some ways it's not nearly enough. Just... just... let's take it a little... slower, OK?'

Brody found he was glad she'd said that.

'Probably a good idea,' he agreed.

'Anyway, I didn't bring my toothbrush.' She laughed. 'Joking, Jack, only joking. Anyway, I've got to go.' She stepped closer again. 'I'm happy I came here this evening, Jack.' Once more she laughed. 'I am. Are you?' She kissed him again. 'Maybe we can do something soon. You can ring me. That OK?'

'Yes, that's OK.'

And then she was gone.

Jack smiled and shook his head, looking about the empty room. Had she really been here at all?

17

Quinn was once again parked outside a house, number 214 Childers Road, Rathgar.

He'd been there two hours now, ever since returning from the Cabin. That had been a waste of time. The volunteers were clearing tables when he'd arrived, mainly sandwich crusts and overflowing ashtrays, and gathering up the scattered decks of playing cards, wrapping them in elastic bands and placing them into a cardboard box. A couple of the last stragglers were leaving, clutching free bags of staples.

'Would you like one?' the small, frail man in the blue nylon housecoat and John Lennon glasses had asked. He was holding a catering pack of table salt in one hand. 'There's a couple left; no loaves though, we can put a couple of bread rolls in instead.' He smiled. 'I'm Brother Kevin.' He extended his free hand, and they shook.

'No, thank you, Brother. I don't want anything. I'm actually looking for somebody.'

'You're looking for someone. In that case, you'll have to tell me who you're looking for, and who *you* are?'

'Oh, excuse me.' Quinn pulled his ID wallet from a pocket, opened it and held it up for inspection.

'Unfortunately, we get your people in here looking for people all the time. But I don't remember ever having met you before.' Brother Kevin placed the pack of salt onto the ground.

Quinn had heard of Brother Kevin. Everyone had. A living saint was what he was most commonly referred to. The Cabin had been established by him, a place for the homeless and those living on the margins of society to spend some time during the day so they didn't have to endlessly roam the streets. Brother Kevin had dedicated his life to the place.

'It says National Economic Crime Bureau on your ID. That's a new one on me. I don't think we've ever had anyone from the fraud squad in here before. Would you mind?' He nodded to the pack of salt. 'I find it difficult to bend.'

'Of course.' Quinn picked it up and followed Brother Kevin to a table, salt cellars on it with their tops screwed off.

'Who exactly are you looking for? And you can put the box down there.' He pointed, and Quinn placed the box onto the table. Brother Kevin began pulling the flaps open, but Quinn could see his fingers were swollen, and he was having difficulty.

'Here, let me.'

'Thank you. I suffer from arthritis.'

Quinn slid his hand under one flap and pulled it open with ease. He did the same with the other.

'I'm looking for JJ Harris. Have you heard of him?'

'Oh, yes. I have.'

Without prompting, Quinn picked up a salt cellar and a plastic scoop and began filling the salt cellar with it. 'You want me to put the tops on these when I finish?'

'No, that's fine. Yes, I know JJ; he does come in here.'

'Has he been in this evening?' Quinn filled the salt cellar and pushed it to the side, started on another.

'This is to do with the body in the lane, isn't it? It was on the news. And I heard he fled from the guards when they went to his flat to arrest him... now, I didn't hear that on the news. I heard it in here; it was all the talk.'

It went through Quinn again, that searing, visceral humiliation. His cheeks burned with it... *It wasn't so bad that he almost killed me, no, that wasn't so bad; what was so bad was that he made me look like a fool, a moron, an imbecile, that's what he did. And no one other than me can make this right. Because if I don't make this right, my career takes the scenic route. I can't have that. I won't have that. Not me. I'm on a fast-track. I'm on my way to the top. So I'm the only one who can make this right. Yes, only me.*

'Has he been in?'

'No, I haven't seen him. I suspect he'll be lying low, don't you?'

'Have you any idea where he might be, Brother?'

'Well, no, I don't think there's many places for him to go to, not really, except his home. He has a home to go to now, so I'd imagine he'll go there.'

'Didn't he always have a home?'

'No. He lived in hostels for a time when he first came out of prison, the last time, that is. He's not the luckiest of people is JJ; it seems no matter how many steps forward he takes, he takes twice as many back... hapless is what I would call him. Yes, hapless. JJ, God bless him.'

Quinn considered he should really be grateful for the fact JJ was so hapless. Because if he wasn't, then right now, the odds were, Quinn would probably be dead.

. . .

QUINN WOKE with a pain in his shoulder from having been lying on his side on the reclined car seat. He hadn't intended to lie on his side; he hadn't intended to fall asleep. But he had done both. That was less than a half hour ago, and now he was awake again. He brought the seat back into its upright position and began massaging his shoulder. His humiliation was still acute, but now his need for a warm bed and a good night's sleep was becoming more acute – for the time being, that is. He checked the green neon dial on the dashboard clock; it read 11:15. He knew it was time to go home. He knew it was time to be logical about this whole business. He knew it was time to go to Jack Brody and ask for forgiveness, ask for his help in making things right again. In short, to swallow his pride. And he knew it was only a matter of time before another zombie showed up knocking on his window.

He looked to 214 Childers Road one last time and wrapped his hand around the ignition key. He was about to turn it when he blinked. The light had just come on in JJ Harris's flat.

Now it was too late, he realised, for logic, that is. Ironic really, that just when he realised that what he couldn't, shouldn't, and mustn't do, he now *had* no choice but to do. Because he was on his own... or was he? He felt it rush through him again, almost lustful, a desperation to make things right, to vindicate himself, to restore respect, to become, once more, the man on a fast-track, the person his peers looked up to.

Quinn was about to open the car door when a voice screamed in his head, *Nooooo*.

He plopped back onto his seat, squeezing his eyes shut, pressing his head back into the headrest.

What. To. Do.

This wasn't stand-off fraud detection data mining any longer, or algorithm utilisation, or anything else he was used to. Sitting at a computer for hours on end in an office alone, peeling back the complex layers of a fraud and digitally ferreting through endless mazes until finally, *bingo*, he found the golden egg and emerged triumphant. No, this process, the sitting for endless hours alone in a freezing car, was different. But he could still emerge a hero. Because that was what he was used to.

Yes, this was very different, and he had to be careful. A computer terminal couldn't shoot you, after all. But inside that flat when he'd stupidly knocked on the door there had been a man with a shotgun. A real shotgun. A shotgun that had blown a hole in a door and almost his head. In that world, if you weren't careful, you didn't get to live very long. No.

Then the answer to what he had to do came to him. And the answer was plain and simple.

Quinn reached for his phone and rang Brody.

'Yes,' Brody said, picking up. He listened to Quinn and said, 'Stay right there. Don't move. I'll be right over.' He hung up and made another call, requested an Armed Response Unit, told them the location and rushed out the door.

Quinn was sitting in his car just like he said he would. He opened the door when he saw Brody approach and got out, stood on the pavement. 'We'd need to be quick. The light's still on.'

'Keep your voice down.'

From behind Brody, Quinn saw what looked like two shadows flitter into the side of the pavement against the railings, becoming lost in the darkness beneath the overhang of trees.

'Who're they?'

'I said keep your voice down.'

'Sorry.'

'ARU. And they knew you were here. Been keeping an eye on the place. They spotted you.'

'They did?'

'They did. I don't have time to get into it. But good info, thanks. Now, you just wait here. We'll be back.'

'No.'

'What'd you mean, no?'

'I'm going in too. Please. There's a way. From the side. I checked. The door's no good, one push... please.'

Brody thought about it for just one second.

Out of the darkness stepped one of the shadows, a rectangular motif on his helmet identifying him as a member of an Armed Response Unit, an automatic carbine slung across his chest. 'He already messed up once. Not him. We don't need any problems.'

'I won't mess up again.' Quinn stared at Brody.

'I don't have time for this,' Brody said.

'I need to do this. Please. Let me. Give me a chance.'

'OK. But like a limpet, you stick to me. Understand?'

'I understand.'

The shadow grumbled, but Brody ignored him.

'Let's go,' he said.

A bus trundling past masked the sound of their approach across the gravel. Quinn pointed to the steps leading down to the basement door. The shadows took the lead and descended, weapon stocks against shoulders, seeing everything through their weapons' sights, the door at the bottom springing open with nothing more than a nudge from a booted foot. Helmet torches lit up the room like daylight. A mat was in the centre of the room, the outline of a curled body inside a sleeping bag lying on it, beside it a backpack. The room was deathly silent. They looked at the sleeping bag. No movement. Silence might not be all that was dead.

A muffled cough came from inside the sleeping bag then, as the body twisted, coughed again, and a head appeared out the top, hands over its ears, a pair of dazed eyes reflecting back at them in the light of the torches. Brody recognised the face, Christy something-or-other, a junkie and low-level dealer. He opened his mouth to speak, his head a perfect replica of Munch's *The Scream*. The first shadow placed a finger to her mouth, and Christy something-or-other closed his again. As they passed by towards the steps up to the hall on the other side, the body moved like smoke out of the sleeping bag, gathered up its belongings and wafted out the door, disappearing into the night.

They went into the hall and started up the stairs. Music was playing somewhere, not loud enough to drown out the sounds of the old staircase timbers creaking beneath the weight of the four mules. A baby cried, but just once, like it had woken from a dream and had been immediately comforted by the sight of its mother's face lying next to it.

They reached the landing and stopped. Light was seeping out along the edge of the boarded-up entrance to JJ Harris's flat, and flooding through a section at the bottom where a plywood panel had been pulled from the wall.

The lead ARU hand signalled to Brody and Quinn to remain where they were. Both ARUs then approached the door. The lead one turned, did not pause or hesitate, and in one fluid movement kicked the plywood panels in. 'ARMED GARDAI. DON'T MOVE. DON'T MOVE.'

And then...

Silence.

Brody waited... it seemed like forever before he heard the word, 'CLEAR.'

She was on her knees when he and Quinn went in. Not because she was being arrested and had been instructed to adopt this pose. No, she was on her knees because she was holding a corner section of floorboard in her hands. Brody walked over to find out why. He didn't have to bend too far down to see. Between the floor joists underneath where the floorboard had been lay a scattering of street bags of skunk. He turned his attention to the girl. But she was looking to somewhere else behind him.

'Hi, Paul,' she said.

'Hi, Susie.'

Brody looked at Quinn. 'You know each other?'

18

Early the next morning, a SOCO officer arrived at The Elms, Ballsbridge, where Considine was waiting for her. The SOCO officer was Jennifer Flaherty, whom Considine had met a few times in the past. Considine had heard her name mentioned recently on the gossip vine, that she'd newly separated from her husband. But Flaherty showed no signs of being upset about this. She was jovial and smiling, probably either a very good actress, or maybe she really was enjoying her new-found freedom like she'd said she was. They exchanged pleasantries and went inside, where Flaherty immediately set about her work.

There were good prints everywhere: on the wardrobe doors, the bedside lamp and the bedside locker, the worktop in the kitchen, the handles on the cupboards above it, on the cutlery drawer, and on the cutlery inside the drawer, on the electric kettle, on the array of make-ups in the bathroom... everywhere. In fact, the SOCO was spoilt for choice. And they were all good-quality prints too, well preserved and dry within the cool, temperate environs of William Anderson's studio flat.

After she'd lifted the prints, the SOCO used her scalpel to take scrapings from the tufts of the electric toothbrush in the bathroom, tipping the dandruff-like flakes carefully into a glass vial. She was glad there was an electric toothbrush. On a recent job she'd had to take scrapings from a toilet brush.

When she'd finished, she spent some moments transferring a print sample from the clear tape used to lift it into her mobile scanner. She pressed send, and a spinning wheel icon appeared on the small screen. It would compare the print with the fingerprint taken from the victim in the laneway. Considine watched everything silently from the doorway of the room. She knew the SOCO would not be able to compare a print like this from a scene if it weren't of such high quality. The scanner pinged, a surprisingly loud sound for so small a machine. But then again, these were usually used at roadsides, so they had to be loud. The SOCO brought the scanner close to her face, peering at the screen. Considine waited, feeling herself tense, her heart rate kicking up a gear. It seemed to take forever, the seconds dripping by like cold molasses on a summer's day.

Eventually the SOCO spoke.

'We have a result...'

'WHERE'S HE NOW?' the Old Man barked, tapping his fingers on the desk.

'Outside. But...'

'But what?' The tapping grew louder.

'He rang me. He wasn't going in alone. He knew. He'd learnt. He didn't go in alone. Instead, he rang me.'

'I don't care if he learnt. He learnt too late.' *Tap, tap, tap.*

'Boss...'

'No, Jack, I don't want him. Send him back to where he came from.' *Tap, tap, tap.*

'Boss...'

'What, for God's sake?'

'Everything alright with you?' Brody asked.

'What kind of question is that?'

'Just you seem a little...'

'Just a little what?'

'I don't know, boss, you tell me.'

'Nothing's wrong with me. And that's just the way I like it. Don't try to change the subject.'

The Old Man look tired, black rings like half tyres beneath his eyes.

'OK,' Brody said, 'then just give the lad a chance. You remember what you told me when I joined the unit?'

'That wasn't so long ago, Jack, remember, so don't go all sagey on me.' *Tap, tap, tap.*

'You told me our strengths were only as good as the sum total of our weaknesses, that we were all learning on this job... even you. Something like that anyway. You remember?'

'Well, it sounds like you don't fully remember yourself. So how do you expect me to?' *Tap, tap.*

'I remember the principle of it,' Brody said. 'That's what matters.'

'You do, do you? And I said that? Or something like it?' *Tap.*

'Yes.'

The Old Man fell silent. The tapping stopped. His face no longer resembled a tomato.

'OK,' he said. 'OK. But one more fuck-up and he's gone.' His voice was calmer. 'The appeal threw up a name, is that right? A William Anderson?'

'Yes, it did. But we don't know if it's him, not for certain.'

'And when will you know?'

Brody's phone started ringing in his trouser pocket.

'Sorry, boss.' He took it out. 'It's Considine; she's at Anderson's address.' He pressed the phone to his ear. 'Yes?'

He listened, then covered the bottom of the phone with his hand and looked at the Old Man. 'I know now, boss. It's Nicola; she's just confirmed. It's him. The body in the lane. It's William Anderson.' The Old Man nodded. Brody uncovered the phone and spoke. 'Good work, Nicola. Dig into William Anderson's employee file, find his next of kin and have them notified. Thanks.' Brody put the phone back into his pocket and started getting to his feet.

'Wait,' the Old Man said.

Brody settled back into his chair again.

'Boss?'

The Old Man said nothing for a moment, then: 'Brody, someone wants to kill me.'

'Just so I'm clear,' Brody said after the Old Man had finished speaking, 'this Daniel Willow, with two *l*'s, as in the tree, went down for thirty-five years for killing four people, a couple and their two children in an arson attack on a… what? A holiday home.'

The Old Man nodded. 'Yes, in Seabay.'

'And because? I didn't catch that part.'

'That's because I didn't tell you. He never said.'

'And it was considered an accident initially, is that right? But you demanded a more thorough forensic examination?'

'Yes,' the Old Man said, 'back then they didn't have what they have now. So we had to bring in a specialist from the UK. There was resistance to that, the expense, but I stuck to my guns. Willow was renting a holiday home next door to this family. No one thought he was the type to do such a thing, newly married, a gorgeous wife. But I had an instinct. And I was right. I got the bastard.'

'And he never forgot it.'

'Seems that way. He's been released on parole from the Midlands Prison, although no one told me.'

'And you're sure it's him?'

'Oh, I'm sure it's him. I've had a look at the release photo from the prison. I didn't recognise him the other evening, what with the beard, and it's been over thirty-five years...'

'When was he released?'

'The day before yesterday.'

'He's gotten straight into it, then, hasn't he?'

'He's had nothing else to think about all this time.'

'But,' Brody said, 'if he's on probation, you can have him shipped right back inside, yes?'

The Old Man shook his head. 'It's not that easy. I can't leave myself open to the possibility of pursuing a personal vendetta. It'll take more than my word to do that, have to catch him actually at something...'

Brody raised an eyebrow.

'That could be arranged.'

'I'll pretend I didn't hear that.' But the Old Man didn't sound too sure.

'Well, what, then?'

'I've been given protection, a Special Detective Unit detail assigned to me, but it only kicks in when I leave the Phoenix Park. I've told Alice to stay home and not open the front door for anyone; it doesn't extend to her... I don't want anyone else knowing about this, Brody.'

'Of course.'

The Old Man looked past him towards the window.

'He's fooled them all,' he said, 'probation board, counsellors, even the bloody governor. A leopard never changes its spots.' He looked back again. 'I'm worried, Jack.'

The Old Man didn't need to tell him that. Brody already knew.

19

Brody mulled over what the Old Man had said back in his office, and felt a little helpless. What to do? Nothing, that's what. Not until the Old Man told him what to do. He took a breath, focusing his mind on what he needed to do right now. And that was to find William Anderson's killer. Simple as.

He glanced at his watch, just gone half past ten, a time, he considered, when working people might be thinking of having a coffee break. The first name up on Anderson's address book was Colm Preston. Brody picked up the phone and dialled the number. It started to ring. He was relieved. It was a real number. Brody was relieved again when it was answered, a male voice saying, 'Hello.' It was a real person.

'Is this Colm Preston?'

'It is Colm Preston. How can I help you? Who's this?'

The voice was so high pitched it was practically singing.

'My name is Detective Sergeant Jack Brody of the Major Crimes Investiga...'

'What? What?' The voice dropped like it had been shot out of the sky, hitting the ground and fragmenting into a thousand frightened pieces, cutting him off. 'Major Crimes. What's this about?'

'I was going to say, the Major Crimes Investigation Unit. Are you free to talk, Mr Preston?'

'Major Crimes...? How did you get my number? What's this about, I asked?'

'We're investigating a murder, Mr Preston.'

'Jesus Christ. A what? A murder? What's that got to do with me?'

'Well, I don't know. The victim's name is William Anderson. Do you know a William Anderson, Mr Preston?'

'I don't know any William Anderson. Why would I know him? William who? Anderson? Why? Why are you ringing me about this?'

'Your name is in his address book, Mr Preston, that's why.'

'It is?'

'It is. And your telephone number. And your address. And your email address.'

'They are?'

'They are.'

Preston fell silent; there wasn't even the sound of static on the line.

'Mr Preston, are you still there?'

'Y-yes. I'm still here. Of course I'm still here. Look, I can't talk right now.'

'When can you talk?'

'I can meet you. I work in the Docklands.'

'The Docklands?'

'Why'd you say it like that? Do you know me? What's your name again?'

'Detective Sergeant Jack Brody, of the Major Cr–'

'The Major Crimes Investigation Unit. You told me that already. I heard. I'm not deaf. And how do I know you really are who you say you are? How do I know that? I only have your word for it. How do I know this isn't all just a scam?'

'You want to ring me back? Did my number show up on your phone when I rang just now?'

'It did, yes.'

'It's also in the Garda directory. You can check.'

'I don't want to ring you back. OK, OK. In the Docklands, there's a food van, a Citroen panel thing...'

'I know it.'

'You do? OK. Half an hour, OK? I'll park near it. I'm driving a lime green BMW.'

'Fine, Mr Preston. I'll see you there.'

He hung up and thought, a lime green BMW, shouldn't be hard to spot.

Brody left his office and walked down the hall to the unit room. Voyle was in there along with Martin Sheahan and Quinn. Sheahan's desk was next to Voyle's, while Quinn sat at his temporary desk in a corner on the other side of the room. Brody had the feeling it might as well have been on the other side of the world. He'd told Quinn he could have the day off if he wanted, but he didn't. Voyle was talking on the phone and didn't sound happy... 'The National Bureau of Criminal Investigation is conducting an investigation into stolen plant equipment in your region... well, I don't know... perhaps you'd need to look at that yourself, sir... if you want to take it like that, then you can. I have no control over how you feel, none... yes, I do happen to know your rank, Superintendent Quigley, yes... Mine? No problem. Detective Garda Voyle, Stephen James, number seven five six one.'

Voyle slammed the phone down, glanced at Brody. 'Boss.'

Brody walked over to him, held out a page from a notepad. 'This will take your mind off things. Name and number from a list in William Anderson's address book. Take Marty and pay this man a visit. Got that, Steve?'

Voyle took the piece of paper. 'Got that,' he said, looking at it. 'Senan Richardson, hm.'

Brody caught Paul Quinn's eye. 'You. With me. Now.'

They went into the car park, walked to an unmarked and sat in. Brody started the engine.

'We're going to see a Colm Preston. His name is in William Anderson's address book.'

Quinn nodded, but didn't say a word.

BRODY AND QUINN drove from Garda HQ along the quays, passing the Guinness brewery on the other side of the river, for which a thirty-four-year-old Arthur Guinness had signed a nine-thousand-year lease in 1759. Now, while there was still almost nine thousand years to run on said lease, Arthur Guinness had been dead for almost three hundred years. Brody always considered time a relative thing. The tail end of a tropical storm had turned the sky a strange pumpkin orange, tapering to yellow along the edges. The Liffey was high, signalling the tide was in, but the wind was strong enough to whitecap the surface and push it back out again.

Dublin is an old city, founded by wild Nordic raiders who first began by fortifying ditches and clearing mud from the riverbanks so that they could tie up their boats. A primitive form of dredging. Thus Dublin began as a wild outcrop on a wild island nation isolated in the cold waters of the Atlantic on the furthest outreaches of what would become known as Europe. An island that would never be considered part of any New World, an island destined to always be part of an Old World. Modern Dublin tries its best; it tries to be sassy and invigorating and different, tries to mix the old and the new into something special. But Dublin's cast has already been set, and it seems to be merely biding its time, tolerating its cloak of modernity, but waiting for the day when, eventually, it can throw it all off again and go back to what it always had been. Because Dublin has its own beauty, its own indelible character and charm. Dublin demands to be loved for what it is, not for what it might be.

Quinn didn't say a word on the drive over. Not a word. And Brody was comfortable with that. But he knew, however, that Quinn wasn't. He fidgeted a lot. He scratched a lot, usually at his head or the underside of his chin or his armpit. He looked out the window a lot. And he turned to Brody a lot, like he was waiting for something, expecting something, but didn't know what.

A sliver of white mixed in with the orange of the sky, and the sun broke through, turning the cityscape outside into a picture-perfect postcard.

Brody pulled into the same Docklands car park he had pulled into the evening before and cut the engine. He turned to Quinn.

'How are you?'

The lad stopped fidgeting, sitting still in his seat. He slowly turned and looked at Brody, like what he had been waiting for had arrived, but it wasn't what he had been expecting.

'This is doing you no good,' Brody said. 'Or me. Or anybody else. Let it go. Put it behind you. It's over.'

The lad spoke. 'I can't. It's not... over, that is. He's still out there. No one else will put it behind them either. They'll remember.'

'You're not that important. They'll forget.'

'They won't. They hold on to this stuff like I owe them money. I've seen it... Sergeant Jennings, you remember him?'

Everyone remembered Sergeant Jennings. He'd made a mistake. A raid on a house and an officer had been shot. Luckily, the officer hadn't been killed, but Jennings, who was responsible for coordinating the operation, had. He shot himself afterwards with his service revolver. There were many other stories just like that one.

'You're not Sergeant Jennings.'

'I feel like I am.'

Oh, shit, Brody thought.

THEY REVERTED to silence until a lime green BMW turned into the car park. Brody and Quinn, sitting in their mud-splattered Hyundai saloon minus its hubcaps, stuck out like sore thumbs, or two plainclothes cops sitting in an unmarked. The BMW pulled alongside them. Ordinarily, a car like that might imply its owner had a few bob to spare. But this BMW's prestige lay merely in its name. As for the rest of it, the car would be instantly relegated to the bargain corner of any dealership it was offered for sale in. And the man who got out looked like the car itself, like he had seen better days. He wore his raincoat open with a blue suit underneath, and it billowed in the wind, revealing the suit fabric to be shiny from wear. The raincoat itself was scuffed at the cuffs, and one of the shoulder lapels was missing. Colm Preston appeared to be mid-fifties, not very tall, heavy about the middle and bald on top, wearing black, thick-rimmed glasses. Brody raised a hand and indicated to the rear of the Hyundai. Preston didn't move. Brody sighed, took out his ID wallet, held it open against the door glass.

Preston got in, Brody twisting round in his seat to look back at him. Up close, Brody realised he had made a mistake in calculating his age, he wasn't as old as he'd thought, and shaved a decade off. It wasn't raining, but Colm Preston's skin glistened, and his breathing was fast.

'Mr Preston?'

He nodded once, a quick, nervous gesture, and leaned forward, folding his arms around his knees.

'I'm Jack Brody, detective sergeant, and this is Paul Quinn, detective Garda.'

'Is this to do with that body found in the lane?' Preston panted. 'It's all over the news.'

'Yes,' Brody said, 'it is.'

'And my name was in this person's address book, is that right?' He took a gulp of air, as if trying to calm his breathing. 'This William Anderson's?'

'I'd prefer to ask the questions, Mr Preston. But yes, that is correct.'

'There could be any reason for that.' Still panting, but his efforts at controlling his breathing were beginning to work. 'I'm in sales, you see, office equipment, furniture too.' He stopped and took another gulp of air, continued, 'We also do a line in indelible marker pens. The kids love them. Maybe he bought something from me.'

'Maybe,' Brody said, 'or it could just be a coincidence that he worked in the Docklands too. A small world, as they say.'

'What's that supposed to mean? A lot of people work in the Docklands.' Another gulp of air. 'Thousands and thousands.'

'Yes,' Brody said. 'Anyway, William Anderson had another name...' He paused, watching Preston's face carefully for any reaction as he said it. 'Tamara.'

Brody didn't need to study his face carefully to see the reaction. It was immediate and undeniable. Preston couldn't even speak. He opened his mouth and stared, the colour draining from his cheeks like water down a sinkhole. But he'd stopped panting. In fact, Brody was certain the man had stopped breathing. For a moment he stayed that way until his mouth opened wide and he sucked in air with a low swishing sound.

'Tamara. Dead?'

Brody nodded. 'Yes, well, William Anderson is dead.'

Preston looked away, cocking his head to one side like a confused canine. Then he turned back to Brody. His breathing had regulated; his expression was one of an intense, all-consuming study.

'But... that can't be. No, that can't be at all...'

Brody realised the man wasn't talking to him, he was talking to himself, trying to work it out.

'Tamara,' he said, '*was* a woman, you see. This has to be some kind of mix-up... is it?'

Brody glanced to Quinn. The lad was sitting twisted in his seat too, his legs folded beneath him, his back leaning against the door, eyes pathetic and mournful. But the lad took his cue.

'I'm afraid not, Mr Preston. We've identified Tamara as William Anderson through items of clothing and photographic analysis. Tamara never existed. William Anderson existed.'

Brody was impressed.

Preston flopped back into his seat with such force that the car shook. 'Oh Jesus H Christ. Oh no. *Oh Jesus H Christ.*'

'How did you come to know the person you believed to be Tamara?' Brody asked, because he couldn't ask how Preston had come to know William Anderson. Preston didn't know William Anderson. He only knew Tamara. You had to concentrate.

Preston turned away and looked out the window. Outside, the wind had stopped blowing, the sky orange and yellow only along its very edges now. Four seasons in one day, or maybe five. Preston had started panting again. He squeezed his eyes shut, said between breaths, 'Will this... get out?'

And there it was, the first concern of every suspect Brody had ever dealt with: themselves.

'Where did you meet Tamara?' Brody asked.

Preston pressed his head against the door glass. 'I can't believe it; she was a man. I just can't.'

'No?' Brody said.

Preston took his head from the door and turned it to Brody, his eyes opening and flashing with raw anger.

'Do I have to fucking spell it out?' Managing not to break once for air as he delivered the sentence.

Brody asked himself if that raw anger was enough to have him slice William Anderson's neck wide open *and* rip out that knuckle in his throat? Maybe.

'Calm down, Mr Preston, just answer my questions, please. Where did you meet Tamara?'

'In a bar.'

'What bar?' It was Quinn.

'The Time Machine.'

'On Capel Street?'

'Yes.'

'When was this?' Brody asked.

'I don't know, some months back.'

'How did you meet her?'

'What do you mean, how did I meet her?'

'It's self-explanatory,' Brody said. 'How did you meet her? Did you approach her? Did you ask her to dance? Did she approach you? What?'

'Her? Why are you referring to him as her?'

'It's confusing otherwise.'

'I was a little drunk, OK; it's kind of hazy. Yes, I approached her. She was really, you know' – his eyes flicked between both of them, like he was sharing a boy's secret – 'sexy, very sexy, I mean, like, really, *really* sexy. I didn't think a woman like her would be interested in a man like me. She was awesome. Shit, I can't believe she's dead. I can't believe she's a man.'

'Are you married, Mr Preston?'

'No, I'm not.'
'Have you a girlfriend?'
'What's that got to do with anything?'
'Just curious. Have you?'
'No.'
'Do you live alone?'
Preston dropped his eyes to the floor and said softly, 'I live at home. With my mother.'
'I'm sorry to ask this, Mr Preston, but do you ever dress in female clothing?'
'Certainly not. I do not dress in female clothing. Never.'
'OK. Tell us about Tamara? You met in the Time Machine. What happened next?'
'I asked her for her phone number. She gave it to me.'
'Did you go someplace after?'
'Well...'
'Did you?'
'Well...'
'Well's not an answer. Did you or didn't you?'
'Not really. Like I say, I was a little drunk.'
'Where did you go, Mr Preston?'
'Someplace. We went someplace, OK. I'm not sure exactly where, a park, a garden, I'm not sure; we went in there and...' Preston stopped and looked at the floor again.
Brody got the picture.
'How many times did you and Tamara see each other?' Quinn asked.
'A few times.'
'How many times?' Brody asked.
'Maybe six times.'
'And the last time?'
'I don't know. Maybe a week ago.'
'That recent?' It was Quinn.
He's getting more confident, Brody thought.

'And you never realised? Like, really?' Quinn found it very hard to believe.

Preston shook his head.

'No.'

'How was that possible?' Quinn pressed. 'You were being intimate with each other, weren't you? Well, weren't you? You were having a relationship with Tamara.'

Preston looked up, anger flaring like burning oil wells in his eyes once more. 'What's. That. Got. To. Do. With. Anything.'

'It's got a lot to do with everything,' Brody said. 'If you were in a relationship, then you were emotionally involved, and if you were emotionally involved, then you cared, and if you cared, you might have cared enough to get so angry that you did something that you regretted when you found out that Tamara was not who she said she was. She wasn't Tamara, because Tamara didn't exist... You do get angry, Mr Preston. I can see that for myself.'

'No,' Preston said, and Brody saw his eyes start to well up. 'I would never harm her. I could never harm her. Because I... I... I loved Tamara. I still do... Are you going to arrest me?'

'Not at the moment, no,' Brody said. 'Have I a reason to?'

'Oh, Jesus. Does that mean you might in the future? I loved her, don't you see. I really did. She was the kind of woman that I always, always wanted to be with.'

No one spoke.

'Mr Preston,' Quinn said gently, 'um, you seem to forget, Tamara wasn't a woman, Tamara was a man.'

'Oh shit,' Preston said, and buried his face in his hands, starting to sob.

'You think he did it?' Quinn said when Preston had left and gone back to his car.

'I don't know. Maybe. Maybe not.'

Brody started the engine and pulled away. Quinn's phone rang. Brody listened as he answered. '... Hello... Oh, yes, Brother Kevin... Really, he is, is he? ... Now? ... OK... We'll be right there.' He hung up. 'JJ Harris's at the Cabin. You know it? It's a drop-in centre.'

'Oh, I know it,' Brody said, 'of course I know it,' and pressed his foot hard onto the accelerator.

But they were too late. Harris had already gone by the time they arrived. They met Brother Kevin outside on the pavement. It was an unspoken rule that the police never entered unless they absolutely had to; it unsettled the clients. And the place was now full of clients.

'He just came and went,' Brother Kevin explained. 'He took a bag of food, and that was it, he was gone again... How are you, Jack? Long time no see.'

Jack could see through the grilled window into the Cabin, full of mostly men, but there were some women in there too. Brody knew many of the faces.

'I'm fine, Brother Kevin. You?'

'Good, Jack, thank God. Good. JJ looked a bit agitated, by the way.'

'He did?'

'And rough, unshaven, poor man, like he's sleeping on the streets again.'

'Did he say where he was going?'

Brother Kevin shook his head. 'He probably doesn't even know himself.'

Both men looked at one another, the policeman and the monk, the policeman knowing the monk walked a fine line between holding the trust of the people he served, his clients, and talking with him.

'Thank you, Brother.'

They went away again, and for the next half hour, Brody

and Quinn did what policemen the world over do when looking for someone. They drove around. Brody was practised in seeking out wanted people. Because he could think like them. It was almost an art form in itself. And because most wanted people were criminals, they generally weren't that smart to begin with. They always seemed to think that the best way to remain hidden was to hide. It wasn't, although there's a certain logic to it. Because, just like a game of hide-and-seek, there are only so many places to actually hide, after all. Also, as in hide-and-seek, the one who's hiding always ends up getting caught. It's just the way it is.

No, what they don't seem to grasp is that often the best way to remain unseen is to actually, well, make sure that you are, seen that is. To not hide in the first place. To always, at all times, remain in plain sight, except to do it, for example, in the centre of the biggest crowd you can find. That way, you blend in, and, hey presto, you've done it, you've actually disappeared. But that seems beyond the logic of your average criminal. Just does. Goes against their every basic, animalistic, criminal instinctive cunning. They have to run, into the most deserted of places, and there they stand out. It doesn't help that criminals, for the most part, are incapable of thinking outside the moment. They are opportunists. When on the run like JJ Harris was right now, they spend their time literally scurrying from one hiding place to the next. Like rats.

And just like rats, sometimes you had to set a trap to catch them.

'That girl, Susie,' Brody said, 'you have her number?'

'She gave it to me, yes.'

'That means you have it?'

'Um, I have it somewhere, but I didn't put it in my phone.'

'I want you to ring her... Listen up, this is what I want you to say...'

Brody knew that to secure an objective he sometimes had to bend things, call it what you will, the rules, the truth. The overseers of standards, the watchdogs, came down hard whenever it was discovered an officer had. Officially, it didn't exist – much. But it did exist. It had to exist. It always would exist. He instructed Quinn to tell Susie the charge of possession would be dropped against her if she did what he asked of her.

'And what is he asking of me?' Susie said, when he'd found her number and rang it.

'I want you to contact JJ Harris, Susie...'

'I don't have his number.'

'OK, Susie, bye.'

'Wait, I can get it. What then?'

'Get him to meet you. I don't care what you have to tell him. And when you get him to meet you, you tell me about it. That's what I'm asking you to do.'

'Maybe...'

'Maybe's not good enough, Susie. I need this done today, as in right now; Harris's out and about as we speak.'

'Can you do something for me?'

'I just told you what I'm doing for you.'

'Something else.'

'I'm not doing enough, Susie, already, is that it?'

'It's nothing to do with any business or nothing, it's personal. My partner. My ex-partner that is. He's been round. He's scarin' me.'

'And?'

'He thinks you and me are doing it. He saw you leavin' my gaff. His head is twisted, his thinking, y'know. He's obsessive. About me. It's getting worse. I'm worried.'

'Wait,' Quinn said, 'did I hear you right? He thinks that you and I are... really?'

'Yeah, really. He thinks we're shaggin', he does.'

'That's fucked up. Look, Susie, say nothing to him, because anything you do say is only going to add flame to the fire...'

'What you mean?'

'It's a saying, Susie, it means you're only going to make matters worse. Lock your door if he comes round again–'

'He will be round again.'

'–and ring the guards. They'll be there in a couple of minutes.'

'I don't want to ring the guards. What'll they do?'

'Either that, or what, he breaks your door down? Which would you prefer?' There was a clicking sound. He took the phone from his ear and looked at Brody. 'She's hung up on me.'

They were parked in a corner of Smithfield's, that huge cobbled stone square near the river and home to Irish Distillers and, in recent years following redevelopment, a popular tourist destination. Brody watched the glass elevator travel up the side of the chimney viewing tower at the visitor centre opposite.

'I agree,' Brody said, who'd heard every word. 'That is fucked up. Anyway, what business is it of his what she does or doesn't do when they're not together anymore?'

'You tell *him* that. Anyway, I think she's lying, I think they are – together, that is. I swear I could hear him in the background. He knew I was on the phone.'

'Now that's what I call adding flame to the fire,' Brody said.

'As long as he doesn't knock her about.'

'You told her what to do if he starts.'

'I did.'

'Not that you needed to. She knows.'

Brody started the engine.

'Let's take another spin round.'

20

'Hello, Alice Maguire speaking.'
'Well now, who else would it be? Of course you're Alice Maguire.'
'Who is this?'
'It's a bad man, mammy, that's who.'
'Willow! My husband told me about you...'
'Did he now? I'm flattered, I really am.'
'Please leave us alone, do you hear?'
'I hear very well; are you questioning my hearing?'
'I'm hanging up now.'
'I'm coming, mammy. I'm coming to get him...'
'Don't call me mammy. How dare you?'

He could hear the fear in her voice, and the sound of her breathing, fast and shallow, before the line went dead.

He laughed, looking at the pictures he'd pinned to the wall in the flickering light of a candle: pictures of Chief Superintendent Maguire, there, striding across the courtyard at Dublin Castle in full dress uniform, and again, sitting behind a long table with other officers at a press conference, and there with Alice – his wife, whom he'd just spoken with on the phone; despite it all, she seemed like such a nice lady – both dressed to the nines at some dinner dance or other. Lots of photographs. No surprises there, the chief super had quite the profile, after all. He placed the tip of his cigar in the candle flame, puffing on it until it glowed bright orange, exhaling in a thick cloud of smoke. The most recent photograph – he'd taken it just the other evening on his mobile... who would have thought he'd be able to master such a device, and after all this time too? And organise to have it printed out too. He'd snapped it as the Old Man had walked into the park with Riley. But it was taken from behind, so it didn't show his eyes, not like most of the others did. It wasn't the same without the eyes.

His lips curled down as he clenched his mouth, tight, so tight it looked like his gums might push right through his cheeks as his eyes appeared to sink into his head, dark and hooded. He extinguished the candle flame between two fingers. He liked the darkness, especially at a time like this, when he felt as he did, when the cauldron of rage inside him was beginning to bubble and hiss. He averted his gaze, turning the tip of his cigar towards him, his face becoming an orange spectre in the darkened room, slivers of light seeping through the boarded-up windows. As the cauldron began to overflow, the hissing, bubbling, rage leeching out of him, through his very skin, he turned the cigar again, away from him. Reaching out his arm, he held the tip of the cigar against the photograph he'd just placed there, the lacquered paper beginning to burn. Then he smiled, watching the flame as it spread from photograph to photograph, within seconds spreading beyond, the whole wall catching fire. He laughed, looking on as it spread to the ceiling and along the other walls. He'd always wanted to burn those photographs, because it was the next best thing to killing the person in them. Now he could do both, of course. As the last remaining wall caught fire, he laughed even harder. Oh, how times had changed. The photographs were gone. There was only him, Chief Superintendent Tom Maguire, left. And soon he would be gone too.

The flames were rapidly encircling him. He laughed harder still, the circle of fire almost complete. He waited until the very last moment, then jumped through before the opening disappeared in flames, and walked calmly away. Willow was temporarily satisfied.

21

Considine turned into the narrow gateway of the pretty two-storey stone house with the red brick surrounds on its windows and front door, and pulled up. Properties around here went for three million euro up. With the addition of add-ons, like a swimming pool, room extension, and maybe a conservatory, or sometimes all three, and also, in the case of at least two, an underground car park, the price could shoot all the way up into the eight-million-euro ballpark. Yet Mrs Anderson's home was the same today as it was when she'd moved in over fifty-five years ago, the same red-brick Victorian pile over granite basement and granite steps leading to its red front door with its gleaming brass knocker. Same as it was when it had come out of the box. Yet the street had changed in more ways than one. Most of the houses were no longer family owned. In fact, there were only two that still were, Anderson's and Hession's, the latter being a doddery old ex-government minister who lived alone further along. The rest of the houses were now occupied by law firms, medical practices, advertising agencies and the like, as well as embassies and diplomatic missions for a total of four foreign governments.

'It's too big for me now,' Margaret Anderson said, leading Considine across the tiled hall and through an archway into a large, sunny room with a view through its bay window of the gardens outside. The room was immaculate, and Considine imagined Mrs Anderson didn't come in here too often, except maybe when she was entertaining visitors, like now. Considine thought it more likely the old woman lived in a separate, smaller part of the house, easier to keep clean and warm. Of course, this was all conjecture on her part. Maybe Mrs Anderson had a great cleaner and used this room every day. But she doubted it. The house had the feel of a quaint, country house hotel about it.

'Would you like something, dear, tea or coffee? Although I'm not certain that I have coffee. I'll have to have a look.'

'No, no, Mrs Anderson. Please don't go to any trouble for me. Thank you.'

'Fine, dear, it's no trouble. But if you're sure?'

'I'm sure, thank you.'

The elderly lady sat in one of two settees positioned facing each other on either side of a fireplace that had a heater in it with artificial coals and a blue flame. Considine sat in the other. Mrs Anderson was a small, bird-like woman who carried herself with a regal bearing, Considine thought. She wore a blue dress belted around her slim waist, and a Celtic brooch pinned high on the front, near the shoulder. Her hair was snow white and perfectly coiffured, her lips thin streaks of red lipstick.

Considine had obtained her details from William Anderson's work record: on it she was listed as next of kin.

But something seemed off. Mrs Anderson had shown no surprise when Considine had spoken to her on the phone, no surprise when she'd told her she wanted to call to discuss her son. Considine was beginning to wonder why.

'William's my middle son, dear,' she said now. 'I have three boys, Thomas, William and Robert. I moved in here with my husband, Robert Senior, back in, oh...'

'Mrs Anderson, I'm sorry to interrupt, but I need to speak with you about your son William. I'm afraid I have...'

'I know he's dead. William's dead, isn't he? It's the body they found in the laneway, that was him, yes?'

The old woman was balanced on the edge of her seat, her back stooped slightly, two delicate hands flattened against her knees, the nails painted in the same colour as those lips.

'Mrs Anderson... you already know?'

'Yes, dear. I know.'

'But how?'

'Because I recognise my own son. On Facebook... Yes, I use Facebook; don't look so surprised.'

'That's not why I'm surprised, Mrs Anderson. I'm surprised you recognised your son, that's why I'm surprised, and you didn't inform us.'

'I'm sorry, dear, but no, I didn't.'

'Why, Mrs Anderson? It's taken quite a lot of effort to identify William and then for us to find and contact you.'

'Yes. Yes, I know. I know. I'm sorry. My son was murdered. I know. I wanted it all to go away, that's why. I just did. I knew it was him, but at the same time, I'd convinced myself that maybe it wasn't, that it couldn't be him, that it had to be someone else. But I knew, I knew, and I'm sorry. I didn't want to ring the guards. Well, I did want to, and I tried, but I just couldn't bring myself to do it; it was easier to just pretend. I'm good at pretending.' She paused. 'Also, and it's a terrible thing to say...' Her voice trailed off.

'Yes, Mrs Anderson, what's a terrible thing to say?'

'That I'm not surprised, that's what. It's like I've always

known it was going to happen. Let me put it this way. Do you know about his... um, peculiar lifestyle?'

'Well...'

'That he liked to dress up?'

Considine nodded. 'Yes, we know.'

'He picked up men when he dressed up like that. Straight men. He told me all about it. We were best friends. A mother shouldn't have a favourite, I know, but William *was* my favourite. In some ways he was like the daughter I never had. We had a great relationship, we really did, and that's such a special thing, don't you agree?'

'Yes, I'm sure it is.'

'I warned him it was dangerous. But I think that was part of the attraction for him.'

Considine nodded.

'They have all sorts of things these days, dear, don't they?' Mrs Anderson said.

'What do you mean?'

'Well, dear, strap-ons and suchlike?'

Considine's mouth fell open all the way to the floor, and she wasn't even aware of it.

'Oh, don't look so shocked, dear. I'm a child of the fifties, not as boring as you'd think; they led the way to the swinging sixties.' She smiled. 'Don't you agree with me, that he played a very dangerous game? And I told him this too. Oh indeed, I did. I was always telling him that. And his reply was always the same, "Don't worry, Mother, I can be very imaginative when it comes to these sorts of things; they never even know." I told him he'd need to be very imaginative, and he'd laughed. He loved the thrill of it all; it was so different to anything in his normal life. He found that stifling, boring, oppressive. He hated it.'

Considine stared. She realised her mouth was still open. She closed it and thought, *Strap-ons.*

'You had a very close relationship with your son, Mrs Anderson. I imagine he must have told you things. Did he?'

'Oh yes, dear, he did, he told me everything. Well, except the gritty details, that is, and I didn't want to know those. But we were very close. I used to be close to Robert, my other son, too, but since he married that... well, there's no other word for it, that tramp... Betty the bicycle I call her. But that's a whole other story, isn't it, dear?'

'You don't like her, your daughter-in-law.'

'I think you can guess. And I don't want to talk about her anymore. I have enough to be dealing with, don't you think? It's family stuff; everybody has to deal with family stuff, don't they?'

'Yes, of course.'

'And don't think that I'm not broken-hearted by this terrible news. I am. More than you'll ever know. But I've been expecting it; as I say, I felt this day would come. In some ways it's a relief. But not the horrible way he died. No. I never expected that. But what I mean is that he's free, that he doesn't have to pretend anymore. That he can be in peace. Finally. Death has brought him over the River Jordan, dear. Am I making any sense?'

Not much, Considine thought, but found herself smiling anyway.

'You can't think of anyone, anyone specific that is, who might have wished your son harm, Mrs Anderson, can you?'

'You mean beyond all those angry straight men who might have had a surprise?'

'Yes, Mrs Anderson, anybody, that's what I mean, anybody at all.'

'Well, then yes,' without any hesitation, 'I can.'

'And who might that be?'

'It's a terrible thing to say, but his younger brother, Thomas. He hated William; he always did. It broke my heart.'

'Was Thomas ever violent towards him?'

'Yes. He pulled a knife on him once when they were teenagers. Don't know what would have happened had I not come into the room... actually, I do, know that is, now that I have the value of hindsight, now that I know what Thomas is capable of. He would have stabbed William, I have no doubt whatsoever. Families bring out the worst in people, don't you think, and the best. With Thomas, it was always the worst. And he has form, dear.'

'He does? What kind of form?'

'He's been to prison.'

'For what reason?'

'Well...'

'Yes, Mrs Anderson?'

'Well, dear, he stabbed someone to death, that's why.'

22

Voyle and Sheahan arrived at Senan Richardson's place of business shortly after lunch. Voyle had been delayed. The Old Man had come into the unit room just as they were leaving and barked, 'My office. Now!' When he went in, the Old Man, who seemed unusually agitated lately, was standing behind his desk, a finger stabbing through the air at him. 'Well, my lad, you've gone and done it now. Lucky for you Quigley rang me and not the commissioner. He says he's friendly with the commissioner, by the way' – the Old Man's voice had dropped, and for the first time Voyle began to think that maybe he wasn't as angry as he seemed – 'but they all say that. Anyway, Voyle, where were your social skills? I thought you had some.'

'I have plenty of social skills, boss, but that lazy bollocks...'

'Whoo, whoo, that's enough. And was that any way to talk to a superintendent? Oh yes, he may be lazy. Oh yes, he may be a bollocks. But you don't, you just don't, you *don't* ever tell him that to his face, you know that. So what you're going to do is ring him up and apologise. You will grovel, my lad, and you will lick his boots. That's what you're going to do, and then I can go to the canteen and get myself some lunch and eat it in peace.'

'No, sir, with all due respect, I won't be doing that. No.'

'Oh, yes, my lad, you will.'

And, of course, he had.

But Voyle was still smarting from having had to do it.

'Hey, Steve, in there, we're passing it.'

Voyle saw the sign just in time, 'Richardson Engine Re-Manufacturers and Reconditioned Alternator Specialists', swung the steering wheel and brought the car through the open gateway. They drove into a yard surrounded by razor-topped wire fencing, the carcasses of old vehicles scattered about everywhere. A dog barked, and Voyle saw the black beast tied up in a corner.

'He a client of ours?' Voyle asked, pulling up next to a VW Tiguan that looked far too new to be sitting on concrete breeze blocks the way it was.

'No,' Sheahan said, 'there's nothing on him that I could find.'

'Hm, I find that hard to believe.'

Voyle cut the engine. Sheahan had just come back from a couple of days' break in Connemara with his fiancée, Marissa. His skin was a healthy pink from the clean air and whatever else he'd been up to down there.

'Hey-up,' Sheahan said, pointing through the windscreen at a man emerging through one of two open double doors in a garage at the top of the yard. In his right hand was a huge spanner, and as he strode towards them, barrel chested, with a shaved head, he flicked the spanner from side to side in his hand. He was almost at the car when he suddenly slid the spanner into a side pocket of his overalls. Voyle and Sheahan relaxed and got out of the car.

'What can I do for you two gentlemen?' The man smiled.

'We'd like to speak to Senan Richardson,' Sheahan said.

'Aye, you would, would you? And what's it in connection with?'

'We're guards,' Voyle said.

The man looked them up and down. 'I'd never have guessed. No, never. But that's not an answer. So the question stays the same, gentlemen. What's it in connection with?'

'A car theft ring we're investigating,' Voyle said, and was surprised at how quickly his little joke wiped the smile from the man's face. 'Vehicles stolen to order, that sort of thing, and chopped up for their parts.'

The man's eyes followed Voyle's as he glanced to the side, to the Tiguan, and it seemed like the man was the only person who could see what he was seeing there.

'You look like you've seen a ghost,' Voyle said. 'That answer your question? So, Senan Richardson, where is he?'

'You're talking to him. Wha'ya mean, a car theft ring?'

'Car theft ring,' Voyle repeated, deciding to keep it going a little while longer, 'thought we'd talk to you about it.' He hadn't expected it to go anywhere, he'd only meant it as a sarcastic joke, but now that it was going somewhere, he'd go along with it.

'Yeah, but that's nothing to do with me.'

'Of course it's not,' Sheahan said, joining in. 'Of course that's nothing to do with you.' He took a chance, pointed to the Tiguan. 'What about that yoke there? I can check the VIN number on it if you like. You'd have no objection to my doing that, now would you?'

Sheahan had a soft, folksy way of talking, love and peace, but his words had a certain authority to them at the same time. He very rarely needed to repeat himself. People heard him the first time. It helped that before becoming a guard, he'd studied law, was actually one year off from being called to the bar. It was also his intention to return and finish his studies at some point, to resign from the force and become a full-time legal eagle, having gained the unique perspective being a police officer offered. Studying law had also made him study his voice, and he had purposely practised giving it the gravitas he was displaying now.

'Come with me,' Richardson said, and it suddenly looked like there were ghosts everywhere.

They followed him to a portacabin hidden behind the garage and out of sight from the road. It was dirty inside, the air smelt of oil, and its windows hadn't been cleaned in years – if ever. Looking through them was like gazing into a sandstorm. On the wall behind the desk was a year planner with a picture of a girl in a bikini along with the words: *Low Profile Racing Tyres from Zuitto, A Smooth Hard Ride – Every Time.*

'I can't concentrate,' Richardson said. 'You've got me rattled about this car ring thing.'

'We have?' Voyle said, like he hadn't noticed. 'What a pity.'

'Yes.' Richardson appeared to see another ghost in a corner of the room where he was staring. 'I mean, really, is there an investigation? You said there was. It's Noone, yeah?'

Voyle pursed his lips. 'I can't talk about an ongoing Garda investigation, Mr Richardson, you understand. Maybe it's Noone; maybe it's not.'

'No, but, you know…'

'Yes, we know?' Voyle said, knowing he knew nothing at all.

'He's a bastard, a vicious bastard. I take in maybe a couple a week, something like that, that's all. I have to. If I don't… well, that's another matter. OK, if I don't, he'll be round here and have my head in a vice grip. Yeah, he's a vicious bastard, and he's done that before. But I don't have anything now, just so you know. But I will soon. He sends them, and I chop them, but he doesn't pay me nearly enough.'

'And if he did pay you enough, would that make it better?' Voyle said.

'Well, of cou...' Richardson began before catching himself.

'No, you wouldn't have a problem, would you?' It came to Voyle then. 'Noone, eh?' He was aware the Criminal Assets Bureau had been after a Noone for a couple of years.

'Noone, yes?'

Voyle and Sheahan exchanged glances.

'Yes, we know about it,' Voyle lied.

'The Lynx Garage...'

'Yes, the Lynx Garage,' Sheahan said knowingly. 'Out on...?' with a click of his fingers.

'The Longmile Road. Yeah, that's the one.'

'Yeah, that's the one,' Voyle said.

'You'll find stuff, some high-end gear if you look today. Has to be today. Because he'll get rid of it. All stolen in the last twenty-four hours. Noone will be there too. You go to the Lynx, you'll see what I mean. And get Noone off my back. I'm a legitimate businessman me. You understand?'

'Of course, Mr Richardson,' Sheahan said.

Richardson leaned forward and spread his hands on his desk, oil-stained, calloused hands, like the meeting had concluded to everyone's satisfaction.

'Only thing is,' Voyle said.

'Only thing is?'

'Well, the only thing is, that's not why we're here.'

RICHARDSON LOOKED up at Voyle like he'd suddenly switched to speaking Mongolian.

'What did you just say?'

'You heard me.'

'You wouldn't want to believe everything you hear, Mr Richardson,' Sheahan added in that pally, folksy way of his.

'Look, fellas, what the fuck are you on about?'

'Do you know a William Anderson, Mr Richardson?'

'Who?'

'William Anderson. Do you know him?'

'I know lots of people... like seriously, you're not here for, you're here for... William Anderson? I don't know any William Anderson. Who's he?'

'Well, apart from being dead, he was also known as Tamara. Did you know any Tamara, Mr Richardson?'

'Dead?'

'Yes, dead. Murdered. Well, William Anderson was murdered, aka Tamara.'

Just when it looked like he'd seen all the ghosts there were to see, Richardson looked like he'd seen another one.

'Dead,' he squawked, his eyes widening. 'Dead?'

'As in all life expired. Murdered, Mr Richardson.'

'This is wrecking me head, lads, like jasus, this is; am I on a bad trip? Seriously, am I? You came here, but you didn't come here for what you said you came here for, you came here for something else, this William Anderson character, but he's not William Anderson, he's Tamara. Is that it?'

'Something like that,' Sheahan said.

'Tamara?'

'Yes, Tamara.'

'What makes you think I know this Tamara?'

'Your name and number are in her address book. Or rather, William Anderson's address book.'

'They are? Tamara... what's she like, this Tamara?'

'On her Facebook page she's got a rock chick vibe, pink lipstick, black hair.'

'Oh, like Chrissie Hynde?'

'Yes, but more, I don't know, more... refined. I think you know Tamara, Mr Richardson... your reaction just now.'

Richardson took a breath and rubbed his chubby hands over his face.

'I can't keep up with all this. Tamara. I did meet a Tamara... I thought something was up with her alright.'

'Like?'

'I don't know.'

'She was a man,' Sheahan said. 'Tamara was a man, Mr Richardson. Maybe it was that.'

Richardson didn't show any surprise. 'Yeah, maybe, I kinda guessed it.' He shook his head. 'It's all making sense now.' He appeared a little more relaxed.

'What's making sense?' Voyle asked.

'I remember.'

'You remember?'

'Yes, I remember.'

'What do you remember?'

'I remember her.'

'You don't own a Volvo estate, 05 D reg, by any chance, Mr Richardson?'

'A Volvo estate? No, I don't own a Volvo estate.'

'Do you have access to one?'

'I have access to a lot of different yokes. I don't know.'

'But it's possible?'

'It's possible... why?'

'You were saying, Mr Richardson,' Voyle said, 'just to go back, that it was all making sense. Tell me. What's all making sense?'

'I met Tamara in a bar in town.'

'You remember the name of the bar?'

Richardson scrunched up his face. 'The one with the bicycle wheels hanging from the ceiling, the, the... the Silver Wheel, yeah, that's it. The Silver Wheel. It was karaoke night.

She sang "My Way", was very good too. Yeah, making sense now, and her voice, wow, what a baritone. I mean it was, it was really good. Like, way *deep*, you know. I know now why that was. But I didn't care, and I don't now either. Shame she's dead though.'

'He, Mr Richardson.'

'Whatever.'

'You didn't care that she was a he?'

'Tell you something too for nothing, she looked better as a woman than a lot of women look as a woman, if you get me.'

'So that's where you met her, the Silver Wheel,' Voyle said. 'Where exactly is that?'

'Just off the docks, near the East Wall, not far from the Dockers Pub, you know, the place where U2 liked to drink and all the posers go to now... right knobhead place it is too, thirteen euro for a bleedin' drink.'

'OK. You met Tamara in the Silver Wheel. Then what happened?'

'What do you mean, then what happened? What do you *think*? Then what happened?'

'Well, I don't know,' Voyle said. He looked at Sheahan. 'What about you, Marty, do you know what happened next?'

'I'd rather not speculate, your honour; it's open to all sorts of interpretations.'

'I'm a single man,' Richardson said. 'I've got nothing to hide. Me and Tamara got a taxi back. Back here. I used to have a camper van, yeah, and we went in there... Look, do I have to spell it out exactly what we got up to?'

'No, that's alright.' It was Sheahan.

'But Tamara was a man.' It was Voyle.

'So? Did I care?'

'And did you?' Voyle asked.

'No, I was having too good a time. I'm sorry to hear Tamara's dead. That's sad. It really is. But it's not what I really care about right now. I'll tell you what I really care about right now, will I?'

'Tell us.'

'About that fucker Noone. Lynx Garage. That's all I care about.'

23

Two fire engines screamed past in the bus lane as Considine drove back to the Phoenix Park. Ahead, she could see a plum of thick black smoke rising into the sky. A couple of minutes later she was passing a blazing building, set a little way in from the road, the fire engine crews scrambling to unload hoses and get their pumps going. The building was familiar to her, as it was, she supposed, to a lot of mules in the metropolitan area. It was the old Garda Complaints and Procedures building and had been derelict for some time. If she remembered correctly, the Old Man had worked there once. She shook her head. There was talk of it being turned into an interpretive centre. But that wouldn't be happening now, at least not for a very long time.

He did have form. At her desk in the unit room she went through Thomas Anderson's Pulse history. He'd contested the murder charge he'd been convicted of, pleading self-defence. The incident was a messy, drunken street brawl when he was nineteen years old. In the end, he was convicted of manslaughter and went down for three years, so his self-defence plea had held some water after all with the jury.

She thought it a little odd his mother had not told her he was a junkie. Of course, maybe she didn't know, but Considine doubted it. Mothers can be very selective in what they choose to know and not know about their children, and their husbands too. Sometimes it's easier to have your arse in the air and your head in the sand rather than have to deal with anything as awkward as reality. But Mrs Anderson didn't seem to have any problem with knowing her son William was a gay transvestite who liked to cruise the bars and pick up unsuspecting straight men. Strap-ons! Considine shook her head again. For God's sake, like, for real? Every straight man's worst nightmare, she imagined – if they actually thought about it, that is. Most probably didn't, because why would they? It was too far out there for them to have to seriously, consciously consider. And she'd never heard it mentioned by any man she'd ever known. Maybe there were a lot of men like William out there, so good at appearing to be women that men didn't realise. Or care. Now there was a thought.

Yes, Thomas Anderson was a junkie, and Considine thought it odd that his mother had never mentioned it. Considine wondered about giving her the benefit of the doubt, that she didn't know. But then she decided, nah, she had to know.

His last permanent address was a flat in Rathmines, on Laird Road, which Considine knew was a stone's throw from Childers Road in Rathgar, where Harris lived.

Coincidence?

Considine had a problem with coincidences. Most police officers did.

But that address, in Laird Road, was a few years old. Thomas's addresses had since alternated between the Back Lane, Benburb Street, and Merchant's Quay. All locations of homeless men's night shelters. Addresses that were also listed on JJ Harris's Pulse record.

Coincidence?

Nah, she decided again, that was stretching it too far. She felt certain that Thomas Anderson and JJ Harris knew each other. Had to. The homeless world was a small one, despite media reports to the contrary, and everyone knew each other. Intelligence told her Anderson liked to hang out along the boardwalk between the Ha'Penny Bridge and Capel Street Bridge in the city centre. And with this latest information, Thomas Anderson became another person of interest in this case, or, more simply put, a suspect.

She added it all to the case file on Pulse and placed a general alert that he was to be lifted as soon as possible, and one of her team notified.

The clock struck six o'clock. She stood and grabbed her coat from the back of her chair. Considine was going home and wanted plenty of time to prepare. To not rush. Because although it might be every day that she attracted the attention of at least one man – or sometimes a woman – and while it might be every other week that a man – or sometimes a woman – gathered up the courage to ask her on a date, it was once in a blue moon that she actually accepted.

And tonight was a blue moon.

THEY WERE JUST HEADING BACK to the station when she rang. Quinn put the phone on speaker, same as he had last time, so Brody could hear.

'Paulie,' Susie said. Quinn glanced to Brody. Really, *Paulie*. 'I hate talkin' to him. You know I do, Paulie. He's such a creep. But I did it, I spoke to him like you asked me to. I did it for you, Paulie.'

'Thanks, Susie, I really appreciate it.'

'I know you do, Paulie; you can make it up to me again, yeah.'

'Where is he, Susie? Right now, that is. Where is he?'

'Meet me at the Canal, the back of the 'joy. He's meeting me, has something for me. I told him half six, yeah?'

Quinn gave a wry smile, the back of the 'joy, or Mountjoy Prison, as if it were Cleary's Clock.

The dashboard clock gave the time as three minutes after six.

'We'll be there.'

'Don't come plodding down like typical peelers so he's time to scarper. He'll know I set him up then. You'd better think of something so that doesn't happen, yeah.'

'We'll think of something, Susie. Thank you.'

'You can make it up to me, Paulie, yeah.'

He hung up, and Brody did a U-turn on the busy road.

They pulled into the kerb along Dorset Street, near the Barley Mow pub, and stood on the canal bridge, looking down along the towpath that ran alongside it.

'What now?' Quinn said. 'She doesn't want us to spook him, remember.'

'I'm thinking about it,' Brody answered.

IN THE GATHERING DARKNESS, the dim lights along the canal, together with the lights from the cells at the back of the prison, shone small and yellow, reflecting on the waters of the canal.

Brody could make out two people sitting on a bench further along. The towpath after dark was not a place for people to sit on benches and linger beneath the charms of Mountjoy Prison's walls, unless they were up to no good themselves, that is.

'Must be them,' Brody said.

'Must be,' Quinn agreed.

'Let's walk. I lead; you follow. Make sure you maintain a good distance from me. When I've ID'd him, I'll move in.'

'Straightforward enough.'

'Good. Let's go.'

They went down the incline from the street and onto the towpath.

'Hang back and give me a head start.'

The priority was not to give the rat any reason to scurry off into the nearest sewer. If need be, Brody could handle Harris on his own until Quinn got there.

A woman walking towards him carrying two bags of shopping kept her head down, eyes resolutely staring at the ground as she passed. There was no getting away from the fact that the male brand had become palpably toxic of late.

He walked quickly. He could see a female sitting, her legs crossed, at the very end of the bench, and the tall, gangly outline of Harris above her, standing on the grass strip between the bench and the towpath. Brody was almost upon them. Harris had his back to him, and Susie didn't seem to notice his approach, instead looking along the towpath towards Quinn.

Brody looked at Harris and became uncertain. Two more steps and he drew level just as Harris turned. Brody heard him speak casually to Susie, and stopped, took out his phone and looked at it, buying time. 'A full moon is a very romantic thing,' Harris said, 'don't you think, Susie?' He turned his back to Brody again.

And then Brody was certain. That the person standing there wasn't Harris at all.

He kept on walking.

QUINN SAW BRODY HESITATE, stop and take out his phone, look at it for a moment, before walking on. He had been about to break into a run, to catch up and assist his boss in the arrest. But now that Brody was walking on, he dropped his head and kept on walking too. He raised his eyes and peered ahead into the darkness. Quinn wasn't even certain it was Susie who was there. He had just passed them when he heard the familiar voice. 'Paulie. Hey, Paulie, over here.'

Quinn stopped. Why was she calling his name? And if that wasn't Harris with her, who was it?

He stopped, turning. 'Hello, Susie.'

The man with her smiled and stepped towards Quinn, offering his hand. More confused than ever, Quinn took it without thinking, just as the man yanked savagely on it, and because he had not been expecting it, Quinn stumbled and fell. As he did, he outstretched his free hand to cushion the impact, and the fist smashed into his face as he went down. He heard something crack, and with it an explosion of pain and an eruption of hot liquid poured from his nose, his eyes involuntarily flooding, so he couldn't see. He squeezed them shut and blinked, trying to clear them, but it was no use. And thus, completely helpless and temporarily blinded, he fell to the ground and felt the foot stomp on his head, again and again and again.

BRODY SPUN round at the sounds, the unmistakable whiplash of flesh on flesh, delivered vicious and fast. He knew it was a punch. With it came the cracking sound of snapping bone. The punch had found its mark. As he turned, he heard a dull thud, like a football that had not been inflated properly bouncing on hard ground. He knew what this was too. Not because he recognised the sound. No, but because he could see the darkened figure's foot coming down on the other darkened figure's outline lying prostrate on the ground beneath it.

A prostate figure he knew to be Quinn. Brody was filled with an instant and all-consuming rage and had crossed the distance as the foot came down once more, fast enough for it not to have made impact with Quinn's head yet. He rammed his own foot against it. The figure stumbled, yet immediately recovered, placing his feet wide apart as he faced Brody, so he was anchored securely, an old trick. In short, a seasoned street fighter. But this would not be enough. Not now. Because now, unfortunately for him, he had more than met his match, Brody being the consummate boxer: disciplined, intelligent, calculating. Brody vaguely recognised the person standing before him, who, even as he shook the knife out from his sleeve and flicked the blade from the handle that glinted in the lights of the towpath lamps and those from the back of the 'joy, had no chance. A small knife, and ugly, like the person holding it, who now began jabbing it in the air toward Brody. Brody saw the ugly smile cross the ugly face. A voice from beside him distracted Brody just enough, and he felt something pull on him, and he looked away, saw it was Susie tugging on his jacket. 'Don't be pickin' on him,' she cried. 'Don't be pickin' on him.' Brody didn't know what she meant, as he heard the unmistakable whiplash sound of flesh on flesh again, delivered vicious and fast. And the sensation against his cheek was like being hit by his old, cantankerous schoolteacher, from many years ago.

Sometimes, and they say it happens just before you die, your life can pass before your eyes. When Brody was sucker punched by Susie's boyfriend now, his life didn't pass before his eyes. No, but in a nanosecond he was right back there, in the classroom of the teacher whom everyone called 'Slapper Sullivan', a person singlehandedly responsible for traumatising a generation of boys from the town Brody had grown up in. In that nanosecond, he remembered little Liam Rooney, the gentlest human being you could ever hope to meet, cowering before Sullivan's open hand as it came down across his cheek and then the other cheek, and on and on. But Brody had never been traumatised by Sullivan; it had only made him angry. Maybe that was the same, but an anger he had learned to blow off in the ring.

Except for now.

The knife came again, seeking to exploit Brody's vulnerability. It would have been enough – had it been anyone else, that is. But this was Brody, and with the ease of a button being pressed, his training took over. Indeed, he was scarcely aware of it as he swivelled onto his right heel, crouching low, so low, like he was performing a Russian dance squat routine, his back straight, in a sublime example of fitness and dexterity. And the blade passed right over him. Then he sprang up again, *surprise*. In the moment it took for his assailant to swing back, to appraise what had happened, Brody had launched his fist. He brought power up from his leg, combined it with power from his shoulder, then his arm, transforming his fist into the head of a sledgehammer, his arm the handle. His timing was perfect, the face square on, as he slammed that sledgehammer into it.

The man squealed in pain, his face exploding in a hail of blood and shattered bone. And Brody felt satisfied. He felt satisfied for his little friend Liam Rooney. And he felt satisfied for himself, though for Rooney it was too late. He'd killed himself at nineteen.

24

Like a lot of beautiful people, Considine didn't think about it, wasn't even aware of it, didn't even *know* it sometimes. Yet, at the same time, she was aware of it; she did *know* it. Of course she did. How could she look in the mirror each day and not know? This was why she didn't wear make-up, the reason she dressed down at work, hiding her curves, seeking no attention. But also, Considine was a practical person – very practical – and too busy getting on with life to even think about it. Such is the preserve of beautiful people, they don't even *have* to think about it. Yet despite Considine's ambivalence, despite her not noticing her beauty, other people did – all the time. In fact, it was what they first noticed about her.

Many men had tried – and a few women too – but usually Considine wasn't interested. Because she was beautiful, she didn't know what it was like not to turn heads.

So, in asking her out on a date, Danny Reagan had to be confident, very confident. Considine knew this. Though, confident men usually turned out not confident at all. They merely pretended to be. She always thought that truly confident men were subtle and understated about it, and truly confident men were extremely rare. Danny Reagan seemed the perfect combination, the perfect balance of humility and confidence – displaying both at the same time. Also, she couldn't help but notice that Danny Reagan was beautiful, like her.

Yes, Danny Reagan seemed to have it all.

Which made Considine wonder. Why the hell was he asking her out? If Danny Reagan was so perfect, why the hell was he still single? But then, she realised, he could say the very same about her. Anyway, she was inclined to overthink matters in situations like this. She decided to try not to. But now, what she definitely didn't like was sitting at this restaurant table waiting for him. She'd been on time; if she had an appointment, she was always on time. She didn't play games. He was five minutes late. Where was he?

I should leave, she thought. *I really should.*

But yet, she didn't; she remained. When he entered the restaurant a couple of minutes later, she knew the reason why. Yes, Danny Reagan seemed to have it all. That man was beautiful. She should at least pout and show some displeasure, who cared if it was childish. He'd get the message. But she didn't. Instead, she smiled and waved. He smiled in return. Came and stood next to her. Touched her lightly on the shoulder.

'I'm, like, really so, sooo sorry. Really. This doesn't look good. Our first date and all, and I'm late.'

Our first date, Considine thought, *he's subtly confident there'll be another.*

'Are you mad at me?' he asked.

Well, I would be, but shite, that cheeky grin.

'I don't know you well enough to be mad at you. Pissed off should cover it.'

He laughed and sat down.

'It was a Zoom with the Japanese office. We overran. Couldn't help it. Again, really sorry.'

'Apology accepted.'

'Thank you.' He looked around. 'Now where's the waiter? I need a drink.' He caught the eye of a server. 'Hi, Piotr, my usual, please.'

'Looks like you've been here before.'

'Yes, I have.'

Hm, she thought. The truth was, his apology was a moot point. An apology is only relevant if someone has been wronged. Considine realised now that Danny Reagan had actually done her a favour. Yes, Danny Reagan was late, but if he had cared, he wouldn't have been. He would have left that meeting, or at the very least made sure it ended on time. Really, that's what he should have done, for their date, for their first date, as he called it. And if there's another, I'll decide, and I'll decide what *I* get out of this.

She smiled. *Yes, I know what I'm dealing with now. But that's OK.* Danny smiled back. She smiled the whole time, because Danny Reagan was really the most beautiful man she'd ever met since, well, since... like, forever. She smiled as they ate – beef wellington for him, pan-fried sole for her – she smiled until her jaw hurt. Over coffee, she smiled.

'What age are you, Danny, I never asked?' She didn't have to make the effort; the smile was just there now.

'Twenty-seven, and how old...?' But his voice trailed off.

'Tut-tut, you should never ask a lady her age, Danny. Don't you know that?'

'Ahem, feeling suitably chastised right now. Sorry.'

Actually, Considine was eight years older. But she didn't care about that. She didn't care about anything. And there was a freedom in that.

She shook her head, as if trying to rid herself of the cobwebs of long-forgotten lust. It had been a long time, after all. But it was still there, and it was stirring, letting her know it was there.

She lifted her demitasse and held it to her lips. It had been a mistake meeting Danny. In one way, that is. She knew that now. But it was going to be one of the best mistakes she'd made in a long time, and she was damned if she wasn't going to enjoy every last minute of it. In that sense, this wouldn't be a mistake. Oh no.

'A penny for them.'

She placed the demitasse back onto its saucer and looked into his eyes, those gorgeous green eyes with their flecks of yellow.

'Guess,' she said.

For a long time they just sat, staring at each other. At last he spoke.

'That you're enjoying your date with me? That you like my company?'

'Oh, yes, I'm enjoying being with you.' *My, my, mirror, mirror on the wall, who is the fairest one of all? Indeed.*

She nudged the demitasse away with the tip of a finger.

'Tell you what,' she said, 'let's have coffee back at my place.'

He smiled. 'OK. But why not mine? I only live around the corner.'

It was all making sense. It was the reason he'd picked this restaurant in the first place. She could see it now, an endless trail of females making the short trek to Danny's bed. It was why he didn't have to tell the waiter his tipple of choice, he'd already known.

She lowered her eyes mischievously. 'No, I've got work in the morning. I like to wake up in my own bed.' She raised her eyebrows.

'Oh, in that case. Well, yes, that's fine. Your place it is, then.'

'Good,' Considine said, and pushed back her chair. She stood. She was wearing a short, black dress and high heels, her long legs stretching off into forever. She saw his eyes widen as he looked at her.

'A penny for them,' she said, and laughed.

RILEY WAS RESTLESS. The Old Man opened the kitchen door and let her out into the back garden, stood watching her as she scampered off down to the end to relieve herself, her eyes reflecting the light like tiny red lasers, but otherwise completely lost to the darkness. Alice was sitting at the kitchen table, watching. He knew she could see it, and was glad that she hadn't commented. There was no need to comment. She knew why he had the service revolver all senior officers were allowed to carry if they so chose holstered to his waist.

'Riley, girl,' he called, 'come on.'

Riley walked slowly toward the house and stopped in front of him, looked up as if to say, 'What, this is it?'

'Come on, Riley,' he said gently, 'there's a good girl; come inside.'

She passed in, her head low, tail not moving: not happy.

FROM THE DARKNESS at the end of the garden he watched as the Old Man closed the door, then heard the soft clinking sound as he locked it.

Willow smiled. All was ready. It would not be long now.

FOR THE SECOND time in almost as many days, Quinn was back in A&E. Brody remained with him. It was almost midnight when he was released. This time Quinn had had a portion of his head shaved to allow the doctor to sew up the wound with six stitches. His nose was broken too. But at least it was straight. He didn't look pretty. But neither did Christy Foley – the name of Susie's partner, ex-partner, or whatever he was. Brody realised he had arrested the petty criminal years ago when a uniform beat officer. Anyway, Susie definitely wouldn't be seeing him for the foreseeable future. His new home would be behind the walls he'd been sitting in front of a couple of hours before – the 'joy.

Brody yawned and climbed the stairs to bed. For the first time he allowed himself to think. Think of this day. Of what it meant.

No one had mentioned it to him, and he was grateful for this. They had either forgotten, or chosen to forget – because they knew, knew that he did not want any reminding. Either way, he was grateful. And although sometimes he did not remember himself, because his mind seemed capable of blocking it out, he knew he could never forget. What this day meant.

He undressed and lay in bed, his head resting against the pillow, tried to focus on his breathing... *in ... out ... in ... out ... in ... out*. Anything to help him forget. His eyes grew heavy and slowly closed, sleep falling on him like a web, drawing him in, then carrying him away.

Caoimhe came to him. She had not visited him for such a long time. She came to him now, and he noted how she was dressed, jeans and a heavy lumber shirt. He asked her why. She said it was snowing outside, and she had to go into the forest. She liked the forest, it wasn't scary or anything, and there was no need to worry for her. No, she said, worry for yourself, as I do too. He asked her why she was going into the forest. She told him it was a new beginning. That on the other side she would emerge into a new world. Brody smiled; he didn't believe in any of this wishy-washy stuff. But she told him yes, it was true. He asked her if there were other people there. Yes, she said, there were lots of people here. Think of all the people who've already died, she said, millions and millions, billions even. Yes, there's lots of people here, because after all, everyone has to die, don't they? Then her image began to fade, as did her voice... *It's time for you to re-emerge as well*, she said. *It's time for you to leave the forest, to come out and live again, Jack. You must! It's time for you to live again without me. From now on I won't be visiting so often, Jack. Remember, you've got to live. I'm the one who's dead. Not you. You're alive. Live, Jack, live...*

His eyes snapped open. The room was in darkness. He thought of his dream, so real like it wasn't a dream, but he knew it was. This wishy-washy stuff could mess with your head. Yes, it could. Yet strangely, he felt rested even though he felt like he couldn't possibly have slept at all. Like he'd closed his eyes only a moment ago. Hadn't he? He checked the time on his phone and was surprised. It was just after seven. He had slept all night. Brody pulled back the duvet and stepped onto the cold wooden floor. He crossed and opened the curtains, looked out, and blinked.

It had snowed during the night.

25

Considine was the last one in. She arrived at the unit room fifteen minutes late, at quarter past eight. Unusually for her, she wore make-up, but still looked wrecked.

'Did I miss something?' She looked at Brody, who was standing at the top of the room, and her eyes slid to take in Quinn, who was sitting at his desk that wasn't his desk, like he'd just gone two rounds with a bear. 'What the fuck happened to you?'

'A jealous boyfriend,' Brody said.

'A what?'

'You can read all about it on Pulse.'

'Haven't you started yet?' It was the Old Man, appearing in the doorway. 'Well?'

'Just about to, boss.'

'What the fuck happened to you?' the Old Man barked, pointing.

'A jealous boyfriend,' Brody repeated.

'Can't he answer for himself? Well, lad?'

'It was, sir, a jealous boyfriend… in a roundabout way.'

'A jealous boyfriend...' The Old Man looked thoughtful. 'You mean, *your* boyfriend?'

'W-what?' Quinn spluttered. 'No. I'm straight as an arrow, me. The straightest arrow you'll ever see. *Not* my boyfriend. No.'

Brody quickly filled the Old Man in, who waved a hand through the air, cutting him off. 'Whatever, can we just get this started?'

Brody caught Considine's confused expression. 'Didn't you get the message?'

She said nothing.

'Never mind. The body in the lane, William Anderson. This is where we are with it...' And he went on to bullet point their progress so far. He was not doing this just for the benefit of the unit, but for his own benefit too. The investigation had only really begun to heat up after William Anderson's body had been identified. Unfortunately, this was after the first twenty-four hours, the hot period, and now, with the passing of that crucial time period, they were playing catch-up.

But Brody had signposts. He didn't know where these might lead, but each would be followed, each avenue would be explored, each cul-de-sac gone down. And fittingly, in light of these metaphors, they needed to find a car.

'We need to find the car,' Brody said, and heads nodded. 'But first, I imagine, we need to find Harris, because Harris will lead us to the car... Nicola, go talk to Robert Anderson, the victim's brother, OK?'

'OK.'

'Steve.'

Voyle nodded.

'Go and find Thomas Anderson, the other brother. The boardwalk might be a good start. And take Quinn with you.'

'Quinn? Boss...'

'Yes. Quinn.'

Voyle and Brody looked at one another.

'OK, boss. Take Quinn. Got it. I know Tommy, little shit, from my time with the Drug Squad.'

'Good. Bring him in for a chat. Although, if he had something to do with this...'

'I know,' Voyle said, 'then he won't be sitting around on the walk like a Buddha asking people for two euro, like he does. I wouldn't mind, but *two* euro.'

'There are two other names in William Anderson's address book. I'll look after those, for now. As you'll see on Pulse, I've put a screenshot up there; there's also a set of initials after each name. We've identified two of them as bars, S W, the Silver Wheel, and T M, the Time Machine. We haven't figured out the other two yet. Keep your evenings free; myself and Quinn will visit the Silver Wheel; Voyle and Marty, you take the Time Machine.'

'Something wrong, Marty?' the Old Man asked when he saw Marty Sheahan's face drop.

'No... well, um, I just had tickets to *Carmen* at the Bord Gais, that's all.'

Sheahan glanced to Considine. Who looked away quickly. Sheahan was on his own; she wasn't going to swap and go to the Time Machine in his place if that's what he was after, *Carmen* or no *Carmen*.

'*Carmen*, eh,' the Old Man said, 'very cultured, Sheahan, have to say.' He gave, what was lately, a very rare grin. 'Sorry to take you away from that. But when you're working down the Four Courts in a few short years' time, and earning in an hour what you now earn in a week, you can think back to the sacrifices you made that got you there...' The Old Man shook his head. '*Carmen*, honest to God. Oh, and by the way, well, it's more than a by the way, I suppose, overtime is approved...' He gave Quinn a sympathetic look. 'That includes you too, Quinn, your caper outside Harris's flat the other night, and last night too, that I just got the gist of. Just fill in your overtime sheets, everybody; I won't quibble.'

Sheahan suddenly looked a lot happier with that news.

A uniform appeared in the doorway and pointed to Brody.

'You looking for a fella called JJ Harris?'

'I am.'

'Kevin Street was just on. He handed himself in.'

'He didn't?'

'He did.'

'Don't quibble, Jack,' the Old Man said. 'Take your luck wherever you can get it.' He clapped his hands. 'This day seems to have got off to a good start.'

IT HAD SNOWED AGAIN. When Brody went into the car park at the rear of the MCIU, another flurry stopped just as quickly, leaving the sky a canopy of cold, hard, but beautiful blue. He thought of his dream once more, of Caoimhe. Did it mean something? Part of some readjustment maybe? Something bubbling up from way down deep in the bedrock of his subconscious, a final coming to terms with the reality that Caoimhe had gone, gone forever.

Marty Sheahan drove, and Brody looked out the window before closing his eyes and feeling the searing pain of loss pass through him. He opened them again, thinking of how ridiculous it was, nothing but pure coincidence that it had snowed, just as it had in his dream... well, it was, wasn't it?

He forced it from his mind, clearing the decks, and looked straight ahead through the windscreen. They crossed the river at the Rory O'More Bridge and went along Watling Street, turning left at the top onto Thomas Street, close to the heart of old Dublin, The Liberties.

Sheahan was a good interviewer. He was clinical; he was

concise. He always carried a little notebook, separate to his official notebook that is, and one that, during an interview, he was constantly writing in. He said it was an efficient way of exposing lies. Because lies very rarely held up under his clinical questioning. He would refer to something, no matter how apparently innocuous, said just moments before. Everything was in the pages of his notebook and immediately available, unlike the tape or digital recorder, which had to be rewound and played back. That was enough to give a person time to think. The old ways were sometimes the best ways.

Kevin Street Garda station was a new building, a striking structure of curved glass and granite. Next to it was the yard and the old station complex of buildings that had been in use for almost two centuries as a police barracks. Before that it had been the site of the Palace of St Sepulchre, the official residence of Dublin archbishops for over six hundred years. The very old alongside the old, and the old alongside the new, a coexistence, a bridge from the past to the present. But to Brody, Dublin would always be Old World, even if, with the new Kevin Street, the Office of Public Works, who'd designed it, seemed to have got the balance just right.

JJ Harris looked like a broken man. The last time Brody had seen him was in a courtroom where he'd been escorted to from prison to answer fresh charges on something or other. That was maybe fifteen years ago. He'd already looked old back then. Now, looking much older again, with every year, every day, every hour, every minute of his miserable existence in fact, etched onto his hollow-cheeked face. He watched them with nervous, skittish eyes as they entered the interview room and took the seats in front of the interview table. He watched them as Sheahan placed his little notebook onto the table. He watched them as Brody unzipped his jacket and then unbuttoned the sports jacket beneath. He watched them as Brody took off the zip-up and draped it over the back of his seat. He watched them with eyes like pinball machine balls endlessly whizzing round and round. It was only when Brody clicked the recorder to life and had read the preamble that he finally relaxed, his eyes settling into dark, calm lagoons.

'I don't care,' he said. 'Just send me back to prison. I want to go back to prison... for a time, until everything blows over. Give me my old job back making fruit boxes in the workshop. I don't want to be outside no more. I've had enough. Please send me back to prison. And I'll do it right next time.'

'Nice to meet you too,' Brody said. 'Now, I'm sure we'll be able to fulfil your wishes, but let's play a game of questions and answers first.'

Harris curled the long, bony fingers of a long, bony hand, tipped with long, dirty nails. A claw, a criminal scavenger's claw, which he used to scratch behind one ear, in a slow, ponderous, calculating gesture.

'Yes, let's go through it.' It was Marty, his voice slow, dropping an octave, gathering up gravitas, like it would in a courtroom one day, a Bic poised over the page of his small notepad.

'Yes, let's go through it,' Brody agreed. 'You know...'

'Yeah, yeah, I know what it's about. You've been looking for me. It's all over the news. I didn't kill that fella... I didn't even know him. Me. Look at me. I'm a broken man.'

Brody had to admit, he did agree with that observation.

'Brother Kevin told me it was best to give myself in. He's right. So here I am. I give up.'

'Let's talk about the car,' Marty said.

'Huh?'

'The car. You know about the car. Your car.'

'Oh, that. *That*. What's that got to do with me? I haven't seen that car in years. I got it when I came out of prison last time. A credit union loan, yeah, they have them for helping ex-prisoners like me who want to start a business, yeah. The most stupid idea I ever had, that was. Like really, I could sue them for giving me that bread. It didn't work out. Of course it didn't. Lee Marvin was born under a wandering star, but I was born under a cursed star. That's the only thing I've had plenty of all my life – bad fucking luck.' The calm lagoons were not so calm anymore, instead turbulent, darker, and full of self-pity.

'Are you finished?' Brody asked.

'Ah, fuck you,' Harris spat.

'JJ, JJ, we've kept this polite so far; don't go and spoil it now. The car. Where's the car? I asked you.'

'I sold it. OK? I bought it for seven grand, sold it for three, can you believe that? Well, actually, two thousand nine hundred and fifty, the fella said he'd take the fast-food delivery signs off the sides if I dropped the fifty. How was I going to take them off? I was left with nothing but a credit union loan, sixty a week for two years. Jesus Christ, a fella can't get a break.'

'Fast food, you said.' It was Sheahan, his voice the same, low monotone, full of authority and a shoulder to cry on.

'Yeah, pizzas and stuff.'

'Pizzas and stuff,' Brody said, 'a small truck of a car like that for pizza and stuff. Yes, I can see how that might have worked.'

'Ah, fuck you,' Harris spat again, and shifted in his seat, turning away from Brody and towards the one who understood him. Brody was pleased. It was always more unnerving for a suspect to find themselves interviewed by two detectives rather than one. A single detective had to be both tough and tender, a difficult tightrope to walk. Pull on either end too tight and the rope might snap. But with two, if played properly, it could be a psychological pincer movement, a yin and yang of polar opposites working together to achieve a common result: snap, they'd caught a common prey.

'Look, JJ,' Sheahan said, 'this isn't easy for you. I understand that, JJ, I really do.'

Harris's shoulders dropped, and he seemed to fold into his chair. 'No, it's not,' his voice a whine.

'So let's get this over with as quickly as possible; what do you say to that? Yes?'

He nodded. 'Yes.'

'Where is that car now?' Brody asked.

'I sold it. I told you.'

'To whom?'

'I can't remember; it was five years ago.'

'Think,' Brody said, 'because that car is still in your name. You just think of that, JJ, good man, think of the implications of what that might mean. And the implications of blasting a shotgun hole through that door and nearly killing one of my officers. Yes, plenty of implications.'

'It's OK, boss,' Marty said in that calm way of his. 'He's thinking. Let him think... aren't you thinking, JJ?'

'What's he mean by that? The implications?' Harris looked at Sheahan, his only friend in the world.

'The question you need to ask yourself,' Brody pushed, 'is this: yes, you might want to go back to prison, but do you want to spend the rest of your life in there? Of course, maybe you do, but I'd imagine the novelty would soon wear off. Yeah?'

Harris looked like he already knew the answer to that question.

'It's a murder, JJ,' Marty said, his voice, even now, a soft comfort blanket, 'you know that. We need to find the car, JJ.'

'And I'd also like to know why you blasted a hole in the door?' Brody pushed from another angle. 'Don't forget that.

And for what, a few bags of weed? It could've been my head along with the door.'

'Yeah,' Harris said, 'for a few bags of fucking weed. That's right. So? Your rep is everything in this game, and I thought you were...'

'What? Someone else?' Brody finished the sentence for him.

'Maybe?'

'Where's that shotgun now, JJ?' Sheahan asked. 'Could you tell us that? Because we can't just forget about it, have it circulating out there.'

'It's in the river.'

'I don't believe you.' It was Brody. 'The river. What river?'

'Tough if you don't believe me. It's in the river.'

'Where? What river?'

'I don't know. A river. The river. Some fucking river.'

Brody leaned forward on the table. 'Where? In what river?'

'I don't know. The river. The river. The fucking river. OK?'

Sheahan smiled. 'Where, JJ, couldn't you just tell us, please? Save us all this palaver.'

'OK. OK.' Harris paused. 'Chapelizod Bridge, OK? Somewhere round there, in the shallows, yeah, in the reeds, I weighed it down with a block in a watertight bag, OK? It's not even my gun. It belongs to... jeez, it belongs to somebody else. And the gear belonged to somebody else too. Everything belonged to somebody else.' He covered his face with his hands. 'Oh, Jesus. I'm fucked. Just take me back to prison.'

Brody could see why he wanted to go back inside so badly, but it was beyond him why Harris thought he'd feel safer in there. He might feel safer, but he wouldn't be, far from it. He pushed hard again, knowing he was almost at the line now.

'The car. Think. Tell us about the car.'

'I don't know about the car. I told you.'

'Come on, JJ,' Sheahan said gently.

'I don't know – honestly. I don't know.'

'I think you do,' Brody said. 'And yes, let's try honestly, good idea. Tell us about the bloody car.'

JJ swung his head to him and looked straight into Brody's eyes. But those lagoons of his held no bitterness now. Instead, suddenly wide and childlike, like wanting nothing other than to please.

'You! You won't give up, will you?'

'No,' Brody agreed, 'I won't.'

'I sold it to a fella. There.'

'Who?'

Harris opened his mouth, but closed it again.

'Who was it, JJ?' Sheahan said, like talking to a child. 'You can tell us. Go on.'

Harris opened his mouth again. They waited. And then he spoke. He told them whom he'd sold it to. At that moment, Brody imagined a piece of jigsaw falling into place, and with it the sound of the two pieces joining together: *click.*

26

Quinn was just about to hang up when the phone was finally answered, a voice that said, 'Yes?'

'Mr Shane Martin?'

'Who's this?'

'Is it?'

'Who's this?'

'Detective Garda Paul Quinn, that's who.'

'What do you want?'

'Are you Mr Shane Martin? Please answer the question.'

'Yes, it's me...' A voice in the background spoke, a female voice. *'Shane, what's keeping you? And who's that on the phone?'*
'I'm sorry. I can't really talk right now. What's this about?'

'A murder investigation, Mr Martin, the victim, a William Anderson...'

'William,' he said the name so softly that Quinn almost didn't hear it.

'Yes, or Tamara.'

'Yes, or Tamara. I know. I heard...' As the female voice sounded again, *'Oh, excuse me, sorry, Shane, I didn't realise you were still on the phone.*' Shane Martin spoke louder this time, and Quinn knew it was because someone was listening. 'Oh, of course, yes, no problem. I don't mind you ringing like this. We'll catch up with that sometime today; it'll give us plenty of time to prepare a presentation. Is that alright by you? Drop in anytime. I'm at the office all day.'

'Yes, Mr Martin. That's fine by me. Where exactly is your office?'

'Oh, you've forgotten, have you? It's 15A Burgh Quay. I'm sorry, but I really have to go now. I'll see you then. And the presentation will work out great, don't worry. Everything will be fine.'

'OK, Mr Martin, I hope so. I'll see you soon.'

VOYLE HAD ENTERED the unit room while Quinn was speaking on the phone. He thought the lad had a good telephone manner, he'd give him that. He leaned on the lad's desk and listened to everything that was being said. When Quinn put the phone down and looked up at him, Voyle smiled and stepped back. He'd been moaning about Quinn a lot lately. Maybe the boss was right; maybe the lad did deserve a break.

'Good work,' Voyle said. The lad smiled too. He hadn't been getting any smiles or compliments from anyone lately. He began typing on the keypad of his computer.

'Shane Martin, 15A Burgh Quay,' Quinn said, pointing to the computer screen. Voyle stepped closer and looked. The screen was filled with the image of a grey-haired man, clean cut with the exception of a thick moustache, smiling out at them.

'Spit of Will Ferrell, that fella,' Voyle said. 'What'd you think? In that movie, what's it called...? *Anchorman*, except for the grey hair, that is.'

'He's art director of an advertising agency, Magic Mushroom Creatives.'

'Magic Mushroom what? That can't be a real name. Can it?'

Quinn tapped the ribbon of text beneath the picture. 'It can. See it there.'

Voyle peered. 'No shit. Grab your jacket, kid; we're going to the boardwalk.'

THE BOARDWALK IS on the north side of Dublin, in the C district of the North Central division. It was originally designed as a tourist and cultural amenity in celebration of the 2000 millennium. The idea was a good one, and for a short time it worked. Coffee docks and ice-cream kiosks and public seating attracted strollers, young families with buggies, courting couples, skate boarders.

But it didn't last.

The drug alter world shifted to consume the boardwalk, its darkness settling on it, and for a brief moment the two worlds, the one of darkness and the one of light, collided. Strung-out junkies began to appear sprawled across the public seating, street alcoholics drinking from cans of cider and bottles of sherry began to occupy the tables at the coffee docks. The world of light, of the strollers, the tourists, the skateboarders, the mothers pushing buggies, retreated and was extinguished.

Now the coffee docks were boarded up. Regular Garda bicycle and foot patrols swept through the area, temporary torchbearers of the light, but the darkness slithered behind them, restoring everything again once they'd gone.

Steve Voyle and Paul Quinn had already been through it once; now they came off O'Connell Bridge, turned left and entered the boardwalk for a second time. As quickly as the snow had come, it had disappeared again, leaving the boardwalk glistening, with a fresh, earthy smell in the air, the sky a camouflage of black and grey swirls. Blowing off the river was a stiff, cold breeze. A seagull, its big wings outstretched, drifted on the air beside them, squawking angrily before tapering its wings and diving away.

Four seasons in one day – or maybe five.

It was 10:30, and everything had the semblance of normality about it. The alter world, while it was everywhere around them, was at the same time mostly invisible now. People, normal people, walked along the boardwalk, but they walked quickly, wary, their gaze ahead, choosing not to see, or ignore it. Mothers pushing buggies were nowhere to be seen.

Voyle knew that many of the figures sitting alone or in small groups on the benches along by the wall, or hunched over the railings, seemingly gazing into the water, were watching them. They knew who they were. Voyle knew many of their faces too, their gaunt, emaciated, sunken faces. But he did not want any of them. No one really wanted any of them.

Fat James was not like them. There he sat, by the wall, next to the Bachelors Walk entrance. He was watching them too, but the difference was he made no secret of the fact. Fat James was a businessman. He didn't use drugs. This was his patch, a lucrative city centre location, no overhead, captive market, cash business. Fat James was a minor kingpin. He supplied the runners who supplied the addicts. The runners were mostly addicts themselves, dealing to fund their own habit. Fat James ruled the entire boardwalk, and he came here each day to make sure it ran smoothly. He came here to make sure there was no competition. He came here to make sure everyone paid their bills on time, even if there was always one idiot who didn't. Fat James couldn't allow that. Everyone knew the price for fucking with him. Which was why very, very few people ever did.

Despite there being hardly any sun, Fat James wore sunglasses, mirror lensed. Voyle could see himself and Quinn walking towards Fat James in those miniature TV screens. Fat James's short stubby arms were outstretched, lying across the backrest, the ankle of one fat foot resting on the fat knee of the other leg, profiling an expensive Nike Air. His build was like his name, but nonetheless his face was handsome. He liked to spread his ample self about too, with children by three different women. He was dressed in the ubiquitous tracksuit, in this instance a navy Nike top and bottom, and an orange Nike baseball cap.

Fat James liked Nike. Voyle wondered if Nike would, if they could, pay Fat James a fee not to wear their gear, same as they paid celebrities to wear their gear. The same principle, only in reverse.

"Uh-huh, the local constabulary," the minor kingpin said when they stopped in front of him. His voice was raw and raspy, like he was using, but he wasn't. It had something to do with an operation on his tonsils as a child. "Officer Voyle and...' He leaned forward, pulling his sunglasses down along his nose and peering over them at Quinn. 'Tut-tut-tut, now if I was ever to look like that, I'd hang up my fucking gloves, I would; be ashamed to come out of the house, I would, for deffo.' He pushed the glasses back up again. 'Anyway, gentlemen, what takes youse out and about on such a fine morning? Taking the air, is it? Or maybe youse is looking for something a bit stronger? Wouldn't be the first of our brave boys in blue. Indeed, some are my very best customers they are.'

'Save it, big fella,' Voyle said. 'I've heard it all before. Thomas Anderson, you know him?'

'Should I?'

'You sell what he buys, so you tell me.'

'How the fuck would I know his name, then? I don't know

any of their names. I know them as Doper and Peddler, Knob Head and Jack Head, Smelly Arse and Lock Jaw. I don't know their names, their real names, that is. I don't want to know their bleedin' real names.' He gave an exaggerated shudder. 'They're junkies, for God's sake. Spare me.'

'That *is* his name,' Voyle said. 'His real name.'

'Exactly. And I don't know it.'

'Chap has a distinctive tattoo on his arm,' Quinn said, 'a zombie, with *flesh eater* written underneath.'

Fat James showed off his Joey Essex teeth in a wide smile. 'Well, why didn't you say?'

Voyle looked at Quinn. 'Does he? How'd you know that?'

'There's a photo on Pulse, that's how.'

Voyle was impressed. Yes, the lad was definitely improving.

'Hop Along,' Fat James said.

'Hop Along?'

'Yeah, cos the way he walks or something. I don't know. Looks like he's hopping along.' He pointed. 'Well, whatta ya know. There's the man himself. The star of the show. Have a look for yourself.'

Voyle turned, saw someone in a long coat moving up the incline from the boardwalk onto the street, moving in a quick saunter, like he was rising onto the tips of the toes and falling back onto the heels of his feet, up and down, up and down, or hopping along.

'You mean… what? That's him?'

As Quinn took off in pursuit.

Fat James laughed. 'Yeah, that's him. Not as quick on the uptake as your friend there, are ya?' nodding towards Quinn, who was tearing up the incline now. 'But you'll never catch Hop Along. I mean, you can try, but look at him go; the man is a human missile. Go, hoppy go!'

Voyle took off too. When he reached the street, Quinn was standing there.

'Where'd he go?'

'Can you get out of my way?' A passer-by glared at Quinn as he stepped around him, looking at his swollen nose and shaved head with the stitches. 'It's bad enough we can't use the boardwalk without you people coming up here too.'

Voyle waved him on.

'I don't know,' Quinn said, throwing his hands up in a gesture of defeat. 'It's like he just disappeared into thin air.'

And instantly it was back again. Voyle looked at Quinn like he was something he'd just picked up on his shoe.

27

Robert Anderson was a jeweller. Now, there are many types of jewellers. There are those who sell cheap and cheerful glitzy rubbish and who can stretch to changing a battery on a watch, but beyond this, they are no more jewellers than one who can darn a sock is a haut couture seamstress or tailor.

But Robert Anderson was the real deal; he was a real jeweller.

Considine knew this when the woman who answered the phone said, 'Robert Anderson Fine Jeweller's, how can I help you?' She sounded like someone at a fine jeweller's should. Someone at a cheap and glitzy emporium wouldn't say those words when answering the phone, or sound the way that woman had – if they answered the phone at all, that is. Still, when she put the phone down, Considine did a Google search, discovered Robert Anderson had attended the prestigious HEAD school in Geneva. No doubt then, he was a proper jeweller. There were two Robert Anderson shops, one at the bottom of Grafton Street, Ireland's premier shopping boulevard, and one at the top. Robert Anderson was described – mainly by himself – as not only the nation's foremost exclusive jeweller, but horologist as well, regularly sought out by the rich and famous for the most important, intimate purchases of their lives.

Horologist? Why couldn't they just say watchmaker?

Anderson sounded in a hurry when she spoke to him. 'I can fit you in around half ten,' he'd said, his accent one that exuded the very best of Hibernia English, devoid of status but dripping with class. 'Yes, half ten, how's that sound?'

'That sounds fine, Mr Anderson. I'll see you then.'

'No, please, call me Robert.'

THE FRONT of Robert Anderson's shop was a rich tapestry of marble and tile, with dark wood stretching between the bay windows to the stained-glass panelling above. He wore a dull grey suit, white shirt and dull grey tie. He was a little short of six feet, Considine guessed, slim of build, with black hair receding on either side of a central tuft above a high forehead. His office was at the top of rickety stairs, and he went up the steps with a quick fluidity of movement, then waited at the top for Considine. The place reminded her of a church, above the recessed ornate ceilings to where no one could see, where dark stairs creaked their way to clock and bell towers, grimy and covered in bird shite. He was standing on the landing, but he didn't stand erect; his head was stooped between two curved shoulders, like he was permanently peering into a display cabinet. And like in a church where no one could see, at the top of the rickety stairs boxes were stacked, stencilled along the sides with *Made In China*. An old display case stood beside an open door, and through the door was a plain desk, a large curtainless window behind it. Through the window Considine could see the ornate metal arm stretching out from the wall and holding the curved top of the big clock that hung there.

He went through the door and said, 'Come in, come in.' He moved to the desk, but there was no chair. Instead, he sat on the windowsill, or perched would be a better description. 'There's a stool somewhere.' He pointed off to the side vaguely.

'That's OK. I'll stand. Mr Anderson, I'd like to say how sorry I am about the death of your brother. We notified your mother, by the way.'

'I know, it was she who notified me.'

'And you have another brother, Thomas.'

'Yes... ah, Thomas. The less said of him, the better.'

'We know of his history, Mr Anderson.'

'Please, Robert.'

'OK, Robert.'

'Thomas is pathetic. I hate to say that of my own brother, but he's a complete waste of space. He's a junkie. Plain and simple. Did you come here to talk about him?'

'No. Not specifically. We're looking at all angles.'

'I don't mean to be rude, but why did you come here? Specifically?'

'To talk to you, that's all. Can you think of anyone who might have wished William harm?'

Robert stood and rubbed his arse, moved to the end of the room and cleared some papers from a stool. He carried the stool and placed it behind his desk.

'Are you sure you don't want this?'

Considine shook her head. Truth was, she was so tired she could fall asleep, and standing was helping her stay awake. Danny Reagan had left shortly before dawn, and it was only then that she had been able to finally snatch a little, and proper, sleep.

'Look, I'm sorry. This is having a devastating effect on my

mother and myself. We all loved William. You know of his lifestyle, I'm sure.'

'Yes.'

He chewed on his bottom lip. 'Personally, I have no problem with it myself, what he did or didn't get up to. But...' He gestured about the room.

'But it might lead to unwanted attention is what I'm saying. Put it like this... can I speak frankly? Detective Considine, isn't it?'

'Yes, it is, and of course you can speak frankly. I'd encourage it.'

'I mean, very frankly.'

Uh-oh, Considine thought.

'Look, if someone were to put down, as they say colloquially, "the hand" and find a dick instead of a vagina, that would count as a nasty surprise, would it not? Every man's worst nightmare indeed. And it might be enough, if it were the wrong kind of person that is, to... you know, react badly, very badly indeed. Maybe William met the wrong man is what I'm saying. I often worried about that.'

'It's a possibility.'

'Because it's possible, isn't it?'

'Yes, it's very possible. Like I say, it's a possibility.'

'Mother is taking this harder than it might appear, and me too.'

'I thought she seemed very pragmatic about it all.'

'Oh, yes, that's Mother for you. And me too. But she and William were thick as thieves, the two of them. Best of friends. Not like mother and son at all. More like cheeky sisters. William brought out the child in her, the frivolous side. God knows, Mother needed it. But life must go on.'

There was an awkward silence.

'Like I just asked, you can't think of anyone who might

have wished your brother harm, can you, Mr... I mean, Robert?'

He gave a weak smile. 'No, William was loved by everyone. He really was. We were close. What with Thomas's drug habit, whom we didn't want anything to do with, by the way, it had the effect of bringing us closer together as siblings. I really appreciated having him as my brother, my good brother.'

'Thomas and William had a specially strained relationship, didn't they?'

'They had no relationship. And I don't have a relationship with Thomas either. Anyway, they hadn't seen each other in years, far as I know.'

'Would Thomas cause him harm?'

Robert pursed his lips. 'Well, yes, he's capable of it. I never really considered that possibility... until now, that is.'

A voice called out from the bottom of the stairs outside.

'Mr Anderson, the Piliski watch collection, I need the key.'

'Be right down, Joseph.' He looked at Considine. 'You may think it's odd that I'm at work like this, but it keeps me busy. I need to be busy; it stops me thinking. I hope you understand?'

She nodded. 'Yes, I do understand.'

He smiled. 'I'm sorry, but I have to go; is there anything else?'

'That's everything for now. I'll be on my way. But if there is anything you can think of, could you please let us know?' Considine took out a business card and handed it to him.

'Of course,' he said, taking it. 'Yes, of course.'

'Thank you, Mr... I mean, Robert.'

'Let me show you out.'

She followed him from the office and down the rickety

stairs. At the bottom he turned. She was surprised to see he had been crying.

'As I say,' he said, wiping the front of a hand across his eyes, 'we're taking this harder than might appear.' He smiled. 'But life must go on.' He opened the door and held it for Considine. She stepped out onto the busy, full-of-life street.

'Yes,' she said, 'it must,' and walked away.

28

Riley sniffed at the bottom of the front door, went into the living room and stood with her paws against the windowsill, looking out. A gentle breeze blew in through the open back door, through the kitchen, and along the hall. Riley turned her head to sniff, then cocked it to one side, like she was confused. Something passed the front window, and she turned back towards it, but too late, whatever it was was gone. Riley pressed her head against the glass, her eyes turning into the corner of their sockets as she peered out. Then she turned and bounded from the room.

Alice pegged the corner of the sheet to the washing line as Riley ran out the open kitchen door towards her. She failed to see someone emerge from the path at the side of the house, her attention taken up by Riley, who was almost upon her now.

'Riley, girl, what is it?' But Riley changed direction at the last minute and wheeled away, Alice's gaze following her. But it was too late.

Alice cursed, knew she had made a terrible mistake. She

had left the house, the morning giving her a false sense of security, a full laundry bag and the good drying conditions something else to think about. She should have listened, right down to the letter, which was a big ask, because she never did what she was told. But it was different this time. She should have stayed inside with all the doors locked. It was too late now. The man who had burnt a family of four to death, and wanted to kill her husband, was standing right in front of her.

Daniel Willow was dressed in a fleece top, cargo pants and hiking boots. His beard looked like it hadn't been cut in months, but his hair was neatly trimmed. His eyes, she noticed, never blinked and were black, cold and cunning.

'Let's go inside, Alice. I don't like standing out here like this. Don't make a sound. It really would be a shame.' He glanced to Riley, who was wagging her tail, but not leaving Alice's side. The dog seemed confused about Willow now.

But Alice got the message.

When they were inside, Willow closed the kitchen door. She heard him turn the key in the lock. She detected the smell immediately, unmistakable: petrol.

'No doubt he's told you all about me,' he said, pulling back a chair from the table and sitting down, indicating for her to do the same.

'This is my house. You don't tell me to sit in my own house. How dare you!'

'Oh, it's going to be like that, is it? Right then. Alice, sit the fuck down. How about that? Otherwise... well, I'd have to think about that, but it wouldn't be nice. Much better that you just sit and speak when you're spoken to. Do you understand, *Alice*?'

She did and sat, resting one hand over the other on her lap.

'That's more like it, Alice. You and old Maguire have any children?'

'Mind your own business, and his name is Tom.'

'Have you?'

'Yes.'

'How many?'

'Two.'

'Grown up, of course.'

'Yes.'

'Any grandchildren?'

'Yes.'

'How many?'

'Three.'

'Would you like to see them again?'

'What's that supposed to mean?'

'Would you?'

'Of course.'

'Then you do just as I say and you will. If you don't, Alice, I'll kill you. Do you understand?'

'Yes.'

'Good, Alice. Now make us both a cup of tea, a couple of biscuits too, nothing too chocolaty, OK?'

Alice got up and did what she was told.

29

Senan Richardson was in the grease pit when they called the second time, looking up at the underside of a large, blue SUV above him. In one hand he shone an inspection lamp into the wheel arch, while turning a monkey wrench with the other. He didn't hear them come in. He cursed under his breath, and Brody could see his arm straining against the wrench, which seemed to be stuck.

'Mr Richardson,' Brody said.

Richardson's head came round the back end of the SUV, peering up at them.

'And you are?' looking at Brody. Then he noticed Sheahan. 'Oh, you again. Coppers. What you back here for this time?'

'Come up, Mr Richardson,' Brody said. 'There's someone else who wants to speak to you.' Richardson hesitated, then put down the inspection lamp and wrench. He disappeared momentarily under the SUV, appeared again on the other side and came up the steps from the grease pit, walked over to Brody.

The officer from the Criminal Assets Bureau appeared at Brody's side, held an official piece of paper out to Richardson.

'Here you go, sunshine. Search warrant. Combined operation between the Criminal Assets Bureau and the Drug Squad. Any questions?'

'You didn't tell us *you* bought the car,' Marty said. 'The Volvo that myself and my partner, my other partner that is, asked you about, the one a murder victim was dumped out of the back of. We've found out you purchased it. Now, why would you keep that information from us? Well?'

Richardson looked at Brody. He was rubbing cleaning grease from a big bucket onto his hands and lower arms in a corner of the portacabin, the oil turning to a black slime. He washed it off in a small sink and began drying himself on a dirty hand towel.

'Look, this place is full of cars. They're everywhere, like apples in an orchard. How am I supposed to remember every last one of them?'

'You weren't asked about every last one of them,' Brody answered. 'You were only asked about one of them. The 05 D Volvo. And here's another thing: how come I never heard of you before? I've been around a while. How's that possible?'

Richardson threw the towel onto a small table with a dirty kettle on it and a couple of filthy mugs.

'Jesus,' he said, 'I'm a law-abiding citizen me, that's why. I can't believe this.'

'Believe it,' Brody said.

'What happens now, then?'

'We decide who brings you in is what happens now, us, or somebody else.'

'Well... they won't find anything here.'

'You don't sound too sure.'

'Well, I am.' But Richardson sounded even less sure now.

'Again, I ask myself,' Brody said, 'how is it that I never heard of you before?'

'Look, maybe, OK, probably, I sold that car... A Volvo, 05 D, you said?'

'Coming back to you all of a sudden, is it?' It was Brody.

Richardson looked furtively around the room. 'Seriously, those outside, can't you make them go away...?'

'I think it'll be me,' Brody said, 'the one who brings you in, I mean. Because right now, your name is the headline on the front page of this investigation. It's a murder investigation, I'll remind you, Mr Richardson. I think we can dispense with the niceties. Throw the bracelets on him, Marty; he's coming with us.'

'Aw, Jesus, no. Please. No. The car. I'll tell you about the car. Please. Let me go through the book first.'

'The book?'

'Aye, the book. I have a book. Sales and purchases. It's right there, in the drawer. Everything goes in the book.'

It was a ledger book. It took Richardson a while to find the entry, but he found it, a barely legible scrawl, but it was there.

'See,' he said, pressing his finger into the page, 'I have it.'

Brody and Sheahan peered over Richardson's shoulder.

'What, is that the name?' Marty said. 'Davis?'

'No, Dixon. Look, Miles Dixon. I keep everything, names, you never know...'

'Yes, you never know. Like now.'

'I was thinking more of parking tickets myself.'

'Why didn't you change ownership to this Miles Dixon?' Marty asked. 'That's down to you, isn't it? To tell the truth, this is all beginning to confuse me a little.'

Brody answered that question. 'Because JJ Harris never changed it either, did he, Mr Richardson? You couldn't change it even if you wanted to. It's still in JJ Harris's name. Isn't that why? That could be a lot of parking tickets.'

'That car was off the road,' Richardson said. 'This record here is my record. I bought the car from JJ, see, and then I sold it on to Miles Dixon. Nothing too complicated about that, is there?' He glanced at Marty, went on, 'An auld boy, this Dixon, lived somewhere down in Kildare, aye, I remember, wanted a big yoke for going around the farm...'

'You suddenly remember a lot,' Brody said.

Richardson was on a roll.

'Yeah, I do. He said the seat of the tractor was hard on his hips. So the Volvo was ideal. In fact, I don't even think Harris had the certificate of ownership. He'd lost it. He didn't care about shite like that. That's another reason why I didn't have it, don't you see?'

'Somewhere down in Kildare,' Marty said. 'Well, that narrows it down. Come on now, Richardson, where down in county Kildare?'

'I don't know... I remember he mentioned something about going to the bank in Kilcock to take out the money. How big's Kilcock? Can't be too hard to find out about him, two detectives such as yourselves.'

The door opened, and the female officer who'd served the search warrant came in along with a male colleague. 'So far,' she said, 'we have a stolen Lexus Hybrid and an Audi A6, two carrier bags of unknown pills and one carrier bag of skunk, hidden in a manhole beneath a pile of old car seats... we've only just started, so off to a good start. I have a feeling there's more to come.'

This time the bracelets did go on.

'Tell them,' Richardson said, squealing, 'that I'm assisting you with your enquiries. Go on. Tell them. I'm working for you. They can't do this. Tell them, for God's sake... here, take those off of me. I have a business to run. Tell them! You can't do this. Why're you doing this? And who'll feed the bloody dog?'

The blood drained from Richardson's face, the white of his skin against the black oil and grease streaks on it reminding Brody of a zebra. A suddenly very quiet zebra as he was led out of the portacabin.

'He's right about one thing,' Brody said.

'And what's that, boss?'

'Kilcock is small, only a pinprick on a map. If what he's saying is true, then this Dixon man really shouldn't be too hard to find.'

They took the M4 motorway from Dublin and twenty-five minutes later turned off at the Kilcock exit. A couple of minutes after this they were pulling up in the small town square. A small town with two banks. At the first, an AIB, the teller told them there was no account in the name of Miles Dixon. She wasn't from the town, she said, 'But give me a minute, and I'll ask around.' She came back and told them no one knew any Miles Dixon, sorry. They thanked her and left. The second bank was a Bank of Ireland. This time they met the assistant manager, who explained that the actual manager had a doctor's appointment, but, 'Will I do?' His name was Oliver Clarke.

'Yes,' Brody told him, 'you'll do.' Clarke brought them into his office and typed Miles Dixon's name into his computer.

'I haven't been here very long. Don't really know what's what yet. If Mr Geraghty were here, he could tell you immediately, but he has a...'

'Yes,' Brody said, 'I know, a doctor's appointment.'

'Of course, yes, I already told you.' He peered at the computer screen. 'Spelt D I X O N, yes...?'

Brody nodded, not knowing any other way to spell Dixon.

'Well, yes, here he is... I think.'

Brody felt an invisible elbow nudge into his stomach. He waited.

'Miles Dixon, address of Coolrain, Kilcock, Co Kildare. Yes, this could be him, couldn't it?'

'His date of birth, please,' Sheahan said.

'Oh yes, of course, twenty-first of February, nineteen twenty-nine.'

'Our man,' Brody said, 'has to be.'

'Only thing is, gentlemen, he died back in 2019. His account is closed.'

No surprise, Brody thought, with a date of birth like that. 'Could you find out how we get there?' Brody asked. 'To this Coolrain?'

'Stay here, please; shouldn't take me long.'

'Thank you.'

A COUPLE of the older staff remembered Miles Dixon. They described him as a 'lovely man', quiet and reserved, who lived alone on his farm just outside Kilcock. As far as they could tell, he'd never married.

The farm was bigger than Brody imagined. At least the house was. They parked at the end of the long, straight driveway leading up to it, climbed over a locked metal gate and began walking towards the house. Sheep were passing over the driveway, moving from one field to the next. The driveway was mucky, and the two detectives had to walk along the ditch to get past some of the worst spots. Despite the man having not been dead for very long, the property had already been half devoured by bramble and ivy. It was a two-storey farmhouse with a black slate roof, looking for all the world like something from the cover of a Stephen King novel. Tall trees pressed in all around it, and crows cawed to each other as the invaders approached. They rounded the side of the house onto a yard at the rear, ahead a collection of outhouses, to their right a lean-to with a pile of chopped wood in one corner, the wood so long there it was covered in moss. Next to the wood was a rusting Massey Ferguson displaying an ancient ZV reg.

'Nothing runs for as long as those old Masseys,' Marty said, who knew about such things, being a farmer's son from the west of Ireland.

They went into the lean-to, and Brody noticed the imprint of tyres from another vehicle that had been parked there, next to the tractor. On the ground was an oil spot.

'It's wider than the tractor,' Marty said, 'but the spacing looks like a car.'

'A big car.'

Marty nodded.

'And not long gone, judging by that oil spot.'

Marty nodded again. 'But what now?'

'Don't exactly know. The story Richardson tells seems to make sense. That tractor would be a killer on old hips, I'd imagine.'

'So the old boy dies, and the car is left here; this is where he kept it, probably with the keys in it too.'

Now it was Brody's turn to nod.

'And then he dies.'

'And then he dies,' Brody agreed. 'That makes sense too. He was old.'

'Very old.'

'Yes, very old.'

'And...' Marty pointed to the empty space.

'And?'

'It's like the song, boss.'

'Remind me.'

'"A Hole in the Bucket". We've come full circle, back to the start, to the beginning.'

'We have?'

'In the song they needed water to sharpen the knife to cut the straw to fix the bucket, but they can't get the water because there's a hole in the bucket. We've been trying to find the car and then, when we get here, it's gone. Someone's leading us along, I think. This is our hole in the bucket.'

Brody thought about that; someone was leading them along, an unseen puppeteer pulling the strings. But hole in the bucket? He shook his head. No, that didn't make any sense at all.

30

Considine went to the Happy Turnip vegetarian restaurant near St Stephens Green after she'd left Robert Anderson, and ordered a jacket potato with coleslaw. She'd only had a cup of coffee and a slice of dry toast that morning before leaving her house. She'd been toying with turning vegetarian for a while now and had recently, finally, committed. Eating in the Happy Turnip was part of a gradual transition to becoming a full-blown grass grazer. What had really switched her onto vegetarianism was a quote she'd heard: *Never eat anything that once had a beating heart.* Well, that'd done it. Now, every time she looked at a piece of meat, she saw Bambi staring back at her.

She sat on a stool at the window counter, looking out. The snow had disappeared, and the streets had dried, the light of a cold sun turning the world into a HD panorama, unlike the hot sun on an August day that made everything fuzzy. Considine liked days like this. Days like this were her favourite.

She thought of Danny Reagan for approximately sixty seconds before, like the snow, it disappeared too. No warm feelings flooded through her, no tingle of anticipation for the next time they might meet. Nothing personal, because Considine rarely felt like that about anyone. Rephrase, she never felt like that about anyone. Although he might not like it, and the Danny Reagans of this world rarely did, he had served a purpose. Quite the role reversal for someone like him, of course, which went without saying.

She yawned, and the phone rang on the counter before her, the number flashing across the screen one she first thought she didn't recognise, but then realised she did. Well, she considered, think of the devil and he's sure to appear – an old Irish saying. She hesitated; she'd missed a couple of calls from this number already. She picked up.

'Hi, Danny.'

'Well, hi there, Nic.' She winced, *Nic, for real?* 'You're not trying to avoid me, are you? I've rang twice already.'

'I know, Danny. I'm working. Sorry. What's up?'

He laughed, a forced rumbly sound, like a distant thunder.

'Well, I got you at last; that's what matters.'

It is?

'I was thinking...'

Uh-oh.

'How about a spot of lunch? You and me? I've just got to see you, I really do. Let's say half an hour, you know Greene's on the Green. It's nice; the food is great, Michelin Star actually. They know me there, only the best.'

'Sorry, Danny, no can do. I'm actually at the Happy Turnip. I've already ordered lunch.'

'Oh, you have, have you? Isn't that the place next to the shopping centre, opposite the park.'

'It is.'

'I can be there in twenty. I actually like vegetarian.'

'Um, of course. You can come here. But I'll be gone, Danny. I told you. I'm working. Sorry.'

'Aw, Nic, don't do this.'

'Do what, Danny?'

'You know what I mean. Play hard to get. Come on, I really enjoyed being with you... you know, last night. I felt we, you know, we had, we *have* a connection. Please... lunch, pretty please. Come on.'

'Sorry, Danny, I told you, I'm working.'

'After work, then. What time? What place? You name it.'

Considine took a breath.

He spoke, his voice low and a little desperate. 'I've *got* to see you, Nic. Really.'

Which is a turn-off to anybody; no one likes a pleader, after all. Danny had begun to dig a hole for himself.

'Why?' she said. 'We hardly know each other.'

'I can't believe you said that, Nic. Look, I know this is crazy. Yes, we've only just met, but I've been thinking about you all morning. I can't get you out of my head, I just can't.'

Probably from about the time that you couldn't get me on the phone.

But she didn't say that.

Then he said something that she didn't quite catch, her attention taken up elsewhere. At that precise moment someone was passing along the street outside. Considine did a double take. It was Robert Anderson. Nothing wrong with that, of course, she told herself, probably going for an early lunch, just as she had... so?

Still, that tall lanky frame, with the bowed head and the curved shoulders like he was leaning over a display cabinet, had a palpable sense of purpose about him. And Considine was a guard, a cop, a peeler, a mule, whatever you wanted to call her. Some were lazy; some were not; some were diligent, while some couldn't care less. But all, to a last man and woman, were as nosy as a bloodhound on a fresh scent.

'Nic,' Reagan said, 'are you listening? Can you hear me? I was thi–'

'Sorry, Danny, I've got to go,' and she hung up. She moved towards the door just as the waitress came with her food. 'Sorry. I'll be back. Keep it for me?'

She'd opened the door and stepped out onto the street before the waitress could answer. Considine scanned the crowd ahead, the street busy with shoppers and strollers out in the cold sunshine. Then she spotted the tall, narrow outline in the grey suit ahead, head bobbing as he made his way through the crowd.

She started after him.

The crowds petered out towards the top of the street, and when she followed Anderson round the corner onto Cuffe Street, she found there was no one else there. If he turned around now, there'd be no buffer between them. She hung back, allowing him to pull ahead, before continuing, head low. Halfway along the street Anderson suddenly stopped. She stopped too. She thought he would turn round and see her. In preparation she fixed a smile to her face, pulled back her shoulders, was about to walk on, to pass him by with a comment about what a surprise it was to see him, and wasn't the weather lovely. Instead, he began looking at his phone, and didn't turn round. Then he put the phone in his pocket and walked on, crossed the road and turned left onto Camden Street. She followed. It was much busier here, and she was able to draw close again. As suddenly as before, he stopped, this time to look in a window, where he lingered for a moment before walking away. She paused as she passed to see what he'd been looking at. It was a jeweller's shop, an array of sparkly necklaces and bracelets in the window, watches from €9.99 to €99.99, cheap and glitzy, although they all looked the same to Considine.

When she looked ahead again, and she'd almost missed

it, she got a glimpse of Anderson as he disappeared into a doorway. She casually walked up and looked at the brass nameplate on the wall next to it:

Aidan Kennedy, Solicitor and Commissioner for Oaths.

She cursed under her breath. That's the trouble with a cop's nose. Unlike popular myth, most times it led nowhere but up a garden path. She didn't know what she'd expected, but this was a complete waste of time.

She turned and made her way back to the Happy Turnip, determined that it wouldn't be a waste of a good lunch too.

31

Shane Martin maintained his demeanour until he'd brought Quinn into his office and closed the door. A bright office, with big windows looking out over Burgh Quay and the River Liffey. A bright office made brighter by white paint and a cream-coloured carpet. On the walls, abstract paintings, mainly of swirling yellows, whites and reds. An office, Quinn thought, befitting a business with the title *Magic Mushroom Creatives.*

When he'd closed the door, Martin pointed a finger at Quinn. 'You rang me at home. My wife was there. She could hear everything. What were you thinking?'

'I don't really see the problem,' Quinn said, sounding unusually confident.

Brody had sent him to speak to Martin on his own. He took this as a vote of confidence and an opportunity to prove to the unit – and himself – that he was up to the job. He didn't want to let Brody down. He didn't want to let himself down.

'This is a murder investigation, Mr Martin. We don't take subtleties into consideration. I could have simply gone and knocked on your front door, you know, and if she answered, your wife, told her why I wanted to speak to you.'

Martin's eyes widened in horror.

'You knew William Anderson; your name was in his address book.'

'I knew him. But I never thought he was putting notches on his belt.'

'What do you mean by that?'

'You know what I mean.'

'So you know he was a man?'

'What?' Martin sat back in his chair, a white, leather, high-back chair. He had on a Hawaiian shirt, which Quinn thought a little out of fashion, but then again, what did he know.

'Yes, I knew.'

'And what about Tamara? Did you know him as Tamara?'

'You mean that nonsense with the dresses and stuff, the wigs... Jesus, that stuff.' Martin shook his head.

'You didn't approve?'

'No, I didn't. He was much better as William, as himself, and I told him so.'

'You did?'

'Yes, I did, I told him I liked him just as he was, as a... man.'

'I see.'

'Look, I'm married. You know I'm married. This is very awkward, to say the least.'

'Where did you meet William, Mr Martin?' Quinn asked.

'The Voodoo nightclub.'

'That makes sense,' he answered, thinking of the V/N entry in the address book.

'Why do you say that?'

'When did you meet him?' Quinn asked, not answering the question.

'You never mentioned he's dead,' Martin commented.

'Didn't I?'

'No. Is that why you're here?'

'Yes, that's why I'm here.'

'I didn't kill him, if that's what you're thinking.'

'I didn't say that.'

'I know you didn't say it, but I bet you're thinking it.'

'We're talking to everyone, Mr Martin; we have to; it's standard policy.'

'Of course. Yes, of course. But I don't want you talking to my wife.'

'We have no reason to talk to your wife... not yet, that is.'

'What's that mean? Not yet. My wife doesn't know anything about... well, you know.'

Martin pulled at the collar of his Hawaiian shirt. Quinn noted his hair was set in an exaggerated quiff; his skin was smooth, soft looking, like he treated it with moisturiser every night. Nothing wrong with that, he knew sales of male personal grooming products were going through the roof. He'd tried some himself. But, for real, his wife didn't know he liked men?

'What?' Martin said. 'You're looking at me like I'm a dirty little poof, is that what you're thinking, is it?'

'Mr Martin, I'm not thinking that. Actually, my own brother is gay. So no, I'm not thinking that; that's your own stuff. For the record, I have no interest in your sexual orientation, none whatsoever, so don't get on your hobby horse, please, and accuse me of that.'

Martin looked sorrowful.

'I'm sorry.'

'How long did you know William Anderson?'

'Not long. Less than a year. We met... I don't know, maybe six times. I still don't understand why he had to write my name in his address book like that.'

'There weren't that many names in it.'

'Weren't there?'

'No.'

'Oh.'

Martin looked away, and when he looked back again, his eyes were moist.

'Where were you on Monday night last, Mr Martin?'

Martin answered immediately; he didn't have to think about it at all. 'Prague. I'm only just back. It was the annual Magic Mushroom Creatives International Conference.'

'By the way, that's some name.'

'It gets us noticed.'

'The Voodoo nightclub, that's where you met him, you say.'

'Yes.'

'Anything you can tell me about it.'

'About the Voodoo? It's a well-known... alternative lifestyles, you know.'

'How did you meet him? Were you introduced?'

'Yes. I don't know exactly how. I didn't like all that drag-queen stuff. But William loved the attention Tamara gave him. She was the opposite of everything he was, but it brought out something in him too, and not always good.'

'In what way?'

'He could be in your face as Tamara, you know, and he seemed to enjoy it... come to think of it, he'd a row with someone not so long ago at the Voodoo. We went there together that time. I didn't like it, the attention, I mean... my situation, you know.'

'Who'd he have a row with?'

'A fella called Larry, one of the managers there.'

'What about?'

'Something stupid. Larry swings both ways, you know,

and he made some kind of comment. I don't think he meant anything by it, something about you can only be one or the other, but you can't be both. I mean, coming from him, that was rich. But he was just being bitchy, that's Larry.'

'And William took exception to this?'

'He got on his high horse, yeah, and Larry just laughed. Then Tamara tried to punch him, I hadn't expected her to do that, but Larry grabbed him by the neck and told him he could snuff him out if he wanted to. He clicked his fingers. "Just like that," he said.'

'Wait. He actually said that, that he could what? "Snuff him out"?'

'Yes, he did, but it was just a silly handbags-at-dawn thing, that's all. They shook hands afterwards, not that night, but they shook hands afterwards.'

The intercom sounded on Shane Martin's desk phone.

'Mr Martin,' the voice said.

'I told you, Zola, no interruptions.'

'I'm sorry, Mr Martin, but it's your wife. She wants to speak to you. I told her you were in a meeting, but she insists.'

Martin's expression was like he'd just burnt his hand on a griddle.

'That's alright, Mr Martin,' Quinn said. 'I'll be on my way.'

Martin covered the mouthpiece with his hand. 'She's been checking up on me lately.'

Quinn got to his feet. 'Perhaps you should tell her. Honesty is always the best policy in a situation like this.'

'I beg your pardon.'

'Perhaps you...'

'Yes, yes, I heard.' He took his hand away from the mouthpiece. 'Put her through, Zola.'

Quinn crossed to the door and opened it, Shane Martin's voice in the background. 'I've been here the whole time,

Julie... no, I'm not... who, he's just a friend of mine, I told you...'

Quinn stepped out. The Voodoo club wouldn't be open for hours yet.

32

The Old Man was chewing on yet another Rennie, kneading the centre of his chest with the knuckles of his right hand. He was standing by the window, Brody by his side, both men looking out across the Phoenix Park, a view little changed in over two centuries. Indeed, this very window was one that people had first looked through during the era when wagon trains were pushing through the Wild West of America. Which reinforced Brody's view, Ireland was an Old World, never a New World.

'You think I'd know,' the Old Man said. 'Like really, you'd think I would have known.'

'About what, boss?'

'The banoffee pie, Brody. I can't take it, I really can't. You'd think I'd have known.'

'Oh.'

He kneaded his chest again.

'This investigation is throwing up results, Jack, everywhere but where we want them... Inspector Mc Guinness, by the way, over in the CAB, commends you on a great result. His result, by the way, but he commends you anyway. And the drugs bust. He's taking that too. But he commends you. Advance three places up the slippery career totem pole for him. But we know the truth, Brody, don't we? And there you have it, the reason why you're still a sergeant. You don't know how to climb the greasy pole, Brody, that's your problem. Look up. Can you see his arse scampering way off into the distance above you?' The Old Man laughed. He rarely laughed.

'I'm happy being a sergeant, boss.'

'I know you are, Brody, just as well. Anyway, this Richardson character... that's his name, isn't it?'

'It is.'

'Funny how we never heard of him. You'd think he'd be a client of ours, what with all we've turned up... what's so funny, Brody? Something I said?'

'Nothing, boss. Just I said it too, that I hadn't heard of him either, that's all. But he is a client of ours now, isn't he?'

'And that Foley bastard.'

Brody nodded. Transpired there'd been a warrant outstanding for Susie's partner, ex-partner, or whatever the hell he was.

'Where are we now with this investigation?'

'Trying to locate this car. I think we came close – today. It's probably burnt out somewhere by now.'

'Someone's pushing the pieces, Brody, and it's not us. We're playing catch-up. Those names, in the address book?'

'Two outstanding. I have Quinn visiting Shane Martin right now.'

'On his own?'

'On his own.'

'You think that's a good idea?'

'We'll see. I hope so.'

The Old Man nodded, but didn't comment.

'Like I said this morning,' Brody said, 'we're visiting the bars...'

'You think you'll get anything from these bars?'

'Maybe not, maybe yes?' Brody shrugged. 'Sheahan would rather go to *Carmen* if you think we...'

'No. No. Do it. He's rearranged his tickets. He cited Garda business, and they scheduled him a different date. Like you say, maybe not, maybe yes. It's worth a try.'

The Old Man pressed his knuckles into his chest again.

'Banana. I can really taste banana.'

THE SILVER WHEEL was a bicycle bar situated on a side street in Temple Bar. Brody had never heard of a bicycle bar before. He didn't know that one even existed. Along with the bicycle wheels hanging from the roof, the walls were adorned with portraits of leading pro cyclists, and the two bartenders were dressed in Lycra cycling shorts and Lycra T-shirts. Apart from these touches, it wasn't a theme bar, just a bar. There was a good late lunch hour crowd, an even mix of men and women.

However...

There was something in the air. Brody could feel it immediately. Like a raw energy. He wasn't sure what it was exactly.

He went to the counter, where a bartender had just finished serving a customer. He looked at Brody, smiled, hands on hips. 'What can I get you?'

'I'd like to ask you some questions.'

The barman had curly blond hair, the spandex cycling top he wore showing off a broad chest and pumped biceps.

'Police?'

Brody nodded.

'You have ID?'

Brody was about to reach for his wallet when Blondie

looked along the counter. 'That's alright. I believe you.' He came closer. 'What do you want to know?'

'Is this a gay bar?'

'Would you like it to be?'

'Does that mean it is?'

The bartender flicked a coaster onto the counter.

'It means whatever you want it to mean.'

'You do food?'

'Of course. Table service only. If you take a seat, I'll send a waiter over... or waitress, whichever you'd prefer.'

'I'll take a drink in the meantime.'

'Of course.'

'A bottle of Heineken, thanks. And while you go about that, you can think if you know someone called Tamara who liked to come in here.'

The barman looked surprised. 'You mean the person who died? That Tamara? That's the Tamara who came in here?'

'There can't be too many Tamaras.'

'No, I suppose not. But still... that's her?'

'Looks like it.'

'Some girl.' He shook his head. 'Oh yes, completely over the top. Got everyone's attention when she walked in here. Men loved her.'

'It's not a gay bar, then?'

'We get a mixed crowd, can't you see?' The barman grabbed a glass and shovelled ice into it. 'Look. It's a bar. We aim to be fluid. We can be anything you want us to be, gender-queer, non-binary, straight, gay, although we're leaning towards androgynous, but it's not quite our default, we don't believe anyone is the sum total of any one thing. We're a combination; we're everything... call it our business model. But like I say, essentially, when you take it all away, we're just a bar. We're here for the money.' He smiled, rubbing the tips of his thumb and index finger together in a money gesture.

'Thanks for the masterclass,' Brody said. 'And Tamara?'

The barman poured some of the Heineken into the glass and placed it on the coaster with the bottle beside it. Someone further along called for a drink.

'I've got to go, other customers, you know.'

'Forget the other customers. Tell me what you know about Tamara.'

'He was queer. So what? And he liked the straight guys. We get them both, although I'm not so sure the straight are all that straight, if you know what I mean? Look, why don't you take a table and order your food. I'll come down and give you a few minutes. If you don't mind.'

Brody nodded. 'I'll do that.'

He ordered the Yellow Jersey meatballs on a bed of creamy French onion pasta. When Brody finished, he pushed the empty plate away. The barman still hadn't shown. He was about to get up and look for him when he came over and sat down.

'I can give you five minutes; it's getting busy.'

An Edith Piaf number was wafting from the sound system. Brody recognised the voice, but not the song.

'It's always busy in here?' Brody asked.

'Yes, it's always busy in here. I'll tell you what, it's never not busy here. Once that door opens in the morning, people are coming and going all day long. Our location, yeah...?'

'Yeah,' Brody prompted when he hadn't added anything further.

'Means we don't have the crazy rents they pay at the top of the street, you know, out on the main drag. So we...'

'Tamara,' Brody said, 'sorry to interrupt you.'

'I was leading to that. What I was about to say is that they come in here at all hours, all looking for the same thing, even when they're not... you get me?'

'No.'

'Even the women are coming in here for the same thing.'

'They are?'

'Yes, they are, even if it's romance, it still amounts to the same thing.'

'It does?'

'Of course.'

'I'm confused,' Brody said. 'What are you talking about?'

'Sex, that's what I'm talking about. That's what people come in here for, even when it's not what they come in here for, if you get me?'

'I thought it was a bicycle bar?' Brody said.

'It is a bicycle bar, a very respectable bicycle bar.'

'It's the only bicycle bar.'

The barman laughed. 'We're everything, I told you. And that's why people come here. It saves a lot of hassle when you know everything is here. It's the way of the future.'

'If you say so.' Brody was even more confused. 'Tamara. Tell me what you know of her.'

'I know nothing of her except that she liked to drink spiced rum and Coke.'

'But you knew her name?'

'Of course. She told me. She introduced herself the very first time she came in here.'

'You know anyone named Senan Richardson?'

He scrunched up his face. 'No, can't say that I do.'

'When was Tamara in last?'

'That's easy. Thursday last week. She always comes in on Thursdays.'

'Why Thursdays?'

'Dolly Parton theme night. I mean, the resemblance was

uncanny; she really did look like Dolly Parton… poor Tamara. Imagine, she's dead.'

'She is.'

'Look, I've got to get back. I hope I've been of some help. Did you enjoy your food?'

'Yes, the food was great.'

'Good.' The bartender hesitated.

'Anything else you can think of?'

'Well, there was something.'

'What's that?'

'Tamara, she never left with the same man twice. Every Thursday. And you know something else?'

'What?'

'That's a dangerous game.'

'Yes,' Brody said, and thought, maybe it was more than dangerous, maybe it was fatal.

33

Willow was sitting in the Old Man's favourite chair, the recliner. Riley had seemed to have made up her mind about him now, clever girl, and was keeping her distance. Alice sat at the table, a vase of fresh flowers in the middle. She had taken them from the garden that morning, gerberas, irises, echinaceas, placed them into a vase and set it on a lace doily she had embroidered herself. Alice loved this room. She loved its view of the garden, loved nothing better than to just sit here quietly, sometimes with her husband, who, after all this time, she loved just as much too. This room held many happy memories.

Until now. Now that it had been sullied. Now evil had visited.

Alice was scared, very scared, but she was also angry, very angry. How dare he? This Willow, with two fucking *l*'s. Alice rarely cursed. But how dare he? She sat, her arms tightly folded across her chest, staring at the floor, unable to look at this monster.

Then it happened, what she feared most, as Willow spoke, softly and calmly.

'I want you to ring your husband.'

She looked up at him.

'The time has come. I cannot wait any longer. Like a good wine, it's time to open it and scent the aroma.' He sniffed loudly, made a motion of placing his nose next to an imaginary bottle. 'Yes, I want to open it. I've waited long enough, too long. It's almost four o'clock.' He pointed to the hallway. 'You can ring him on the landline out there. I spotted it.'

'C-can't you wait until he comes home later?' Alice spluttered. 'It won't be much longer. He never comes home early. Please.'

'And delay proceedings further? No, why would I do that? He who hesitates is lost, as they say.' His voice rose. 'Ring him, I told you. Now!'

Alice, with a sudden calmness that surprised even her, said, 'No, I will not.'

Willow's face creased into shocked surprise.

'What did you say?'

'I said no. I will not be a part in any plan to kill my own husband. I'd rather die myself first.'

Willow appeared speechless, but then recovered: 'If that's the way you want it...'

She didn't answer.

'This is your last chance. If you don't ring him, if I have to continue waiting here until he decides to come home, you know what I'll do, don't you?'

Again, Alice didn't answer.

'I'll simply kill both of you. I'll do him first, and you can watch... or maybe the other way round'd be better; he can see *you* get it... yes. But I'm curious, don't you want to see your grandchildren again? Last chance, Alice...'

Alice looked away, towards the window, and was completely still. She didn't speak.

'Maybe I'll kill your children and grandchildren too; now there's a thought.'

Alice blinked, but still remained silent.

'Going, going... gone. Right, bitch, if that's the way you want it, if that's the way you want it. Two for the price of one it is.'

34

Considine parked in her reserved bay right in front of her door. Home was a one-bedroom ex-labourer's cottage a ten-minute drive from the Phoenix Park. The sales brochure had called it charming, but Considine called it cramped. Still, she liked it, which was just as well, because with Dublin house prices the way they were, she couldn't afford to live anywhere else this close to the city centre.

She got out of the car and had locked it before she became aware of someone standing behind her. Then it clicked into place. The purple Lexus she'd spotted parked further back along the street and had dismissed as coincidence. She realised now it wasn't a coincidence. It was his.

She turned, and Danny Reagan smiled.

'Hi, Nic, thought I'd drop by. That's OK, I hope?'

'Drop by? This is more of an ambush.'

His smile got even wider.

'Aw, come on, Nic. It's me.' He tapped his chest. 'Danny. Ambushed? I'm not ambushing anybody. I just couldn't wait to see you, that's all.' His smile faltered, but he immediately hitched it back up again. 'I mean, I did try to ring, but, you know, you…'

'Sorry. I had no choice but to hang up. Work related. I did tell you I was working.'

He took a step towards her. 'Last night, Nic, I just had to see you. I mean, it was brilliant… well, wasn't it?'

Oh, yeah, Danny, it was the best ever; you're the best ever – Jesus.

'OK, five minutes, that's all. I don't mean to be rude; it's just the way it is at the moment.'

'At the moment. I can understand that. We all like our own space from time to time.'

Whatever.

She stepped past him and opened the door, went straight into the small living room cum kitchen. She put her handbag down on the table, left her coat on, went and filled the kettle.

'Coffee, black. Correct?'

'Correct.'

'Take a seat.'

He pulled a chair back from the table and sat down.

'I haven't stopped thinking about you all day,' he said when she'd placed the coffee in front of him, steam shrouding his face. He lifted it and took a sip. 'Whoo, this is scalding.'

'I like it really hot.'

'Oh, I know you do.'

'Aw, Jasus, can you stop with the smutty innuendo. This isn't the boys' locker room, you know.'

'I'm sorry, yes, I know. Of course. I apologise.'

Considine placed her hands flat onto the table on either side of her mug. Danny Reagan stretched his arm out and was just about to lay his hand on top of one when she quickly pulled hers back.

'What is it with you?' His smile had disappeared, and his voice dripped with hurt anger.

Considine was silent. She'd been expecting this, waiting for the mask to slip. He quickly put the smile back in place.

'I'm sorry. I didn't mean to snap. I'm really sorry. It's just, I really like you, Nic.'

She considered what would be the best way of dealing with this. Subtle or hard. She selected subtle – to begin with, that is.

'That's alright, Danny. But if you don't mind, I've stuff to do, and I'm knackered–'

He looked like he was about to crack another smutty joke. But he didn't.

'–if that's OK.'

If that's OK. Shite, you're asking his permission. Wrong, wrong, wrong.

'I thought we could do something,' he said, 'as in right now. You'll feel better for it. How about a drive over to Dun Laoghaire? We can get something to eat, maybe. Come on... Anything you want, just name it.' He was still smiling, rising from his chair.

'No.'

'What?'

'No. I said no, Danny.'

He didn't speak, and they both stared at one another. He was getting the message, Considine knew, but that didn't mean he was about to accept it.

'Why?'

'Why? Because I'm not interested, Danny, if you must know, that's why.'

She saw it then behind his eyes, a darkness coming down. He was no longer pretending.

'Not interested, hm. You're not interested. You're not interested, what? You not interested in *me*?'

'Sorry, Danny, I'm just not.'
'And what about last night, hm?'
'What about it?'
'We slept together, for God's sake. That's what.'

She closed her eyes and cocked her head to the side, trying to make sense of his words, then opened them again.

'Tell the truth, how many women have you spent the night with and then never bothered to call again? Go on, Danny, tell me. What? Cat suddenly got your tongue. And what, I should feel privileged that I'm not one of them, is that it?'

'You know what you are, don't you?'

'I'd stop right there, Danny, if I were you. We can still part civilly.'

'Whore.'

Considine jumped to her feet.

'Right. Out.' She pointed to the door. 'Go on, fuck off.'

His dark narrow eyes became calculating, a flicker of a smile starting to appear on his face as he made to step towards her. But he didn't move. The flicker died as he stiffened, and she saw his right fist clench. Considine had seen it all too many times before, in too many houses, with too many frightened women. Women who had looked to her, the one in the blue uniform, to be their saviour. Yes, she had seen it all before. And there was only one way to deal with this.

'What is it, Danny, want to give me a smack, is that it? Put me in my place like, is that it? Go for it, then; just you fucking try.' She held her arms loosely by her sides.

Danny smiled, another big, wide smile, and the darkness disappeared as his eyes twinkled.

'Aw, Nicola, what do you take me to be? Some sort of gorilla.' He took a step back. 'I'm going, look, I'm going. I can see myself out.' He turned and stepped over to the door. 'Gee, this house is tiny.' He opened the door and paused, looking about, then up to the ceiling and down again. 'It's like a bloody shoebox.' He looked over his shoulder to her. 'You could have done so much better for yourself, so much better. See ya round, Nic.' He stepped out onto the street and banged the door shut behind him.

Considine took a deep breath and shrugged. Pity he was such an asshole, because he really had been a great shag.

35

Capel Street, a once dull, grimy, traffic-clogged thoroughfare on Dublin's northside, was now home to some of the best restaurants and funky bars in the city.

Voyle wondered why he had never heard of the Time Machine bar before.

'I thought I knew every pub in this city,' he said to Sheahan as they walked through its doors and across the chequerboard floor tiles by the ornate, dark wood counter with its gleaming brass foot rail. Mirrors were everywhere, behind the bar, along the walls; it made the place seem bigger than it actually was, like there were three of everyone in it.

The barman was an old gent with white hair and smooth skin like wax. He wore a long apron and around his thin neck a thin black bow tie. In fact, Voyle thought, he looked like a corpse. The place appeared to be full of people, but both detectives had to remind themselves to divide the illusion by three.

'Good evening,' Sheahan said, 'could we have a word?'

'A word?' the barman repeated in a soft country accent. 'Don't see why not. You two gentlemen don't want a drink, do you?'

'You want one?' Voyle said to Sheahan. 'We can manage a small one.'

Sheahan shook his head. 'Not for me, no, but feel free to have one yourself if you want.'

'I don't either,' Voyle said, 'so, no drinks, thank you.'

'On duty, is it?' the old man said. 'You look like a guard' – he pointed at Voyle – 'but not yourself' – to Sheahan – 'you look like a solicitor.'

'Really,' Sheahan said and laughed, pleased with that. The old codger was a charmer.

'We want to ask you about William Anderson...' Voyle began.

'The body in the lane.'

'Yes, the body in the lane.'

'Or Tamara.'

'Right again.'

'Everyone knows about it now. Terrible. He was a regular.'

'Who?'

'Well, that person, of course.'

'Yes, I understand,' Sheahan said, 'but who was the regular? Was it Mr Anderson, or was it Tamara?'

The barman gave a little laugh.

'Oh, Tamara of course.' He turned and pointed to a stool at the end of the counter. 'Used to sit there. When he, sorry, she, first started coming in here, that'd be about five years ago now, she'd never been in before that, and I'd know. I've been a barman here for twenty years, from way back before the way it looks now, back in...'

'That's a long time ago, alright,' Voyle said, cutting him off.

The barman nodded proudly. 'Yes, it is. Silly name, Time

Machine. It wasn't always called that. It was known as the Shamrock Inn, a proper pub name that.' He lowered his voice. 'They wanted to get rid of me, you know. Thought I wouldn't fit in.'

'I think you fit in very well,' Voyle said. 'Now, William Anderson, or Tamara.'

'I was a bit disappointed, really, to tell the truth...'

'You were? With what?'

Someone called for a drink, and the barman said, 'Excuse me, won't be a minute,' and shuffled away.

'Still don't know how I never heard of this place before,' Voyle said.

When the barman returned, he took up where he'd left off. 'Yes, like I was saying, I was disappointed. I was disappointed because as a woman he really was very, very, how can I put it... sensual, yes, that's it, sensual. Oh yes, she was really sensual. And you'd never guess. I mean, she had me fooled, and it's not easy to fool a barman, it's our business to read people. I couldn't believe it, got the shock of my life, when I, ahem, spotted the...' He pointed to his Adam's apple. 'I'd actually, oh, maybe I shouldn't say, but I'd actually given her the eye myself. Good God, yes, I did. But I had no idea, you understand; really, I had no clue.'

'Of course. I wouldn't worry about it. When was she last in?'

'Oh, that would be... three nights ago.'

The detectives looked at one another.

'That's Wednesday night?' Sheahan said.

'Yes, it is.'

'The night he was killed. You didn't think to tell us, Mr... what's your name.'

'Frank Costello.'

'Mr Costello.'

'Well, no, I didn't...'

'You didn't think it would be relevant, is that it? But you said you knew about the case. You knew he'd been murdered.'

'I did.'

'Well then, you should have known that's when he was murdered too, Mr Costello. Mr Anderson was murdered on Wednesday night. And he was in here beforehand.'

Frank Costello looked at his feet and up again.

'I'm sorry, yes, in hindsight, I should have informed the police.' Someone gestured for a drink. 'I have to go.'

Voyle shook his head. 'No. Get somebody else. We want to talk to you. I spotted a CCTV camera over your front door on the way in. We want to see the footage.'

IN THE BACK OFFICE, the barman, Frank Costello, fumbled with the CCTV system's remote. A screen on the wall displayed footage from outside the pub in real time.

'I don't have anything to do with this normally. Lucy, she does the accounts, looks after this too. She won't be happy if I mess it up; they'd love me to mess it up; they'd have an excuse then.' He pressed a button, but nothing happened. 'Damn thing.'

'Don't you have any other cameras?'

'No. Just the one over the door. The comings and goings, you know. We don't allow cameras inside. Punters wouldn't like it, not if they thought we had footage of them necking someone, a mistress maybe, or Guinness dribbling down their chin and talking shite, which happens all the time... There, I have it.'

'What exactly do you have, Mr Costello? What were you looking for?'

He fumbled with the remote some more, then pressed a button, said, 'This,' and pointed to the screen.

They watched, the image on screen momentarily disappearing, but back again almost immediately, an exact replica, except the date in the corner was three days older. They were looking down onto the front entrance, could see traffic passing along the road in the background, and three women emerging from the pub, walking off into the night. A solitary elderly male followed, turned in the opposite direction and walked, half stumbled, off into the night too. Some moments later Tamara emerged, like a meteorite, the lights catching the top half of her dress, covered in something, row upon row of beads maybe, reflecting it, a sheen of twinkling diamonds. She wore a red dress, with red stilettos, the highest heels Voyle had ever seen in his life, and an explosion of blonde hair running halfway down her back. She walked with seductive grace and feline poise, slinking off into the night and out of camera range.

'She's on her own,' Sheahan said. 'I didn't expect that. Did she normally leave on her own?'

'No,' the elderly barman said, 'there was always somebody.'

'What kind of somebody? You know any somebody who did leave with her?'

'Well, yes.'

'Who?'

'Mr Stephenson, but that's a while ago now. He's a bit sheepish about it.'

'And what about recently?'

'You have to remember,' the barman said gravely, 'we are a city centre pub. Most people in here on any one night I don't know. I have no clue who they are. They just walk in off the street and off on out again.'

'Well, it is a pub, after all,' Voyle said.

'Exactly, and Mr Stephenson is the only one I know that

she left with. There were others, but I don't know who they are.'

'Did you ever leave with her, Mr Costello?'

'Are you serious? You are, aren't you? No, I bloody well did not. I mean, I knew. I told you, that brief time when I didn't know, maybe I would have then... but no, I certainly did not.'

'And how would we be able to find this Mr Stephenson?' It was Sheahan.

'Easy. Last time I looked, he was sitting at the counter right outside.'

He was also half steamed. That was immediately evident. Voyle thought that Tamara didn't seem too fussy whom she took home if this old codger was one of them. He was a small, squat man, whose feet didn't reach the foot rail, perched on a stool, wearing a trilby hat and, despite the heat in the pub, a Crombie overcoat. He seemed to be deep in conversation – with himself.

As Voyle and Sheahan approached, the mirrors offered three different angles, and Voyle had to remind himself that only the one directly ahead of him was the real Mr Stephenson. Voyle sat on the stool next to him, pulling it closer; Sheahan stood behind. Mr Stephenson pointed a finger to underline the point he was making to himself, oblivious to their presence.

'Mr Stephenson,' Voyle said.

The man's head was half slumped again his chest. He slowly raised it, and two foggy eyes attempted to focus, first on Voyle, then over his shoulder to Sheahan. He sat up erect and coughed.

'Yes.'

'We're police officers, Mr Stephenson, and I'd like to ask you some questions about Tamara. You know Tamara, don't you?'

He coughed again, squeezing his eyes shut for a couple of

seconds, then opening them slowly, as if emerging from sleep.

'Now. What did you say? Tamara?' He seemed uncannily lucid all of a sudden.

'Yes, Tamara.'

'Terrible business, dying like that. A lovely girl, yes, a lovely girl.' He shook his head. 'Yes, terrible business.' His eyes weren't so foggy anymore either.

'You know, Mr Stephenson, that she wasn't a girl. Tamara was a man. His name is William Anderson.'

'What? Was she? A he? Whatever.' He appeared to take this news without any surprise. He reached for his whiskey glass on the counter, took a swallow, put it back down again. 'I'm a little tired, busy day, you understand. Anyway, yes, she was a lovely person, Tamara.'

'How well did you know her?' It was Sheahan, moving to the side and leaning his elbow on the counter.

'Oh, you know, from coming in here, we'd say hello, that sort of thing.'

'Did you ever go home with her, your home, her home, whatever?'

Stephenson laughed, a rolling belly laugh. He slapped a hand against his thigh.

'Home with her. Why, you flatter me, gentlemen. Mrs S would have a fit... come to think of it, that's not such a bad thing. Home with her indeed. Tamara would be very disappointed in me if she had. Ha, ha. No. I never went home with her, or, as you put it, whatever.'

'Where did you go when you left here with Tamara? We know you left with her recently.'

'The Tricky Dicky.'

'What?'

'The Tricky Dicky – right across the road. The most silly name, I'll grant you. They do something called Kelaps, a cross between a kebab and a bap. Very tasty. I wouldn't normally have gone in, bit late for me to be eating. Mrs S expects me to be home at a certain time. But Tamara, she – oops, sorry, he – wanted a word. Are you sure she – oops, he – wasn't a woman. Had me fooled, I can tell you.'

'A word? A word about what?'

'Investments, that sorted of thing.' Mr Stephenson placed a hand in his pocket, took out a crumpled business card. 'I'm a financial advisor. See.'

Voyle took the card:

Walter Stephenson, Pensions and Investments Advisor.
IADC accredited.

There was an address and a couple of telephone numbers on there too.

'Ordinarily, she should have made an appointment and come to my office, of course. But, you know, a couple of sherbets and I'm anybody's...' He laughed. 'That's a joke, by the way, under the circumstances, perhaps not one in very good taste.'

'What did you talk about?'

'She said she was coming into some money, and she wondered what she should do with it. That she didn't know who to talk to about it. You know, despite giving the impression of being very outgoing, I got the distinct feeling that she – oops, he – was rather shy and maybe a little lonely.'

'You're very astute,' Sheahan said.

'Thank you.'

'How much money?' Voyle asked.

'She didn't say. It was an inheritance. From her mother.'

'Her mother? But her mother is still alive.'

'Is she? I don't know. A little premature, then, I suppose. Or maybe not, it's important to plan for these things, when you know it's coming. Yes, maybe not so premature after all. I told her – I'm just going to refer to her as *she* or *her*. It's easier. Confuses me otherwise. I told her to invest in fixed bonds and property, maybe. Limerick is a good bet, relatively low prices, good rental income, and appreciation values always on the up.'

'Really?'

'Yes, also County Clare, bu–'

'No,' Voyle said, 'I mean Tamara spoke to you about an inheritance. And that was it? That's the reason you and her went to this Tricky Dicky's, and for a what?'

'A Kebap, a cross between–'

'I know, between a kebab and a bap.'

'That's right. And very good they are too.'

'Anything else you can remember from your conversation with her?'

'Not really. They serve wine at Tricky Dicky's. Tamara ordered a bottle. Everything becomes a bit of a blur after that. I remember getting home though. Mrs Stephenson was not happy. Not happy at all.' Stephenson reached for his glass and drained the contents, held it in the air to signal for another. 'Any of you gentlemen like to join me?'

'No, thank you,' Voyle said. 'But I'll keep the business card, if that's OK?'

'Oh yes, that's OK. I have plenty more. Frank, yes, give me another, make it a double this time, cheers.'

36

It was almost half eight when the Old Man finally got home. He left his security detail outside, but they didn't leave until he'd gone into the house and closed the door. He watched their car drive off through the green, frosted glass of the door panel. He was about to take his coat off and hang it on the coat stand when he paused, cocking his head to one side.

Where was Riley? Usually she'd be bounding out to greet him by now. And where was Alice? She'd have shouted a greeting by now too. The house was so quiet, eerily quiet. And then he heard it, a voice.

'Welcome home, Tom. I've been waiting ages.'

A low, hoarse, chuckling sound followed, and the Old Man turned. He was standing there, Willow, outside the living room door, with what looked like a thin iron rod with a yellow tip in his right hand. It made a crackling sound, and he watched as the yellow tip changed to red, a series of sparkling swirls appearing inside it before two blue, electrical charges extended on either side like a pair of antennae. Willow pointed it, a cattle prod, and stepped closer.

'I know you've got a shooter on you. Put it on the phone stand there. Unless' – he made a jabbing motion – 'you want a thousand volts in your fucking face.'

37

A little past nine o'clock, Brody stepped into one of the three rings at the Northside Boxing Club, at the rear of what were called The Flats, a tough Dublin Corporation housing complex. His sparring partner was Jimmy Nugent, a man even tougher than he looked – and that was saying something. The bulldog, they called him.

'I was just about to close up,' he said as Brody arrived. The club was in a converted courthouse, which was ironic, as most of the men in The Flats had passed through it when in its former guise at least once. It was also deserted. Jimmy was a recovering drug addict, who now dedicated his life to youth work, trying to save kids from going through what he did. And the kids in The Flats needed saving.

'It's either this or a six-pack of beer,' Brody said, 'maybe a couple of shots too, but I detest hangovers, so this it is.'

'And so say all of us,' Jimmy said, his voice like churning gravel, nodding his head towards one of the two rings. 'Want a sparring partner for a couple of rounds? I could do with it myself. Been skipping for twenty minutes. I'm ready.'

Brody agreed and went and changed.

'Nice and easy,' Jimmy said, when he'd stepped into the ring. 'We need to get you up to temperature.' He crouched and bobbed, but not throwing anything Brody's way, giving him time.

Brody shuffled around the edge of the ring, air jabbing, bobbing and weaving, turning in full circles, gaining speed, slowing down, back shuffling, stretching his neck muscles. Then he turned in. Jimmy was waiting for him in the centre of the ring, where he'd been watching his every move.

Brody weaved and threw a jab, a half-hearted jab, merely letting Jimmy know he was there, that he was ready, before stepping in closer, reducing the radius of Jimmy's circle. Jimmy took a step towards him too. They were face on, testing each other. Brody threw another light jab, but lightning fast; it got through Jimmy's defences and hit the corner of his forehead. Then he followed with another. Jimmy didn't like it. He returned the jab, but Brody had back shuffled and was out of reach. Jimmy moved closer, but Brody was still out of reach. Jimmy wasn't. Brody had long arms, and he threw another jab, slow and stodgy, Jimmy brushed it away, not realising it was a ruse.

Splat.

Brody had followed with another, travelling like a missile down the corridor Jimmy had left open in brushing Brody's arm away. But the missile was low yield. This was a friendly sparring match, after all.

But Jimmy didn't like that either. He didn't like it at all. He came at Brody, his head low, fists high, a battering ram, so fast he thought he'd catch Brody by surprise. But he didn't. Brody back shuffled again, and as Jimmy's head came up, just enough, a periscope breaking water... Brody stopped.

Splat.

Jimmy blew air through his nose and made a loud grunting noise as the punch hit home. Brody was familiar with that sound. It meant Jimmy was blooded, and as mad as a horse with an itchy nose – a flaw in any boxer when the red mist descended like that, because it removed control. Which was a double-edged sword. Jimmy Nugent had won fights because of it, but he'd also lost. And when he lost, he usually lost big, and when he won, he usually won big too. His KO, or knockout rate, was currently fifty-two per cent.

Brody concentrated. He knew Jimmy could be dangerous like this. He switched to an out-box style, using his long arms to maintain distance. But Jimmy was having none of it. He came in slugging, not bothering to feint any punches, catching Brody a couple of times. Jimmy only needed to get lucky once.

Brody back shuffled again, stopped, back shuffled a second time. Jimmy came forward, but his movements seemed more measured and precise, low slung, bobbing and weaving. Brody went to the side and sent in a cross punch that glanced off the top of Jimmy's head. Jimmy sent in an uppercut that took Brody by surprise, but it didn't connect; just in time he snapped his head back, feeling the wash of Jimmy's glove on his skin.

Brody went defensive. So did Jimmy. Even Stevens. Then Jimmy sent in a quick jab, testing, but Brody shoulder rolled it away easily. Brody feinted a right, and Jimmy weaved. They faced each other. Even Stevens.

And then, as if in an unspoken communication between them, they moved forward, into battle, toe to toe. Brody was not as fit as he used to be, but he was still supremely fit. Boxing is one of the most intense, energy-sapping sports. To anyone who says otherwise, Brody would tell them to try it sometime, try hitting the heavy for more than sixty seconds, and see how it felt, if they could last that long. Most couldn't.

Brody and Jimmy slugged it out for maybe five minutes, at times offering examples of sublime fighting skills, but for the most part it was messy and ugly. Then Jimmy turned his back and raised his hand in a signal that he'd had enough, as he crouched down, hands on knees, breathing hard.

'Just remember,' he said, between gulps, 'you're younger than me, fella, that's what I'm putting it down to; otherwise I would have clipped your arse to rights, you whippersnapper.'

Brody was a year younger, that's all, but he didn't point this out. Instead, he laughed. And so did Jimmy.

'I needed that,' Brody said.

'Me too. Better than any smack high I ever had, that's what I keep telling the kids.' He stood straight again. 'I says to them, look, if you're going to try drugs 'cause you want to get high and escape your shitty reality, at least give boxing a go, 'cause it's the best bleedin' high you'll ever get. That's what I tell them. By the way, Jack...'

'Hm.'

'Anything you want to talk about. You know, if there is, I'm all ears' – he pointed to them and grinned – 'even if they're cauliflowers.'

Jack laughed.

'No, Jimmy, thanks. I don't need to talk. I did. But I don't now. It's passed. Thanks.'

'I'm glad to hear it.'

'Right, I'll get showered and get out of your way so you can lock up.'

'Don't be such a stranger, Jack. Drop by more often. Maybe we could set up a training class with the kids. You've a lot to give, you know.'

'Maybe. Give me some dates, and I'll see what I can do.'

'Really?'

'Yes, really.'

'That's great, Jack, really great.' Jimmy smiled, a smile that didn't sit easy on a face like his. 'I'll get back to you, OK? With the dates.'

'OK.'

BRODY DROVE HOME along the North Circular Road to Drumcondra, listening to the sounds of the engine and the tyres turning on the tarmac. They were the only sounds in the world. He passed through Hanlon's corner into Phibsboro, listed as one of the coolest places in the world to live by *Time Out* magazine. He passed through another corner, Doyle's, and drove along Phibsboro's main thoroughfare, took a right at the end and went over the canal bridge, the towpath alongside, where he and Quinn had met Susie's boyfriend that evening. Five minutes later he drew up in front of 76 Bishop's Road, home sweet home. He was getting out of the car when his phone rang.

'Yes.'

'Boss.'

'That you, Quinn?' He hadn't recognised the number.

'Yes, boss.'

'What is it?'

'You want to go to a nightclub?'

38

The Voodoo nightclub stood at the end of a narrow, dark cul-de-sac just off the western end of the quays. One time this area of the city had resembled a war zone, with derelict and burnt-out buildings huddled along the riverbanks. It was also home to a seedy red-light district. During the affluent '90s it had enjoyed a renaissance, with whole swathes of buildings demolished and swanky new ones built in their place. But now, the rot was setting in again, the swanky buildings looked old and faded before their time, slowly deteriorating, returning to what it had been before, like weeds reclaiming a neglected garden.

From a distance, it looked like two flaming torches were fixed to the front wall of the club above its entrance door. But as they drew closer, Brody could see these were in fact lights in the shape of torches, with paper trails lending the shimmering effects of flames. The wall was painted all in black, with the exception of a series of white brushstrokes on either side of the open double doors giving the impression of whiskers by an open mouth. Yellow light spilled out of the mouth, and the queue of people entering stretched back to the road outside and had the appearance of being devoured.

'No jumping the queue, granddad...'

'Hey, leave granddad alone; he's kinda hot... over here, granddad, ya fine thing ya.'

Brody ignored the catcalls as he and Quinn approached the door. Two bouncers were standing there, little and large. Brody went up to Little, round and red faced. If someone were to knock him down, Brody thought, he'd simply roll over onto his feet again.

'Not your type of place, fellas, sorry,' Little said.

Brody held his ID out in an exaggerated movement so that those in the queue could see him doing it. There were no more catcalls.

'You have a manager called Larry here?'

'Larry Doherty, yeah?'

'We'd like to speak with him.'

The bouncer shrugged and unclipped the end of the velvet rope from its post and waved them through. 'Upstairs bar, ask for Larry there.'

As they walked along the corridor from the door, the lights got steadily dimmer and the music steadily louder. Brody pushed through the door at the end and entered an epicentre, an intense kaleidoscope of colour, an explosion of sound. Every so often the light threw up a white beam, a split second where everything appeared in crystal-clear clarity. He led the way through the pulsating bodies, found the stairs and went up to the second floor. It was packed with bodies here too, but just not as many bodies. At the bar he pushed his way to the counter and waited to catch the eye of a bartender. It took a while. The purple-haired girl with the piercing in her nose and the centre of her chin who eventually came to him said, 'What's it to be?'

'Larry. I want to speak to Larry.'

'Who're you?'

Brody offered up his ID.

'Wait here.' She went through a door in the wall but was back almost immediately, cleared the glasses on the counter in front of them and lifted up a hatch. Brody and Quinn passed through, and she brought them into what looked like a stockroom, bare concrete floor, bright lights, shelves of liquor bottles, and all along one wall, kegs of beer attached to their lines and connected to gas cylinders and coolers.

There was a man sitting on a keg, smoking a cigarette. He had bleached blond hair and wore a white suit.

'Larry?' Brody said.

He nodded, took a long draw on his cigarette and blew out the smoke in a thick stream.

'You didn't see me smoking, OK, against the rules, health and safety.'

'We don't care about that.'

Larry had the pale, sickly skin of one who sleeps all day and is awake all night.

'What then?'

'William Anderson.'

'William who? Who's he?'

'Tamara.'

Larry winced.

'That bitch, what about her?'

He took another long draw on the cigarette and sucked it deep into his lungs, then angled his lower lip over his upper and directed the smoke to the ceiling, like an upside-down waterfall.

'Exactly. What about her? Did you have a row?'

'Who told you about that?'

'Did you?' It was Quinn.

'I wouldn't call it a row. But we had words.'

'Why?'

'Why?'

'Yes, why?'

'Because someone needed to tell her, that's why. She was usually cool, but sometimes she could be a right pain in the arse.' He looked at his cigarette, it was almost down to the tip, dropped it onto the concrete floor and squashed it underneath his shoe. 'We were frantic busy; you've seen what it's like out there. She was at the counter with her... I don't know what he was, her boyfriend, but they were being very affectionate. I told them to move aside and let the punters in to order their drinks. She didn't like it. That's what it was about. Silly.'

'That's all?' Quinn said.

'How do we know that's all?' It was Brody.

'Because I just told you, that's why.'

'Wasn't Tamara, and her friend, who we spoke with today, by the way, a little old for this place. Your clientele are kids. I bet if we checked IDs, we'd be sending some home, and sending you forward for a court appearance.'

'Hey, you're not going to do that, are you? Everybody gets checked at the door.'

'No, we're not going to do that. But we could.'

'Tonight is student night, that's why, two for one and all that... Tamara was a regular. We get all types in here. Anyone tell you we're not your typical club, we're...'

'Alternative,' Quinn said.

'That's right, alternative.'

'For example, tomorrow night we have an OAPs' behaving badly night. That gets wild, let me tell you. Is that why you're here, over a stupid few words I had with her, Tamara? Really?'

Brody studied Larry carefully, his brown eyes bloodshot and tired, but not devious.

'You don't know, do you?'

'I don't know what?'

'William Anderson. Tamara. He was murdered.'

'He was. Shite. No. I didn't.'

'It was all over the news.'

'I don't watch the news. I'm sleeping. I wish I were sleeping now.' Something seemed to dawn on Larry then. 'Oh, I get it, you think I had something to do with it because you'd heard me and Tamara had had a row. Aha, that's why you're here.'

The silence from Quinn and Brody was an answer in itself.

'Well, you're wasting your time on that one, gentlemen, you really are.'

And Brody had to admit, they probably were.

39

The crackling, spitting inferno lit up the night sky, the occasional *wooooff* as something exploded, the flames bright orange with the thick black smoke curling into the night, obscuring the roadway above. It was 3 a.m. Another hour passed before a vehicle came along. By then, though the fire had lost much of its rage, it was still sufficient to throw off enough smoke to force the driver to slow down. He had his windows open; he always had them open when driving at night, the cold air streaming in to help keep him awake. He knew that smell; it was of burning oil and petrol, of upholstery and rubber. He coughed, closing his windows quickly. Unable to see much ahead, he braked, as the smiling wizard painted along the sides of the truck that promised *Nothing Gets Moved Faster Than A Wizard Delivery* suddenly wasn't going anywhere. He opened the door and climbed down from the cab, folding his arm across his mouth and nose, and went to the edge of the road. It was a twisting road, a crash barrier running alongside for much of it. But not here. Here there was a gap allowing access to a mobile telephone mast, scarcely enough room for any vehicle to pass through. He walked in and stopped. A copse of trees was ahead of him, and behind it the ground gently dipped away, leading, he knew, to a sheer drop into a valley. He fumbled for his telephone, fumbled some more until he'd located the torch app, turned it on, and carefully stepped forward. He held on to a spindly branch as he did so, the ground hard and slippery underneath. He was a professional truck driver, and professional truck drivers came upon accidents more than most. He knew they weren't officially called accidents anymore. They were known as road traffic collisions. Whatever, it was all the same. There'd been a smash.

He thought what he was doing was probably a waste of time, but he had to look anyway. If there had been an accident, or traffic collision, whatever – and he didn't know there had yet, all he knew was that he could smell one – the emergency services had probably been and gone already. It would have been a great help if a temporary sign had been erected, to tell people like him that emergency services had already attended.

He went down the incline and at the end held tightly to another thick branch and leaned forward, peering over the edge. And immediately got all the answers to his questions. Firstly, there had been an accident – a traffic collision, whatever. Secondly, no one had been here but him; emergency services had not attended. Because the remains of what was down there continued to burn, and a fire crew would never leave it like that. He could see the outline of the twisted wreckage, and he held his breath and listened for any signs of life, a call for help maybe. But there was nothing; everything was eerily silent, the fire burning without sound. Not that he had expected any. He hadn't. The poor bastard who'd tumbled down there was dead in that intense fireball. No one survived a fireball. He turned and made his way back up the incline, pressing the number nine three times on his telephone with a shaky hand.

40

Willow was smoking a cigar. The windows in the living room were closed, and the air was filled with the whitish blue smoke from it.

'I've always liked cigars,' he said, whipping it from his mouth, the cap glistening with saliva. 'This is a Havana Regal. I got them shipped to the prison. It helps to have money. You ever smoke cigars, Tom?' He placed the cigar in his mouth and switched the gun back to his right hand, resting the index finger on the trigger. For a man who couldn't possibly have had access to firearms for the best part of four decades, the Old Man thought he seemed awfully comfortable holding it. But what he noticed most was that the safety lever was turned to 'off'. All it would take was the pressure equivalent of lifting a mug of coffee to discharge a round and the time it took to take a couple of sips for all ten in the magazine to be discharged. Alice sat next to him, one hand resting on top of his knee. The air was cold, and, despite everything, the Old Man really wanted to go to sleep. He shook his head as Willow stood abruptly.

'Catch,' he said, pulling the cigar from his mouth, sending it cartwheeling through the air.

The Old Man fumbled to catch it, and it fell against his chest, then bounced onto his crotch. He jumped as it rolled to the back of the sofa. Willow laughed. The Old Man picked it up.

'Now, put that cigar in your mouth and eat it,' he shouted.

'You can't be serious.' It was Alice. 'My husband can't eat that.'

'Do I fucking look like Billy Connolly to you? Eat it, I said. Open up and eat it. Yum, yum. Come on, you bastard. Eat it!'

He trained the Walther's muzzle on him. The Old Man looked from the cigar to Willow.

'No,' he said, with quiet authority, 'I will not,' and flung it at Willow, who raised his arm to deflect it. The Old Man, big fists clenched, rose and stepped forward, but not quick enough, as he felt a sharp, cutting sensation to the side of his face, heard Alice scream. Willow had struck him with the tip of the pistol grip, he realised, feeling hot liquid begin to flow down his cheek. He reached up, felt a flap of flesh hanging there.

'Tom,' Alice screamed. He felt her hands on his shoulders, nudging him gently to sit down again.

'Leave him alone. I give the orders around here.'

'Look what you've done,' Alice screamed. 'How dare you? Look what you've done to my husband.'

The Old Man sank heavily onto the settee.

'Get up,' Willow roared. 'I didn't tell you to sit down. Get up, you bastard.'

The Old Man shook his head, feeling the world suddenly spin, and shook his head again. Across his chest an invisible vice had begun to tighten. 'Jesus,' he said, reaching for it, as the vice tightened, tightened, and tightened again. He heard Alice's voice, but it was like a weak echo, and getting weaker, as the grey light faded, a black horizon rushing towards him.

ALICE SAW the colour drain from her husband's face, retreating before the mottled white that spread down from his scalp as it literally took his life away.

'Quick,' Alice said, pulling his tie off – thank God it was a clip-on – and undoing his shirt collar button. 'Ring an ambulance. My husband is dying.'

'No. No. No. He can't. I am the one who decides. Get out of my way. He can't die, he can't. I've waited too long for this. Get out of my way, you bitch.'

Willow grabbed Alice by the hair, and she felt the searing pain as he yanked her backward. She fell to the ground as Willow stood above her husband before crouching down, then standing again. Finally he ran a hand through his hair and looked up to the ceiling and howled, a long, horrible, tortuous sound, like all the evil in him was venting its fury.

Alice turned and looked towards the empty fireplace. A corkscrew of smoke rose into the air next to it where the cigar stump was burning into the carpet. But she didn't care about that. She looked at Willow again, his back to her, his arms rigid, the gun gripped between both hands pointing at the floor. She had little time.

She crawled on her belly to the fireplace, unhooked the long, heavy brass poker and silently stood. She watched as Willow started to raise his arms, an almost leisurely movement, as if in slow motion, bringing up the pistol and aiming it at her husband. She had even less time now. Alice raised her arms also, her hands gripping the poker, holding it like a short spear, looking along it to the soft centre at the back of Willow's neck. She would only get one chance at this. Her right hand gripped it tight, but she held her left hand lightly around the middle, acting as a rudder. Willow seemed completely oblivious to her, like he had discounted Chief Superintendent Maguire's wife as being any kind of threat.

Alice took a deep breath and held it, then charged...

Willow seemed to sense she was there only at the last second, angled his head slightly, as if he was listening for something... but too late. She plunged the tip of the poker into the centre of his neck, where she'd been aiming, as she began to shriek wildly, a sound from somewhere deep within her primordial self, one she had never uttered before, a throwback to an age of survival of the fittest, of the conquering of the savage beast, which is what Willow was. The poker tip slid through the gap between two layers of bone in the vertebral column as Alice used both hands to push with all her might, sliding it through muscle, which sounded like a finger being pushed against the inside of a person's cheek... *pop*, as the poker jolted and emerged out the other side of Willow's neck.

His arms collapsed to his sides, the gun falling to the floor, and his body gave a violent twitch as he stumbled once, then collapsed, his head bouncing against the tile-covered brick hearth. He lay there prostrate, his wide eyes staring up at Alice, yet through her and beyond, and seeing nothing at all.

Alice ran to her husband, collapsed onto her knees and held him gently.

'Tom, Tom, oh Tom...'

But knew it was too late, the Old Man's body was already tepid and turning blue.

41

Brody's phone rang a little before four o'clock later that morning, and he was instantly awake. He knew it could only mean one thing: bad news. He snatched it up.

'Yeah, Brody.'

He listened and hung up without saying another word, closed his eyes and laid his head back on the pillow. Brody knew there was only one certainty in life: what you fretted about never happened, but what you didn't expect, and never saw coming, always blindsided you.

Like now.

The Old Man was dead.

He began to make sense of everything else he had been told. That Alice Maguire had stuck a wrought-iron fire poker through the person responsible's neck. And that person was dead. A person by the name of Daniel Willow. The Old Man was right to have been worried. Brody couldn't help but wonder if there was anything he could have done. No, he decided, there wasn't.

Jesus!

The Old Man was dead.
Dead!
Brody wanted to fling his phone across the room. But he didn't. That wasn't a good idea. He wanted to pummel the heavy, but he didn't have one, so couldn't do that either. Then he thought of Alice Maguire and imagined her as she stuck the poker into her husband's killer's neck. The fucker! He felt a little satisfied. He wanted to hug Alice, but he couldn't; instead he shouted, 'Good on you, girl!'

AT A LITTLE PAST nine he was in the unit room with Voyle and Considine, numbly staring at his Pulse screen. No one spoke. Police officers, routinely exposed to the worst the underbelly of life had to throw at them, were forced to build up resilience; otherwise they succumb. Yet, sometimes, this resilience manifests itself as rude indifference, coldness or apathy, or all three. But it is none of these. It is simply a coping mechanism, a means of survival. Like now.

The Old Man's death had been dropped on them like a missile. They each were, in their own way, now dealing with the aftermath. And there was nothing they could do. The local detective unit in Donnybrook were in charge; both bodies had been removed to St Vincent's Hospital and were lying together in the morgue, pending autopsy.

Brody knew what the Old Man would say to him right now, *Get on with it.*

And he knew that's what he had to do. He had to get on with it.

An incoming incident alert pinged on Pulse, and he immediately opened it, posted by Traffic at Dublin Castle, tagged to a reg number he was interested in, 05-D-75648. He read what it had to say: there'd been a collision in the Dublin mountains, a body had been found in a burnt-out car at the bottom of a sheer drop at the side of a twisting road, burnt and twisted beyond all recognition. An update had been added to the report by a forensic traffic investigator, who posted that the VIN plate had been recovered and come back for a 05-D-75648, Volvo V70 estate.

Brody, desperate for a diversion, grabbed his jacket, told Voyle to come with him, and they both rushed from the office.

The Dublin mountains overlooked the sprawling Dublin suburb of Tallaght to the east of the city. There was quite the carnival already there when they arrived. Road traffic forensic investigators were mapping the scene, a green laser beam flicking across the road close to a bend, the investigator logging the results on a handheld pad. Two firemen were reeling hoses into the back of their engine. Two marked patrol cars with their roof lights turning blocked the road at either end, while a grey, old Toyota was parked up at the roadside. Brody recognised it as Dr Mc Bain's car.

The young guard standing on the roadway raised his hand as they approached. Voyle showed him his ID, and the uniform pointed at Brody and said, 'What about his?'

'What about his? We're together. Who do you think he is? A stroller along for a gawk? Fuck off.'

Brody took out his wallet. 'Easy, Voyle. That's OK, son, no problem.' He held it out for inspection. The uniform nodded sheepishly, and they walked on.

An inspector from Tallaght introduced herself as the officer in charge. Brody recognised her.

'Hello, Lindsey.'

'Ah, Brody, how are you?' She placed her hands on hips, wide hips that had borne her three strong children. 'I'm sorry, Jack. I just heard about the Old Man. My condolences. I met him once. The man was a legend...'

Brody nodded. She seemed to sense the mood, that he

didn't want to talk about it, and nodded to her left. 'Funny thing,' she said.

He and Voyle followed her gaze.

'Funny thing?' Brody repeated.

'Yes, that gap there. It went right through it. Look.' They stepped over to the crash barrier. 'This went in about seven years ago. Nothing has gone over the side in all that time. Until today, that is. But yet' – she pointed – 'right through there it went, through that relatively small gap, scarcely enough room for it, but barrelling through it goes, doesn't even glance off the barrier or anything else, passes the trees and goes down the incline... there, you can see the tracks, then over the side and *whoosh*, flying without wings, baby. The poor bastard had no chance.'

'Still there? The poor bastard?'

'Uh-huh, Jack. Well, he's not going anywhere, is he?'

'I'd laugh if it were funny, Lindsey, I really would.'

She held his gaze a fraction longer than was necessary. Voyle caught it and wondered if these two didn't have some history. The truth was they had, but it had been a long time ago, and Lindsey Twomey was now a happily married woman.

'We'll see if we can't get down there,' Brody said.

'You can if you go that way.' Lindsey pointed again. 'There's a little trail. Take care. Nice seeing you, Jack.'

'You too, Lindsey.'

'Nice seeing you, Jack,' Voyle said as they moved away. 'Very friendly there, boss. Do you two...?'

'You'll never know,' Brody said, cutting him off at the pass.

The trail was very narrow, made by mountain sheep, and as they descended, the acrid smell of burning grew heavier and sharper, almost viscous, like they could almost reach out and touch it. And with it, the unmistakable smell of burning human flesh.

Dr Mc Bain was the only one down there. He wore a blue tweed jacket and jeans. There was no requirement for him to wear a hazmat suit in this environment, but he did wear shoe coverings and gloves. His hair was pure white, long enough that it almost reached his shoulders, and his bushy eyebrows were two caterpillars above his eyes. He had a thick moustache and wire-rimmed glasses. Brody always thought he looked like an older Groucho Marx.

He and Voyle stopped short of the wreck. The doc was leaning through the space where the front windscreen had been, his arm extended towards the black, smouldering outline behind the steering wheel, like a charcoal recreation of a human body. Except this was a real human body, smoke rising from it like a fine mist. The doc folded back his arm and placed the sample of whatever he'd just taken with his disposable tweezers into a vial.

'This time you do show up,' he said to Brody, taking a pace back from the wreck, bending down and placing the vial into an aluminium case by his feet.

'This time?'

'And young Voyle with you. How's it hangin', Voyle, you getting much lately? No doubt you are, you randy bugger. Aye, Brody, you weren't there last time. In that alley, that is. What was it called, something to do with glucose, although I know that's not it.'

'Sugar. Sugar Lane.'

'Aye, that's the one. Bit more cut and dried that one was. This one, not so... I'm only here because of the link between the two, procedure says I must, but a waste of time. I mean look at him. He's like the one roast I did in my life, burnt to a crisp. I still have to cut him up on the table, so I could have saved myself the journey. Anyway' – he pointed – 'I don't think cutting him up will be of any use either; his insides will have melted, nothing more than dog food by the looks of him. And what's to say if it walks like a duck, and it talks like a duck, that it isn't a duck, a plain old, ugly I'll grant you, duck of an RTC.'

'Male or female,' Brody asked.

'Male.'

'See, you can tell me something. How soon before you'll know if you can ID?'

'What kind of question is that?' The doc leaned down again and clipped the aluminium case shut. 'You've been watching too much *CSI*, Brody. I've told you, that's not real.'

'I don't watch *CSI*.'

'Aye, aye, but it's infected the discourse, as they say. But you're in luck. Normally I wouldn't have known until I had him on the table. But his right hand was clenched tight, a death grip, not unusual when burning to death, even if unconscious. So I snapped a finger off, and it's in that box there. I'll take it back to the lab, and if lucky, it should be enough for a print comparison.'

'Thank you.'

'Oh, there is something else, Brody.'

'And what's that?'

'The seat belt on the cadaver, it melted, but it didn't furrow the skin as you'd expect...'

'Furrow the skin, Doc.' It was Voyle. 'What do you mean?'

'Like a plough when it's pushed into the ground, don't you see? Leaves a furrow behind it. The same principle. There isn't one on the cadaver. That's what I'm saying.'

'Meaning there wasn't pressure against the seat belt at the time of impact,' Brody said.

'No, Jack, it doesn't. There was pressure, of course there was, but listen up, there wasn't sufficient pressure to create that furrow.'

'You've lost me.' It was Voyle.

'If the average body, you imbeciles, is subject to the

kinetic forces at play in a crash of this magnitude, a seat belt will have left its mark. A normal person will involuntarily strain on impact, it's instinct, and the harder they strain, the greater the forward kinetic energy when they are propelled forward. In this case, although the seat belt has melted, like I said, it has done so at an indentation of no greater than two centimetres, and the reason for that is because they weren't straining in anyway whatsoever. And something else, on top of something else. Maybe it's my devious mind. But if that were the case, and if the skin, despite the person not straining, and while the skin was *intrinsically* rigid at the same time, would all combine to repel the forces at play, the result would be minor markings as opposed to anything else, which is the case here.'

'That clears that up, then,' Voyle said, throwing his eyes to heaven, none the wiser.

'Don't get lippy, my lad. Tell him, Brody, for God's sake.'

'What the doc is trying to say–'

'Not what I'm trying to say, what *I* am saying.'

'What the doc is saying is that at the time of impact, the deceased was already dead.'

'Really?' Voyle looked at the doc. 'Well, why didn't you just say so?'

The crash investigator thought it all odd too. He told Brody that Lewis Hamilton couldn't have done it better, gone through that gap like that, yet this driver had.

Brody agreed. While the car might have been driven from the road, could it have been pushed over the side of that sheer drop?

It looked that way. But why?

'And Brody.'

'Yes, Doc.'

'Sorry to hear about the Old Man.'

Brody nodded and walked away.

42

'I didn't expect to see you so soon again, dear.' Mrs Anderson said, opening the door and stepping aside to allow Considine into the hall. 'Especially as you could have saved yourself a trip and spoken to me by phone. Something must be wrong. What is it?'

'Can we go into the living room and sit down, please, Mrs Anderson? I just want a few words. I didn't want to discuss it on the phone.'

The old lady nodded. 'Yes, dear, of course, but it doesn't sound good.'

She sipped on a sherry a moment later, the glass gripped in the long slender fingers of her hand. Considine had declined to have anything.

'If I can do anything to help, I will. What is it, dear? By the way, is everything alright with you? I just can't help but think you look a little... sad.'

'I'm fine, Mrs Anderson,' Considine lied, 'really...'

'Do you mind, dear, but don't call me Mrs Anderson. Would you not do that? Call me Margaret. I think we know each other well enough that you can call me Margaret. Will you do that, dear?'

'I will.' Considine smiled. 'But only if you call me Nicola. I hate you calling me dear. Will *you* do that?'

The old lady smiled. 'You do? You hate me calling you that?'

'Uh-huh.'

Under the circumstances, what Margaret did next surprised Considine. She laughed.

'If this had happened when I was younger, I would have found it hard to cope. I was fragile back then. My marriage was very difficult. But now... do you believe in God, Nicola?'

'Um...' Considine began, and in light of what had happened, considered, there's a thought. She didn't know if she did or didn't. It depended on the day of the week. But right now, maybe she did.

'Anyway, I believe in God, Nicola, I do. Maybe I'm fooling myself, and that's fine if I am, but at a time like this, it's a comfort. Because William will have gone to God, and it won't be long before I see him again, before we'll be together.'

'Oh, don't say that, Margaret. I'm sure you have many good years left. Come on now.'

The old lady shook her head.

'No, I don't, Nicola. I never mentioned, because there wasn't any need. But I'll tell you now. Cancer. Stage four. So no, not long at all.'

Considine considered that news. 'I'm sorry to hear that, Margaret, I really am.'

'Don't be, dear... oops, I mean Nicola. I'm not sorry, you see. I'm tired, Nicola, of living I mean. So no, it won't be that long at all. Aw, you think I'm a silly, doddery old woman. And you're probably right, Nicola, you're probably right.'

'No, Margaret, I'm not thinking that at all.'

A silence fell on the room.

'Now, Nicola, what is it you came to see me about?'

'It's probably nothing.'

'Don't worry if it's nothing. What is it? You can ask me anything.'

'To tell the truth, I don't really know what it is I want to say... I mean, I do, but I don't know how to say it, that's all.' She thought of the Old Man and pushed it from her mind.

'Don't try, then, Nicola, just say it. I promise whatever you say will be alright. I won't be upset.'

'Have you money, Mrs Anderson? That's what I want to ask. Are you wealthy?'

The old woman didn't answer right away. 'Well, I didn't expect that question. No, certainly not, I didn't expect it. Why on earth would you ask me that question?'

'You said it would be alright to ask anything.'

'Oh, it is, dear, it is.'

'And are you? Wealthy, that is?'

'Well, I have a few bits and pieces. At my age I should think that I have to. Some shares, you know, don't know much about shares though, my husband left them to me. He may have been a difficult man, but he was a good provider, a very good provider.' She looked away. 'But I often think I shouldn't have stayed with him like I did. Let's just say there were fights, lots of fights.' She looked back again. 'But I don't want to get into that. It just can't have been good for the children.' She paused, then continued, 'Anyway, I also have a little cash in the bank, Nicola. And there's also this house; that's worth a pretty penny now, I suppose.'

'How much cash? In the bank?'

'Oh, you know, maybe, well, not quite five.'

'Five thousand?'

'No, dear, five hundred thousand.'

'Oh.'

'It's not that much, dear, not when you think about it.'

Only about twice the price of my house, that's all. Yes, everything really is relative.

'What about an insurance policy?'

'Well yes, that too, of course. I've been paying into it for years, which is the sensible thing to do. My husband set that up too. I wanted to leave a little something behind me, Nicola, for my children, even Thomas, despite him achieving little in his life except breaking my heart. But he is my child, the same as they all are. I really have to treat them equally; it's what any mother would do. But tell me, dear, why do you ask?'

'Like I told you, Mrs Anderson, I don't fully know myself.'

'You must have your reasons. Do you think maybe someone is after my money, is that it?'

Considine said nothing. She had the feeling Margaret knew why she was asking about her will, but was choosing to ignore it. It was easier to ignore it; it was easier to keep that head in the sand.

'Well, you don't need to worry about anyone being after my money, Nicola. I can look after myself. Someone once rang me from Abuja, that's the capital of Nigeria, Nicola, did you know that? I knew what they were after, and I told them what to do with themselves, I can tell you. They thought I would fall for that old line, that they had two million sterling ready to deposit into my bank account. Is that the reason why you ask?'

'Something like that,' Considine lied.

'That's very kind of you, Nicola. I've met so many kind people lately. People are very kind, aren't they?'

'They can be, Mrs Anderson, yes, they can be.'

And they can also be lying, stealing, murdering scumbags.

'Will there be anything else, Nicola?'

'No, Margaret.'

'Well, I'd like to go rest now. I always go to bed around

now. You know, strange thing, I feel William is with me in the room when I'm lying in my bed, almost as if he's sitting right by me. I really feel he's with me, so much so that I sometimes forget he's even dead, that's how powerful the feeling is; it's like he's come home to me. I find it very comforting. It makes it all so much easier to feel my William has come home to me. Isn't that the strangest thing?'

'No, Margaret, it's not, it's actually quite sweet.'

'Yes, it is.'

Something passed behind the old woman's eyes, a sudden, visceral pain. And gone again just as quickly.

Considine got to her feet. 'I can let myself out, Margaret. You go to bed.'

43

Back at the ranch, Brody went to the unit room and quickly ran through recent developments in the case. He did not mention the Old Man. There was no need; everyone knew about it; the whole country knew about it. And now, the team knew the details too, that Daniel Willow had recently been released from prison and immediately made a beeline for the person he blamed for his incarceration. Of course, while he wreaked havoc, Willow could not see, refused to see, the main instigator for everything wrong in his life was... da dum, himself. It was an all too familiar narrative. Much easier to blame others for your own misfortune, a scenario the members of the MCIU came across almost every day of the week. Now, the Old Man had died because of it.

They were all angry too, but had to park their emotions – for now. When it was over, they could get drunk, climb a rock face, or punch a heavy until their knuckles bled. Whatever. But right now, they had a job to focus on.

Brody summarised the following bullet points: Motive for victim's murder, unclear, but, thanks to Nicola Considine and information Voyle and Sheahan had picked up at the Time Machine bar, might be related to an inheritance; Mrs Margaret Anderson's will was worth – throwing everything onto the table – over one and a half million euro.

'Who's going to get this now?' Voyle asked.

'The remaining heirs, Thomas and Robert.'

'You mean one of them might be sniffing around dear mother's inheritance, is that it, boss?'

'Might be.'

'It happens. No law against it, is there?'

'No. There's not.'

'Sounds to me like we're back where we started.'

'There was someone outstanding from Anderson's address book,' Brody said, 'Callaghan. Just so you know, he's been discounted. Lives in Australia. And we checked, he hasn't left the country in a couple of years.'

'And of the other three,' Sheahan asked, 'any likely suspects?'

'Anything is possible.'

'Except we haven't got anything on any of them, do we?' Considine put in. 'Nothing that links them to the murder?'

'Noooo, we don't, but they were all intimately involved with the victim. We have that. So theoretically, any one of them could have had motive.'

'Theoretically,' Voyle said, 'of course. But theory on its own doesn't help, now does it?'

'No, it doesn't.'

Brody thought Voyle sounded smug.

'Have you any other ideas, Steve?'

Voyle shook his head. 'No, boss.'

'Right then. And before we get back to things, I know this is a difficult time for everybody, but we need to stay focused; it's what the Old Man would have wanted. OK?'

They nodded. Brody realised he hadn't needed to say that. They knew it already.

THE SHADOWS WERE CREEPING across Brody's office. He sat with the light off. He was trying to mentally order the murder investigation into some kind of sequence. For the most part he could not. So he decided to work backwards. He played in his mind images of Anderson leaving the Time Machine bar, then jumped to the images of his body being dumped from that Volvo in the lane, a time frame of approximately seven hours. Anderson had not left the bar with a potential suitor, but he had met someone. Who? Someone who had stripped him naked and slit his throat, and not necessarily in that order. There were no other marks on the body. None that were apparent anyway. And where had he been killed?

His desk phone rang. He picked it up.

'Brody.'

Silence.

'Brody.'

'Um, Sergeant Brody… how are you?'

Brody loved that accent. Mercedes had a habit of pausing before she spoke. The landline number was generic; unless an extension number was selected, all phones in the unit room, in his office too, rang. They called it a glitch. But one that had still not been fixed. He also knew she had a thing about Voyle, and not in a good way. If she heard his voice, sometimes she hung up.

'I'm good, Mercedes, and you?'

'I could, how you say, eat a horse. I never understand that. A horse. A horse is pretty big, no?'

'Yes, Mercedes, it is.'

'Um, Jack, sorry to hear about the Old Man.'

'Yes.'

A silence followed.

'Anyway,' she said, breaking it, 'Dr Mc Bain asked me to ring. We got a match, Jack, on dental records, to your victim in the car wreck. Good news, yes?'

'Yes, Mercedes, but good news is relative, not good news for the victim.'

'What, Jack?'

'It doesn't matter... and?'

'And, Jack?'

'The victim, who is it? Have you a name?'

She laughed, a warm, frivolous sound that had no place alongside the grim business of death they were dealing in, but he was glad for it nonetheless.

'Oh. Thomas Anderson. That's the name. He's on the system. Mucho bad boy, yes. Oh, and he had enough cocaine and weed in his system to kill a... horse.'

He wasn't surprised. He had expected it. Now he had another signpost: William Anderson and his brother, both dead. William, of course, wasn't even in the ground yet. Yes, that was a signpost. A big signpost. To an inheritance cake left to the last man standing maybe, a man who was not all that he seemed, a man in need of money. But did he need it enough that he would kill for it?

'You still there, Jack?'

'Yes, I'm still here. I'll let you go and eat that horse now.'

She laughed again.

'Maybe you might come and eat a horse with me sometime... I mean... dinner, you know?'

'You pulling my leg, Mercedes. It's not the first of April yet, is it?'

'No. I'm not. I'm serious.'

'You are?' *You are?* 'I'm old enough to be your father, Mercedes, granted, a very young father, but your father nonetheless. You know that?'

'I know that.'
'Thank you, Mercedes, I'm, um...'
'That's a no?'
'Yes. That's a no.'
'OK, Jack,' not sounding in the least put out.
'OK.'

She hung up, and Jack looked at the phone for a moment, shaking his head. Maybe he should pinch himself; did that really just happen? He didn't need to; he knew it had. Mercedes Camacho had really asked him out. That girl needed to get out more.

He brought his thoughts back onto the matters at hand, couldn't help but feel that the wheels of this investigation had begun to finally turn and gain traction. Another thought struck him: if the motive was payday on his mother's inheritance, and Robert Anderson had actually murdered his two brothers, then next on the list might be Margaret Anderson herself. If Robert Anderson had really killed both his brothers, would he now be capable of having the patience to sit back and wait for nature to take its course? If it was the case that he indeed had the patience, then Brody feared there was nothing to stop him literally getting away with this, with murder. And if that in turn were the case, then Robert Anderson was one of the cleverest, most devious bastards he'd ever come across in all of his career. Then, if that in turn were the case too, then how the hell did he make such stupid business decisions.

As he thought about it, he heard the engine whine and felt the wheels of the investigation slip back into the mud, spinning again, not going anywhere.

Damn.

44

At one minute past nine the following morning, Considine dialled a number and waited for it to be answered. It wasn't. She hung up and waited another minute before dialling again. She continued doing this until, eventually, at six minutes past nine, someone picked up.

'Hello, Aidan Kennedy, Solicitor and Commissioner for Oaths,' the voice said, clearly that of an elderly female.

'Hello. My name is Detective Garda Nicola Considine. I'd like to arrange to come in and speak with Mr Aidan Kennedy. Is that possible?'

'Well, yes, of course that's possible. I can give you an appointment; let me check the book.'

'Actually... by the way, who am I speaking to?'

'Veronica, Mr Kennedy's secretary.'

'Hello, Veronica. I'm on Camden Street. I could pop in right now.'

Considine had taken a chance and come straight from the Phoenix Park. She was standing along the busy street.

'Right now?'

'Yes.'

'Actually, I don't think that would be possible... but wait, ah yes, Mr Kennedy does have a free spot, actually, in a couple of minutes, if you come straight away, that is.'

Considine pressed a door buzzer.

'Did you hear that?'

'Yes. Someone's at the door.'

'That's me, Veronica. I'm right outside.'

IT WAS old and musty on the other side of the door, with a long, narrow hallway and a staircase at the end. Ledgers were stacked on the floor against the wall, all along it. To the right was an office; through the open door Considine could see more ledgers stacked against the wall in there. She crossed and stepped into the office, light coming through a high old Georgian window. Considine felt she had walked onto a period TV set, *Upstairs, Downstairs* maybe, even the old lady sitting behind the big ornate desk at the end of the office, dressed in a cardigan with a grey blouse buttoned to the neck and a pair of spectacles hanging around her neck on a loop chain, looked the part. The woman looked up.

'Detective Garda Considine?'

'Veronica?'

'Top of the stairs. He's waiting for you.'

Every step of the old stairs creaked, like the building was a living thing, and Considine was stepping on its bunions.

He sat behind a desk in the cramped, period room, the slanted sunlight through the window at his back igniting the dust motes floating on the air, and the sheen of his old jacket and the sprinkling of dandruff on its collar. He was an old man, very old, his head thin and long strands of white hair like thread combed over the top, the neck shrivelled, with thick veins pushing through like strands of cord. His eyes though, were cobalt blue, quick and hard.

'Take a seat.' His voice was surprisingly youthful, taking Considine by surprise. Maybe he's a young actor who's just come from make-up? She almost laughed at the thought.

He pointed, and she sat in the frayed leather seat in front of the desk, like a captain's chair. 'What's this to do with, miss?' There were no formalities.

Which suited Considine just fine.

'Have you a client, a Mr Robert Anderson?'

The old man's blue, hard eyes weighed her up silently.

'Yes, Robert is an old, valued client of mine. Now, young lady, what's this about?'

'And his mother, Mrs Margaret Anderson. Would she be a client of yours too?'

'Hm.' He pursed his wrinkled mouth. 'Lots of questions. Could I see your identification, please, before we go any further?'

'Certainly.' She took it out and held it for inspection while he donned his spectacles and peered closely at it. 'Hm. Major Crimes. Now, again, what's this to do with, young lady?'

'Is she, Mrs Margaret Anderson, a client of yours too?'

'Yes. Of course. They both are. Have been for years, and Mr Anderson senior too before them. Young lady, you're on thin ice. I don't have to answer any questions. Not until you tell me what this is about. Then I'll decide.'

'Yes, of course, but...'

'But?'

'Soon as I leave here, you'll be on the phone to tell him I've been.'

'I can do that anyway. Very certain of yourself, young lady, aren't you? Of what I might or might not do.'

'You are his solicitor, after all; it's what I'd expect.'

'Two things, young lady. Those ledgers you see piled

everywhere, that's because my practice is closing. I'm retiring. No surprises. Even Perry Mason got old. And number two, I don't particularly like Robert Anderson, despite the valued-client claptrap I just gave you.' He gave a wiry smile. 'I am his solicitor, after all; it's what you'd expect. Technically, he's not my client any longer. I'm passing him on to another practice, my nephew's, actually. So don't worry, I won't be telling that bollocks anything. And I have too much respect for dear Margaret to ever want to worry her. So I won't be telling her anything either. Once again, what's this about? I haven't got all day.'

'It may be nothing...'

'Oh, please, let me decide on that. Just say it out, will you. I'm not getting any younger. I don't like wasting time; every minute counts at my age.'

'It's to do with Margaret Anderson's will. I'd like to ask you some questions.'

'You would? Now, that's a coincidence.'

'It is?'

'Robert was in to see me about it only yesterday.'

Considine thought about that. 'Yes, I know he visited.'

The hard, blue eyes showed surprise.

'You do?'

'Yes. It's what got me to thinking about this in the first place. And something else, but I won't go into that just at this moment.'

'You won't?'

'But I will, once you tell me something. Bear with me.'

'Tell you what, exactly?'

'I don't know. Not exactly. Let's start with this, why did he come to see you?'

The hard, blue eyes widened just a fraction, then looked away, following a thought, then back again to Considine, like he'd decided on something.

'He wanted my advice on buying a property. In Spain. I told him he hadn't the money to buy any property, and I reminded him my last bill was still outstanding too...'

'If I could interrupt.'

'You may.'

'He's a high-class jeweller, is he not? With two shops on Grafton Street. It seemed to me he was doing quite well for himself.'

The old man smiled. Not a smile of mirth, no, but one of *you've got to be joking me*.

'Doing quite well, did you say? You know what he pays in rent for those shops of his? One hundred and seventy thousand a year each, combined total of three hundred and forty thousand. Yes, three hundred and forty thousand. Almost seven thousand every week. Each and *every* week. He's barely treading water. Robert's Fine Jeweller's can't continue. And you know the reason why, don't you? You've heard?'

'Heard what?'

'The wedding ring business.'

Considine shook her head.

'A lady purchased a wedding ring, cost over five thousand euro, ordered specially from Italy, it was. When she went in for fitting, accompanied by her father, seemingly he knows about such things, he claimed it wasn't the ring she'd ordered. He rang an expert who came round and confirmed it was a fake, imitation platinum, apparently. The guards were called. Robert pleaded ignorance and quickly refunded her the money. But he was prosecuted. The father insisted. And that doesn't go away, ever, lingers on like a bad odour. He was fined, the kiss of death, really, when you're dealing with the type of client he was. He's finished now, but he won't admit it.'

Considine thought of the boxes piled on the landing outside Robert Anderson's office, *Made In China* stencilled along the sides.

'It's a dive to the bottom now for old Robert, all the way down, down, down. I hope he pays my bill before he hits bottom. Which can happen at any moment.'

'Really?'

'I told you, he's finished; it's just a matter of when. Look, if he hadn't got so greedy, he'd be fine; the business has been running for over twelve years, after all. But you can't tell Robert anything – not that I did, because I didn't know. But I do know Robert, and his thinking was why pay three thousand euro wholesale for a platinum ring when I can buy something just like it for three hundred? Who's to know? But someone always does know. Robert could only see the money signs. He has the eternal optimism for everything and anything to do with himself. Let me put it like this, if Robert's ship were to ever come in, you wouldn't find him waiting at the quays. No, you'd find him at the railway station, waiting on a train. That about sums old Robert up. Not that he's a particularly bad businessman, he isn't. He just has this knack for fucking everything up. He seems incapable of doing anything else. Might take him a bit of time, but he'll get there.'

'I see...' Considine said, and her voice trailed off.

He watched her. 'Yes, you see what?'

'Why, well, why he might have an interest in, you know, such things.'

Their eyes met, a silent communication passing between the two.

'Hm, yes. I see what you mean. But I don't know. Robert's not a... of course, how can you tell? You can't. Who knows what anyone is capable of? Under the correct circumstances, I mean. But Robert... I don't know. Still, if someone were desperate enough. Anyway, he has a brother, even if I hear he's a complete waste of space. He'd have to get his cut too.'

'Didn't *you* hear?'

'Hear what?'
'Thomas, his other brother.'
'Yes? And?'
'And. Well, he died last night. A traffic collision... apparently.'
'Really?'
'Really.'
'I see. It'll all go to him, then, old Robert.'

They looked at one another again, like both knew exactly what the other was thinking.

45

Despite it being as unlikely as a heat wave in December, all the same, it didn't really matter. Brody had known this was bound to happen. And now it had. The word had come from Assistant Commissioner Padraic Kelly. Who said they didn't need any more. That the news Thomas Anderson's body was the one in that 05 D Volvo was enough. William Anderson had been killed by his brother Thomas, who had a known gripe against him. And by his death, his brother Robert had probably been spared from suffering a similar fate. Because, by this reckoning, had Thomas lived, he would have killed Robert too. 'It just makes sense, to take the whole cake for himself.'

And just like that, both incidents had been placed in the same box, neatly wrapped, and the assistant commissioner was about to place it onto the highest shelf he could find and, hopefully, never have to look at it again.

'This case never made sense from the get-go,' Assistant Commissioner Kelly said, like he'd know. Brody wanted to throw the phone across the room. 'And for the benefit of *expediency*, that's my decision.' Brody absolutely hated that word.

'Really, you can't let it go that easily.'

'I'm not letting anything go easily. It makes sense. The man was higher than the space station on cocaine. He drove off the road; yes, he went through, yes, even if slowly, he went through a chicane of crash barrier and trees; yes, I know all that. Did you think I didn't educate myself on all the details?'

'No, sir.'

'Right then. I don't think he meant to drive off that cliff, or whatever it was. The car was being driven slowly; maybe he just wanted to park up for a while, sober up. Until you come to me with something other than fairy stories, this case is shut. But, Detective Brody, it's not closed. It doesn't have enough to close it either. But there's more than enough for me to believe in what I just told you. And you should too. So this case is shut down. Get onto something else.'

'I want to talk to Robert Anderson's wife.'

'You want to talk to his wife?'

'Ex-wife. They're separated. She may know something. If anyone knows anything about him, it'll be her. I feel it's important. I want to talk to her. Give me a couple more days.'

'It's the weekend.'

'Give me the weekend, then... and something else.'

'What?'

'A search warrant.'

'To search what?'

'Robert Anderson's home and place of business.'

'Have you lost it completely, Brody. You don't have grounds. Jesus, are you mad in the head? Come on now. I'll pretend I didn't hear that. And now, Jack, if you don't mind, I'm busy.'

The phone went dead.

In the unit room, Paul Quinn was sitting at his desk that was not his desk; Voyle and Considine sitting at their desks, ignoring each other; Marty Sheahan waiting on the phone, doodling on a notepad. No one spoke. They didn't notice Brody standing in the doorway. He thought Quinn looked crestfallen, beaten, his first major criminal investigation had turned out to be an abject failure. He looked like a fast-track whizz-kid who had just got shunted into the sidings. And now the unit commander was dead. If this were a ship, Quinn would have been dumped on the quay at the first port they called to a long time ago.

Four telephones rang, a shrill chorus shattering the silence.

'God's sake.' It was Considine, reaching for her phone. 'Can't someone sort these out.' She saw Brody for the first time. 'I could get a heart attack, boss. Anyone could get a heart attack.' She picked up. 'Yes? MCIU.' She listened, covered the mouthpiece with her hand. 'Boss, it's for you, Robert Anderson.'

Surprise, surprise. He crossed to Considine's desk, held out his hand, and she plonked the receiver into it. He put it to his ear. 'Yes?' ... 'Detective Sergeant Brody, is that yourself?' ... 'It is.' ... 'I'll get straight to the point. I've lost two brothers now, Sergeant, my two dear brothers, William, murdered, and now Thomas, in what I think are questionable circumstances, both dead, and Thomas while William's not even in his grave.' ... 'My condolences, Mr Anderson.' ... 'Your condolences. Is that all you can say? I'm sorry, but I want more than that, more than your condolences. I want to know what you're doing to apprehend the person, or persons, responsible for William's death.' ... 'We did everything we could, Mr Anderson.' ... 'Everything you could. What's that supposed to mean? Aren't you doing all that you can now? I heard about the death of your boss, by the way, my condolences. But really. What you just said sounds very past tense to me. What I want to know is what you are doing now?' ... 'I'm talking to you, that's what I'm doing right now, Mr Anderson.' ... 'I beg your pardon. Are you being smart with me? Don't be smart with me. Why aren't you finding those responsible for the deaths of my two dear brothers?' ... 'Do you have information, Mr Anderson?' ... 'Do I what? ... 'How are you so sure the death of Thomas in a traffic collision last night was anything other than an accident?' ... 'Isn't it obvious?' ... 'Nothing is obvious, Mr Anderson.' ... 'Don't give up. Please don't give up, that's all I'm asking.' ... 'I won't give up, Mr Anderson.' ... 'Good, then don't. Now, I'm busy. Goodbye. But I will be monitoring events, don't you worry.'

The line went dead.

Brody saw that everyone was looking at him.

'I got most of that,' Voyle said. 'He's telling you not to give up. The real killer wouldn't be telling you that, now would he?'

Brody was wondering the same thing.

'Paul,' he said.

'Yes?'

'Find out who his ex-wife is, good lad, and come and let me know. Nicola will help if you need it.'

The lad looked away. Brody realised his mistake. Of course he could do this on his own; he didn't need anyone's help.

AND HE DID. And he didn't need anyone's help. And it didn't take him long either. Brody got the sense that Quinn's career from now on would be one where he was forever trying to prove himself, not just to others, but to himself. That wasn't a good place to be.

Anyway, her name was Betty, who now went by her maiden name of Nagle: Betty Nagle. She had a hairdressing business on Ranelagh's High Street called Betty's Cuts. Brody didn't know what he wanted to say to or ask this lady, but he knew that he wanted to talk to her. He went there with Considine, because she had started this investigative thread in the first place. Quinn asked to come along, and Brody agreed, but he sat in the car outside. Only because three was a crowd.

Betty Nagle was not happy. Not happy at all.

'This is very embarrassing. Did you have to come into my place of business?'

Her place of business had ten chairs, but only half of them were occupied. From what Considine had said about Robert Anderson, Brody had not expected this; he had expected someone more... well, dour. But Betty Nagle was not dour. Not dour at all. Instead, she had dyed blonde hair, thick make-up, lips too full to be completely natural, and wore a black lace top with a black bra visible underneath, and tight black leggings. He got the impression she was a woman trying desperately, if not to turn back the hands of time, then to stop them from advancing any further.

'Is there anywhere we can talk?' Considine asked.

'We can step outside. I need a cigarette anyway.'

She held the cigarette at the end of an arm folded across her chest, puckering her lips as she exhaled, blowing the smoke away from herself into the air. Her acrylic nails were of pink and red waves.

'I heard Thomas died. Good riddance. But I don't know why you want to come and talk to me about it.'

'Who are you referring to?' It was Considine.

'That scumbag, Tommy, my ex-husband's brother. Absolute bastard. I hated the sight of him. No, you're wasting your time. I can't help you.'

'Actually,' Brody said, 'we haven't come to speak with you about that; we've come to speak to you about your ex-husband.'

'What, you mean Robert?'

'Why, is there more than one?'

'Are you being smart?'

'No. You just asked if I meant Robert, like there might be another one, that's all.'

She took a hurried puff on her cigarette, exhaled, took another. 'Oh, I see. No, he's the only one. So far, that is. I am seeing somebody though. Somebody special. And he's ten years younger than me.'

She looked at them defiantly, as if daring them to say something.

'Good for you,' Considine remarked, and Betty smiled.

'Robert's a stick in the mud,' she said. 'What possible reason could you have to come and talk to me about him? Have you spoken to Margaret, by the way, his mum? I haven't had the chance.'

'Yes.'

'And she's bearing up well, is she?'

'She, she's taking the news remarkably well.'

'That's good. I'm glad. Margaret's a good woman. One of the best. I really like her.' She took another puff on her cigarette. Brody and Considine exchanged glances, because Margaret Anderson had made it obvious she hated the ground this woman stood on.

'About your ex-husband,' Brody said.

'What about him?'

'Do you two stay in touch?'

'As little as possible, only when it can't be avoided.'

'Do you have children?'

'Yes, one, Rihanna, she's fifteen. And if it weren't for her, we wouldn't want to have anything to do with one another; we wouldn't even speak.' She took another puff; the cigarette was almost down to its tip. She dropped it to the pavement. 'Look. I don't mean to be rude. But I have a business to run. What's this about?'

'Your ex-husband, would you call him a good businessman?'

'Yes, I would. We were never short. I will say that about him.'

Brody and Considine exchanged glances again.

'So he's never been in financial difficulties?' Brody asked.

'Is this what this is about? No. He's never been in financial difficulties. He has two jewellery shops on Grafton Street. In a good week, you know how much they can pull in?'

'No,' Brody said, 'I don't.'

'A good week, they can pull in six hundred K. That's a lot of rinses and blow-dries for me, I can tell you.'

'OK,' Considine said, 'so he was doing well.'

'Yes. Very well.'

'And now?'

'What do you mean, and now? I don't know about now. We don't talk, I told you. Only if it's to do with our daughter, that is.'

She glanced over her shoulder and in through the window of her shop.

'I really need to get back. I've got to do a balayage. I was booked specifically.'

'Does your ex-husband pay you maintenance?' Considine asked.

'Of course, and he's never missed a payment. Why would he? Detectives, my ex-husband is a wealthy man; you don't seem to realise that.'

'Why did you two split up?'

'An affair.'

'Did you know her?'

'Know who?'

'The other woman?'

'You've got the wrong end of the stick, darling. It was me. I was the one who had the affair. With Rick, the one who I'm with now. He's ten years younger than me. Did I mention?'

'You mentioned.'

Betty raised an eyebrow. 'Well, he is.'

ON THE DRIVE back to the Phoenix Park, Brody realised he had to accept that this investigation was at a dead end. It couldn't go any further, he couldn't go any further, because there was nowhere else to go. And contrary to popular belief, it wasn't as difficult to get away with murder as people might think. But there was, however, one important point to bear in mind. And it was this: most murders – and thankfully, murder rates were relatively low on Ireland's green isle – were committed in the heat of the moment and not premeditated. Most people who took the life of another – crime-land hits besides – were usually brought to justice fairly quickly because they were known to the victim, to the family, to partners, spouses, friends. So no, not hard to find at all. That is, if they didn't hand themselves in first, or, like the Old Man's killer, get killed in an actual incident.

But this case was different. The assistant commissioner had said it himself, *It never made sense from the get-go.* But Brody was certain of something: he had no doubt that it was Robert Anderson who had killed both his brothers. He couldn't prove this, of course, no, he couldn't – but he absolutely was certain nonetheless, because he *felt* it.

There was nothing to do but wait. Brody thought of the old saying, chase the butterfly and it flies away, but stand still and it comes to you. Robert Anderson was more Venus flytrap than butterfly, but right now, there was nothing else Brody could do but wait, and hope.

46

Margaret passed away the day after William's funeral. People said they hadn't seen her looking so well in ages. She actually seemed, people whispered amongst themselves as William's coffin was lowered into the ground, happy.

When the home help arrived the next morning, she let herself into the house as normal. But Margaret was not sitting in the kitchen waiting for her, as was usual. So the home help called out her name, but got no response. She climbed the stairs to Margaret's bedroom and found her in bed. She seemed to be sleeping peacefully. But there was no sound of her breathing. When the home help checked, she found that Margaret wasn't sleeping. Margaret was dead.

47

The butterfly came to Brody two weeks after his visit to Betty Nagle at her salon. It came in the form of a phone call. Not from Anderson, but from his ex-wife.

During those two weeks, the Old Man had been laid to rest. His funeral was huge. Just before the coffin was lowered into the ground, the flag of the Republic was removed by a member of the colour party, folded neatly, and presented to Alice standing tall and regal by the grave. She took it and held it close to her chest. The coffin was lowered, the priest sprinkled some holy water, and that was it. The final curtain had come down on the Old Man's life; Superintendent Tom Maguire was gone forever.

Also during those two weeks, Voyle and Brody had spent time down country on the trail of stolen plant equipment. The Criminal Assets Bureau had become involved and requested they attend. Brody realised that Voyle really should have listened to Quigley. Because it wasn't just plant equipment, it was what the plant equipment – or some of it anyway – had been used for, specifically the gouging out of walls of bank cash machines in the middle of the night. There had been a spate of seven, all along the border counties, a total of two million euro taken and hundreds of thousands of euro in structural damage to banks, service stations and supermarkets left behind. Superintendent Quigley had been in over his head, way over his head, that much was obvious. Voyle had even apologised to the man. OK, Brody had made him apologise to the man. The superintendent didn't seem to bear a grudge. To Brody he looked like a man in shock. But when it was over, the superintendent had settled back to overseeing his district where nothing more than domestics, petty thefts and drunk drivers were all that usually ever happened. And that was just the way he liked it.

'This is Betty Nagle,' the butterfly said. Like the last time, she didn't sound too happy now either.

'Hello, ma'am...'

'Christ, did you just call me ma'am? For real, ma'am? Who calls anyone ma'am anymore? I'm not a ma'am. I'm not an old woman. And my name is Betty. Call me Betty, will you? Betty.'

'Of course, yes, Betty. Sorry. What can I do for you, Betty?'

'My bastard ex-husband... who are you, by the way?'

'Steve Voyle.'

'I don't want to speak to you. Put me onto the other one, Brody, or Considine.'

'Can you come round and see me?' she said when Brody picked up.

'Hello, Betty. Yes, of course. I can do that. Right now if you want.'

'Yes. Right now. That'd be good. But not here. Christ, I don't want you steamrolling into my salon again. Meet me down the street, in the little square there. I'll be sitting on a bench. Fifteen minutes. I'll see you then.'

'Fifteen minutes. I'll be there.'

Brody grabbed his jacket, was about to leave the office when he stopped. Paul Quinn's secondment to the unit was over. The lad was back at fraud in Harcourt Street. Brody had promised to keep him up to date on any developments. He gave him a call. The lad asked to come along. Harcourt Street was only a stone's throw from Ranelagh; he could meet Brody. Brody agreed.

He was there when Brody arrived. He spotted him standing at the street corner opposite the square. Quinn smiled as Brody approached. His wounds had healed, Brody noted, his nose straight as a pencil.

'Thanks, I appreciate you ringing me.'

'No problem, I thought you would.' He turned to observe the square, saw Betty Nagel stepping out the door of her salon and walking towards it. She stopped to light a cigarette before continuing on quickly.

'I know I'm like a bad taste in the mouth,' Quinn said.

Betty reached the square and sat on a bench, crossed her legs.

'I wouldn't say that,' Brody said. 'Maybe to Voyle, but I wouldn't mind him. That's Voyle for you, he's either having a problem with somebody, or somebody's having a problem with him... Hey up, she's waiting. Come on.'

Betty Nagel was sitting straight-backed on the bench seat, dressed in black leather trousers, a red T-shirt and a black leather jacket. There was a look on her face, like her lotto numbers had come up – only she'd forgotten to buy the ticket.

'Where's the woman?' she asked as they approached. 'What's her name? Considine?'

'She's on a day off.'

'I was wondering why she didn't answer the phone. Could you sit down? You're making me nervous standing there.'

Brody sat beside her on the bench, and Quinn sat beside him.

'Who's he?' Betty pointed.

'Detective Garda Paul Quinn. He's working on this case.'

'He is? I never met him.'

'Why did you want to see us, Betty?'

'You know he's got some money already, don't you?'

'Who?'

'My ex-husband, that's who. He got an advance from the credit union for burying her. Fourteen thousand. She went down in a wicker casket, more like fourteen euro. And he's getting an advance from the bank too. They have special facilities, if a beneficiary can prove they are, let me get this right, impecunious. In other words...'

'I know,' Brody said, 'broke.'

'You do? I had to look it up.'

'How do you know all this, Betty? Didn't you say he had money?'

'I did. Until that ring thing, that is. You know about that, yeah?'

Brody nodded. 'I do now.'

'Now he's already feasting on his mother's carcass; he can't help himself, he's desperate.'

Feasting on her carcass? He wouldn't have taken Betty for coming up with a turn of phrase like that.

'This has annoyed you?' Brody said.

'No, it hasn't. I'm livid, that's what I am.'

'Why?'

'Why? Why do you think?'

'I don't know, that's why I ask.'

'Look. OK. I had an affair. I was the one who finished the marriage. But I was doing both of us a favour. That doesn't mean it stops right there... oh no. Too much water has passed under the bridge for that. And we have a child together, don't forget that, although he seems to want to.'

Brody sat back. He realised he'd had his back turned to Quinn, shutting him out of the conversation. The lad would be sensitive to that.

'He owes you, Betty, is that it?' Quinn said.

Betty's mouth twisted into something resembling a snarl.

'Yes, he owes me.'

'Explain,' Brody said.

She crossed her hands with their long, acrylic nails and cupped them onto her knee.

'I said I had an affair.' She looked at Brody.

'Yes, you did.'

'But that doesn't give him the right to, to... flaunt it.'

Brody waited, Quinn too.

'Now he's with her. I knew he was with her. I didn't mind... in the beginning, that is. But he's still with her. And now it bothers me.'

Betty looked at him again, her bottom lip beginning to tremble.

'Who?' Brody said.

Her eyes flared. 'Majella. Bitch. My best friend – one time, that is. You know, I think they were fucking each other the whole time, the whole time I was...' Her voice trailed off.

The whole time, Brody thought, that you were fucking Rick.

'It doesn't matter,' she said. 'They just were, that's all. And now...'

Silence.

'And now...'

'And now, they're sailing off into the sunset. I don't think so. He's buying an olive grove somewhere outside Alicante. His latest brainwave. How cosy, he and Majella, my one-time best friend, bitch, walking off into the sunset hand in hand. I don't think so. I. Don't. Think. So. How dare he, after all that he promised me? How. Dare. He.'

Something passed behind Betty's eye. Like a realisation she had said too much.

'What did he promise?' Brody pushed, knowing this chance would never come again.

'He said when she'd gone, he'd look after me. That's what he said. When she'd gone, "I'll look after you, Bet," that's what he said. Well, she's gone, and he hasn't... Bet still hasn't seen anything.'

The wind stirred, blowing some strands of hair across her face. She used the fingers of one hand like a rake to push the strands back behind an ear.

'What haven't you seen?' Quinn asked.

Betty looked wary.

'It's OK, Betty,' Brody said. 'You can tell us.'

She shrugged. 'Why not? Yes, I can tell you. He first mentioned it a year ago, when she was diagnosed.'

'Margaret?'

'Of course Margaret. Robert's mother.'

'On that,' Brody said. 'I want to ask you. You told us what a lovely woman she was, and how much you liked her.'

'Yes.'

'Well, it's not true, is it, Betty? She couldn't stand the sight of you.'

Betty smirked.

'So?'

'Well, why would you say that?'

'Because...'

'Yes, because?'

'Because he fucking owes me, that's because. I had to go along. And he had it coming.'

Brody wanted to smile, but didn't, because Betty sounded like a character in a B-movie crime thriller. And Brody knew at that moment that she was. She was playing a role. It all made sense to him.

'He told you, didn't he?' he said. 'If he didn't tell you, then you wouldn't know, and if you didn't know, you wouldn't be talking to me, that's for certain. But you knew. Because he told you, he told you something, didn't he?'

Betty's eyes widened; then the long lashes fluttered. She ran a hand over her face.

'Oh, God.'

'So why don't you tell us?'

She looked down at those hands, like she was beaten. 'He told me.' Her voice was resigned. 'He'd had a couple of drinks, and he told me. OK, he was half-cut, in fact. And when he's like that, he's liable to say anything. He really is. Anything. I didn't know why he wanted to come round. We don't talk, like I told you. And it's hard to tell when he's like that if what he says is true or not. But then, when he told me, I knew it was. I just knew it was true. I mean' – she looked at Brody and then to Quinn – 'you couldn't make that sort of thing up, no matter how cut you were.'

'Go on,' Brody said, knowing this was very close to the line. He pushed. 'He promised you something, didn't he? And you didn't get it. What did he promise you?'

'No, you're right. I didn't get it. He said, "What if William and Thomas were to disappear, what then?" And I said, "Well, what if William and Thomas were to disappear, what the hell are you talking about? What's that mean?" and he said, "That would leave me as the sole benefactor." And I looked at him. I thought, what does he mean? But at the same time, I knew what he meant. I just couldn't believe it, that's all. I was shocked, I really was.'

'And then what?' Brody asked.

'He told me exactly what was in the will. I mean, that's a lot of money.'

'Yes.' It was Quinn. 'But why would he tell you? He didn't have to say anything.'

'I told you he was half-cut; OK, he was drunk as a skunk. And when he's like that, he's liable to say anything. I told you that. But there was a method to his madness. He said he wanted me to say what I said to you, about what a nice man he was, the good provider he was, the successful businessman he was, and how much I loved Margaret, although I couldn't bring myself to actually say that. You have to admit, it had you fooled, didn't it?'

'Did it?' Quinn said.

'Yes, it did. You might have had your suspicions, but that wasn't enough, was it?'

Brody had to admit it wasn't.

'So,' Brody said, 'what do you think we should do with this information?'

Betty shrugged. 'I don't know.'

'Well, would you make a statement? Would you–?'

'No way,' cutting him off, looking at Brody like he had two heads.

'Why not? He's killed two people. What does it take to convince you?'

'It's his word against mine, that's why. And he's the father of my daughter. I can't.'

'You mean you won't,' Brody said. 'If this had worked out the way you had hoped it would, you wouldn't even be talking to us; you'd have said nothing. Do you feel better now? Having got it off your chest.'

She jumped to her feet. 'I've got to get back.'

'When are you meeting him again? Because you will, won't you? To tell him you've spoken to us, and that he needs to cough up. That's what this is all about, isn't it? You'd need to be careful.'

'He wouldn't hurt me.' But she didn't sound too certain.

'And anyway, he didn't say he killed anyone, what he said was, what if they were to disappear, that's what he said. There's a difference.'

'When are you meeting him again?'

'He's coming to the salon on Sunday night. I go in on Sunday nights to get things ready for opening on Monday. So?'

'So, Betty...' Brody fell silent, thinking. 'You're going to help us.'

Betty shook her head.

'No.'

'Oh yes, Betty, because I have to tell you, you don't have much choice.'

'I'm walking away, that's what I'm doing. And that's ridiculous. No, I won't help you. You hear me loud and clear? I've got to get back. This is... this is police harassment.' She turned and started to walk away.

'Who's going to look after Rihanna?' Brody said after her.

She stopped.

'What did you say? Did you say what I think you said?'

'I said it, Betty. And you need to think about it.'

She turned slowly, began fumbling in her handbag, took out a cigarette and lit up, furiously puffed on it a half dozen times, walked back to him.

'Because you,' Brody said, 'are now an accessory to a crime.'

She froze, pulling on the cigarette, the tip glowing like a furnace, finally pulled it from her mouth. '*Whhhat?*' The word lost to a cloud of smoke. 'I'm not an... whatever the fuck you just called it.'

'Fine, Betty, you can tell that to the judge when the time comes. And when the time comes, who's going to look after Rihanna? Hm? You'd need to think about that, Betty, really, you would.'

Her bottom lip began to tremble, and she dropped the cigarette to the ground, walked over to the bench and plopped herself down, turned her eyes up to his.

'My Rihanna... *Nooooo.*'

'I'm sorry, Betty. Just try not to worry, because she'll be well looked after. They have temporary foster care placements for situations just like this. You know, when both parents are sent to prison.'

'Oh, Christ, *prison*?'

'Yes, Betty, prison.'

'OK. Fuck him, then. What'd you want me to do? Tell me. I'll do it.'

THE OLD MAN'S office door was open. But the Old Man wasn't in there. Brody stood outside. A couple of minutes later Assistant Commissioner Kelly came down the hall, brass sparkling on his Sam Brown belt, a rack of ribbons over his left chest pocket, shoulder full of epaulettes.

'I can give you five minutes.' He passed into the Old Man's office, and Brody followed, but didn't sit behind the desk. Instead, he stood by the window, just as the Old Man used to. 'Now, what is it?'

'I need a special warrant... sir' – Brody felt the informality of 'boss' would not be appreciated by him – 'to plant a bug, sir.'

'You're not asking for much. Who? Why?'

'Robert Anderson's wife. She's meeting him on Sunday night.'

'That again. This'd better be good. I'm not going before a judge unless you have something very good indeed.'

'Robert Anderson discussed his brothers disappearing with his ex-wife,' Brody explained.

The assistant commissioner turned from the window and looked at Brody.

'He what?'

Brody nodded.

'He *what*?' he repeated.

'He discussed his brothers disappearing with his ex-wife.'

'Before they died, that is?'

'Yes, of course before they died.'

'Yes. I thought that's what you meant. Just to be sure. That's good.' He smiled. 'Yes, that's very good. But why do you want to plant a bug in his wife's, his ex-wife's, place of business?'

'Because that's where they're meeting. Sunday night. She told me.'

'Why did she tell you?'

'Hell hath no fury like a woman scorned and all that. He's in a relationship with her best friend; that's annoyed her. But what's really annoyed her is he promised her some cake, and she didn't get it.'

'Cake?'

'His mother's inheritance cake.'

'Oh, that cake, I get it.'

'She's agreed to help us, bo... I mean, sir.'

'She has. How so?'

'By getting him to talk about it. Getting him to admit it. On tape.'

The AC started plucking his lower lip between the thumb and index finger of his right hand. Thinking.

'That'd be something alright if it works,' he said, 'the rat in the trap. But does she know about the bug?'

Brody shook his head.

'No. Only that we'll be listening, she doesn't know how. I don't want her to know how. If she knows how, she might give something away, a look, something...'

'Yes, good thinking, she might.' He picked up the desk phone. 'I'll ring Judge Hanley right now and get it sorted... And, Brody.'

'Yes?'

'Good work.'

48

The woman who rushed into Betty's Cuts just as they were closing for the day was desperate.

'I need a quick wash and blow-dry. I've just got a call. My husband's having dinner with his boss and his wife. They're over from New York. I'd forgotten about it. Completely. Can you believe that? It's this evening. Please, can you do it? Please. It's an emergency.'

'I'm closing.' Betty was unmoved by the woman's plight.

The woman pointed to the price board on the wall. 'Forty, it says there, for a wash and blow-dry. I'll give you fifty. I need this done. Really. Please.'

Betty looked at her watch. 'Make it seventy and I'll consider it.'

'Seventy, for a wash and blow-dry, that's exorbitant.'

Betty raised her eyebrows. She didn't care. She was never going to see this woman ever again anyway.

'Take it or leave it.'

The woman shook her head, but said, 'Yes, I'll take it, but only because I have to.'

When Betty disappeared into the laundry room at the

back to get fresh towels, Garda Denise Ryan of the National Surveillance Unit took great pleasure in fixing the miniature microphone to the underside of the middle chair along the left side wall of the salon. That was enough. The technology in the button-size wire held in place by a powerful magnet could pick up every sound from anywhere in this room. She had been briefed on the case and hoped this bitch Betty did the talking with her ex-husband in here. The warrant allowed an eavesdrop from sixteen hundred hours to twenty hundred hours on Sunday evening. The tap would only be operative between those times. It only took Ryan a few seconds to fix it in place; then she went to the door and silently pulled it open, stepped out onto the street and walked quickly away.

When Betty emerged from the back of the salon a couple of minutes later, clutching the fresh towels, she cursed under her breath. She really should have known, seventy for a wash and blow-dry was pushing it. So the woman had walked. She really should have settled for fifty.

49

A butterfly flaps its wings and the weather changes on the other side of the world. Experience had shown Brody that sometimes it didn't matter what the manual said, sometimes there were no answers. The manual – and he knew this now – was merely a work of well-plotted and planned-out fiction. But nonetheless that's what it was – fiction. Brody had believed for, oh, the first five years of his career maybe, at best, everything in that manual to be true. And when faced with a scenario like described in the manual – and most scenarios were in the manual – he ran through the checklist of how best to deal with it. And it worked. Every time. Which was great. But the manual didn't cover everything. That was impossible. It didn't cover those five per cent of non-conforming, non-predictable incidents that can come out of a clear blue sky and blindside an officer, leaving him knocked for six, if not dead. No, they were not covered in the manual. Although some officers were lucky enough to go through their entire careers without ever once encountering a five percenter.

Brody hung back, but only to gain a sense of perspective so that he could see the wood for the trees, as it were.

50

The white panel van took up station parked against the kerb just down from Betty's Cuts on Sunday afternoon. The driver had driven by a couple of times already, waiting for a suitable parking space to become available. It was a totally innocuous-looking van; no one would ever give it a second glance. The driver spent time in the back setting up his equipment, testing the measurements, setting the bass, treble, balance, just like he would in a recording studio. And he wasn't just the driver, of course not. He was a specialist officer with the National Surveillance Unit. All the members of the unit were specialists. His was in audionics. However, he could not input the code to allow him to switch on the wire until precisely sixteen hundred hours. There was no room for error. Everything had to be set up and ready to go for that time. His greatest fear was feedback. No matter how advanced the technology, feedback was feedback. It didn't discriminate.

When he was set up, he waited. He couldn't leave the van. That was the rule. And in case of emergencies, an empty two-litre water bottle was stashed in the corner. As for any other toilet emergencies, well, that had never happened – yet.

At sixteen forty-five, a knock sounded on the passenger-door window. That was the rule too, one knock. The operative checked through the small glass panel of the divider and pressed a remote, then heard the front doors unlock. Brody got in the passenger seat, because getting in and out that way was less suspicious than using the back door. People expected people to use the front doors. That was the rule too, anything that might attract attention was strictly forbidden. Brody closed the passenger door, and the operative then opened the divider door into the back of the van.

'Jack Brody?'

'That's me.'

'Come in.'

Jack bent low as he moved into the rear. The van suddenly seemed very small with him standing in the back of it, surrounded by banks of equipment. It was like the cramped cockpit of an aircraft.

'There's a pull-down seat' – the operative pointed – 'right there.'

Jack pulled it down and sat; it was hard and uncomfortable, made for someone half the size.

'We met once,' the operative said, 'Trevor Rice.'

'Where?'

'Parkgate, Defence HQ, cyber-security seminar a year or so ago.'

Then it came to Brody.

'You had a beard then, didn't you?'

'And long hair.' He extended a hand, and they shook, his grip strong but not too strong, an honest handshake.

Brody checked his watch.

'We'll go by that clock,' Trevor said, pointing. Jack noticed the digital clock fixed to the top of the side panel opposite. 'Have no choice anyway; it's all synchronised.'

'Cutting-edge stuff.'

'Has to be, my man; we're skirting the edges of personal freedoms here, can't leave ourselves open to any accusations. Sensitive stuff, as you can imagine.'

Brody could. Some politicians would just love to jump on this bandwagon.

'Are we live?'

Trevor Rice nodded. 'Yes. But I cannot record until either of the parties speaks. I can only record then. If there's anyone else present, I'll have to delete what they say.'

Seven minutes to go.

The windows of the van were tinted, but only outside. From inside, Brody had a clear view out, could see further up the street to Betty's Cut, no lights on, silent, no sign of life. He had a thought: maybe she's changed her mind; maybe she's not going to meet Anderson after all. Maybe after his visit she got spooked. Maybe she spoke to Robert Anderson, and he got spooked too. Maybe.

At sixteen fifty-seven, with still no sign of any life, Brody began to seriously consider a no-show. At seventeen hundred hours, five o'clock, still no sign of life, he was resigned to it.

But then.

He saw her walking quickly along the street in his direction, wearing a dress, high at the neck but short on the legs – very short. She didn't have the legs for a short dress. Brody knew the sentiment might be considered sexist, but it was true nonetheless. Betty Nagle had legs like tree trunks. Why she thought that dress was a good idea, he had no clue. She stopped outside the salon.

A scratching sound filtered into the van, sharp and precise. Brody looked at Trevor Rice.

'She's putting the key in the door.'

'It's loud,' Brody whispered.

Rice grinned. 'No need to whisper; sound is only one way. She can't hear a thing.'

'Oh yes, of course.' But Brody's voice wasn't much louder.

They listened, the clip-clop sound of shoes, the rustling of a coat being removed and hung up, more clip-clopping, fading. That was another worry: what if Betty talked to Anderson in a back room, out of earshot?

There was silence; each second pulled and stretched so that time itself seemed to slow down. Then the clip-clopping was back, growing louder and louder, Brody wanted to cover his ears, before it suddenly levelled out. He realised the sound wasn't so loud, it was rather the silence beforehand had been quite heavy. There was a whooshing sound. Brody recognised it as the sound of the air in the hydraulics as one of the chairs was raised, presumably for Betty to sit in. Then came a creaking sound as he imagined Betty turning the chair from side to side as she waited for Anderson to arrive. He wondered if she was sitting in the actual chair with the wire stuck to the underside of it.

The silence again as the creaking noise stopped. Brody looked up, out through the rear window of the van. Anderson was standing on the street outside the door of the salon. He felt his belly pitch, like he was on a rollercoaster that had just suddenly dipped. They had both arrived. Anderson didn't knock; he could see Betty inside through the door. The chair creaked once, then the clip-clop of Betty's shoes. Brody saw the door open and Anderson step inside.

'You're late.' Betty's voice sounded agitated, but clear and sharp, as if she were standing right alongside him in the van. It was weird.

'A few minutes... so?'

Betty: 'A few minutes... *so*? You have a knack for playing down everything, don't you?'

Footsteps, not the clip-clop sound as before, but softer, duller, Anderson's shoes. *Please don't walk out the back.* The footsteps stopped. *Thank Christ.* A whoosh as Brody imagined him sitting on a chair too. There was the clip-clop sound, but no whoosh. Betty had remained standing.

'Make yourself at home, why don't you... how's Majella? Is that what delayed you? Giving her an early bird, were you?' Betty's voice had an edge to it.

'Come on, Bet, there's no–'

'Stop calling me fucking Bet; those days are over. I had an early bird myself. Rick just can't get enough of me.'

Anderson laughed.

Betty: Something funny?

Anderson: You tell me.

Betty: Um. You're pathetic, that's what you are.

Anderson: I have something to tell you.

Betty: You have a lot to tell me.

Anderson: But I have something specific to tell you.

Betty: What?

Anderson: Majella's pregnant. That's what.

Silence.

Betty: That's a joke. Tell me that's a joke.

Anderson: It's no joke.

Silence.

Betty: Jesus. Yes it is. That's a joke. Has to be. What age is she? Forty-two. That's it. Same month as me, February, almost forty-three.

Anderson: No shite.

Silence.

Betty: You bastard. You absolute bastard.

Anderson: There's no need to be like that. I thought you'd be happy for us.

Betty: Rihanna. How is she going to take this?

Anderson: She'll love it. She won't be an only child anymore. She always wanted siblings. We know why she doesn't have any, don't we?

Betty: Fuck you. I could have, I wanted to, but you never showed any interest. You absolute bastard.

Anderson: That's why you got that kid, Rick, to prove to yourself you're not an auld hag. Sorry, Betty, but you are.

There was the clip-clopping sound of feet, and the creaking of a chair, and a sound like the clapping of hands.

Anderson: Ouch. That make you feel better. But hit me again and I'll put you through the fucking window.

Betty: Let my hand go. I said let my hand go. You're hurting me. What? You going to kill me too?

Brody stiffened, took a breath and held it, waiting, hoping... But Anderson only laughed. Clip-clop, Betty was stepping away.

Anderson: What is it, Betty? I don't have a lot of time. I want to be on my way.

Come on, Betty, Brody thought. *Talk. Get him to talk about it. Don't lose this opportunity. Talk...*

Betty: What is it? Seriously. What is it? Don't act thicker than you already are.

You're changing the subject, Betty. Jesus.

Anderson: Tut-tut. I'm not that stupid though, am I? Come on, you have to admit. I'm smart, Betty, and you know it.

Betty: Smart. That's a good one. Everything you ever touched has been a complete fuck-up, even our marriage. You're a dead duck, washed up, fucked up. You're hopeless.

You're losing him, Betty; you're losing him with all that...

Anderson: Fuck you, Betty. What is it? I want to get out of here.

Betty: No, fuck you. I want some of that money.

Anderson: You'll get nothing.

Betty: I'll go to the police. Maybe I already have.

Jesus, Betty, no...

Anderson (laughing): Really, and that's why I'm standing here, is it? Go on then. Tell them.

There was the sound of his footsteps, and Brody silently cursed. Anderson was going to walk out that door without saying another word. He was going to walk out of this investigation. He was going to live happily ever after. Because sometimes there really was no justice; sometimes the bad guys really did get away with it; sometimes they really did get away with murder.

But then.

Betty: Didn't you find it hard? To kill someone. How could you, Robert, how could you do it? It's like I don't even know you. Tell me. It makes no difference now. But I want to know.

Yes, yes, Betty, that's it. Good. Yes, that's it...

Brody heard a sound, recognised it as a creaking spring in the van, the type of sound he'd normally never be aware of. But he was now. If a cockroach were to cross the floor right now, it would sound like a crocodile.

Answer, Anderson, fucking answer.

And he did.

Anderson: It's not that hard to kill someone, *Bet*, once you do it the first time, that is. Not that hard at all, just you remember that. Yes, just you remember that.

Betty: Oh, you going to kill me now, is that it? You pathetic moron, you didn't kill anybody. You're not capable of it. You haven't got it in you.

Yes, that's it Betty, that's it, keep it going...

Betty might not have known it, but she was giving a masterclass in reverse psychology: investigators spent time in classrooms to do what she was doing now.

Anderson: Don't I? You're wrong, *Bet*, you're very wrong.

Brody ran a hand across his forehead; it was moist with sweat.

Betty: I don't fucking think so.

Anderson: Don't you?

Betty: No. I don't.

Anderson: I cut my brother's throat, *Bet*, yes I did. So there. I pushed that car off the embankment with my other brother in it. He was unconscious the whole time, the pathetic junkie. I thought it would be harder to kill William. But it was the other way round. I had to think of so many things to make it look like Thomas had done everything. And it all worked out. See, I'm not so stupid. What do you make of that? You just remember what I'm capable of, *Bet*, just you remember. Well, now you know.

Betty: I don't believe you. You're pathetic, to come out with that one, and for what... to impress me? I should be flattered? Words are cheap. You can say anything you want; how do I know if any of it's true or not?

Anderson: What? Flatter you? Keep taking the happy pills, *Bet*. I'm not just saying it. Does this look like I'm kidding to you. Look. I said look, bitch, here.

There was a rustling sound.

Anderson: At the phone. There. See.

Silence.

Betty: What's that?

Silence.

Betty: Jesus, that's gross. He's... oh my God. How? What? Where'd you get this?

Betty: Oh my God. You...

Anderson: Yes?

Betty: You... you... killed. Both of them. *You.*

Anderson: Give the bitch a round of applause.

Betty: Christ... Oh my God... Oh...

Anderson: Close your mouth, *Bet*. Yes, I did. I told you. And

Bet? Now that you know exactly what I'm capable of... Well, now that you know exactly what I'm capable of, I'd leave well enough alone if I were you. Don't make trouble, *Bet*. You're the mother of my daughter and all that. I'd hate anything to happen to you. You've been warned. If you weren't the mother of my child, you'd already have ended up like these two here.

More than enough.

Brody got his phone. He dialled Considine. When she answered, he said simply, 'Now,' and hung up.

Almost immediately, he could hear the roar of engines outside, moving fast, in high gear, followed by the screech of tyres and the sounds of doors opening, feet running. He got up and went to the back door and pushed it open. The uniforms running towards Betty's Cuts were from Pearse Street. There were eight of them in three cars. Brody watched in disbelief as they all gathered round the front door. No one had gone round the back. He started running over. Considine was banging on the door and getting no response. She pushed against it, but it was locked. She knocked again, banging her palm, much louder this time.

Just as Brody arrived, the door opened.

'Where is he?'

'Where's who?'

Brody barked at three uniforms, 'You, you and you, round the back. Now.'

'I have people around the back already, boss.'

'You do?'

'Yes.'

She pushed her way in past Betty Nagle, and Jack followed. He went straight through the salon and into a small kitchen area at the back. Through a window he could see a gate outside at the end of a small, narrow yard, flapping in the wind. He left the room again. Next to it was a narrow walkway, a door at the end. He ran to it and pushed it open. It led out into the yard. He ran out and across to the gate. Outside it was an alleyway; he saw three uniforms further along, climbing over a second gate. One of them raised his hand towards Brody and shook his head. Well, of course Anderson wasn't there. Because the uniforms were at the wrong gate, that's why.

He looked both ways along the alley. *Shit, shit, shit.*

Brody asked himself: what would I do if I were Anderson? Maybe Anderson got sight of the uniforms in the lane; maybe he'd at least heard them. In that case, he would have taken off in the opposite direction, and that would be to Brody's left. He went that way. The alleyway he was on ran the length of the back of the buildings, curving gently and emerging onto Cullenswood Road further past the square where he and Quinn had met Betty. If Anderson had come this way, he would probably have run away from the village, by turning right. Brody took the chance that he had, and ran this way too. Here the road forked in two; on his left was Oakley Road, on his right, Charleston Road, which led to Rathmines. But Anderson likely had a car parked somewhere and might already be long gone. Brody stopped. He heard the sound of an engine from behind, approaching fast. He turned. A squad car was speeding towards him. Just as it seemed about to pass, it screeched to a halt. The driver's window came down. 'He's been spotted.' The driver was a young female; she nodded ahead along Charleston Road. Brody ran over and got in the back of the Mondeo, was flung into his seat as the car sped away. He grabbed the back of the front seats and pulled himself forward, peering ahead through the windscreen. There were few people about, and none of them was Anderson. Brody decided he couldn't have gone too far, not on foot. Passing a side road, he spotted something out of the corner of his eye. He wasn't sure what, but it was worth the chance.

'Stop. Go back. Turn left.' The squad car screeched to a halt. There was traffic behind, but because they'd been going so fast, the vehicle following had time to safely brake. The squad car reversed, Brody flung forward this time, and screeched to a halt again; as Brody was flung back, the car spun to the left and careered forward. Brody felt like he was a boat in a violent storm. Ahead he could see someone walking nonchalantly along, the street otherwise deserted. A waste of time, he thought. He was just about to tell the driver to stop and go back when the figure started to run. The driver sped up. Just as the car was almost alongside, the figure darted in through the open gateway to a house and disappeared. They stopped and got out, ran through the gateway and saw someone disappearing around the side of the house. They took off in pursuit, but at the last moment, Brody peeled away. 'Stay with him,' he shouted. 'I'll go this way,' and proceeded to run across the front of the property. He went around the side and almost knocked down the man who was standing there. He held secateurs in one hand and a small potted plant in the other.

'Who're you?' sounding remarkably composed.

'Guards,' Brody told him. 'Go inside your house and lock the doors.'

Brody ran down the side and across a patio onto a large garden. The three uniforms were already there. But there was no sign of anybody else.

'Where the hell'd he go?' a uniform asked.

There didn't seem to be any place to hide, apart from the neat perimeter bushes on either side that is, but that would be a tight squeeze. The garden itself was made up of shrubberies and flower beds. Of course, he might be in the house itself. Brody walked over to the uniforms.

'Let's continue on,' he said, louder than was necessary. 'We'll look further down the road. Come on.'

He led the way out again to the front of the house, and stopped, whispered, 'Drive down a little bit, park up and come back. I'll stay here. Got that?'

They got that.

As they moved away, Brody ran over to the ivy-covered porch. He went down the side of it, turned, and pressed himself into the corner. He took a deep breath, held it, and released it slowly, took another, released it even slower, until his breathing became a silent, gentle rhythm. He waited and listened. His only hope was that whoever occupied this house didn't come along. Or a dog.

He waited.

Whoever had run in here had to be somewhere close by still. Didn't they? It could only be Anderson. Couldn't it?

He waited.

Brody half closed his eyes as he listened, concentrating on detecting sound. There was a breeze, very slight, but it was there. He heard the rustle of leaves, and once, the murmur of a passing car, but nothing else.

Until...

He became aware of a tempo amid that gentle sound of leaves, a regular, even gentler *pat... pat... pat...*

He recognised what that sound was. It was footsteps. And they were approaching from the other side of the porch. Brody edged towards the corner. The footsteps stopped. Brody didn't see the collection of empty jam jars by his feet. His right shoe hit them, and they clattered over, some rolling away with a hollow tinkling sound. The *pat... pat... pat...* sounded again, heavier, faster, now running away.

Brody darted out from the porch. The figure was disappearing down the driveway. He ran after it and emerged onto the street at the bottom. *Shit.* Not again. The man had disappeared. Brody looked along the street. To his right he could see the squad car, and it was a long way down, the driver's door open. They were taking their time. He hadn't told them to go that far. Hadn't he told them to walk back?

A searing pain suddenly exploded in the back of his head, and his vision shook and blurred. The short plank of wood that had just been smashed across the back of his head broke in two. Anderson dropped it and started to run. It was like Brody's eyes were coated in Vaseline, the world reduced to nothing more than smudged shapes and colours. From the searing pain in the back of his head, he felt hot liquid trickling down the back of his neck, like lava from a volcano. He saw the smudged shape move out from behind him, and Brody knew this might be his only chance. He took two blind steps forward and launched himself through the air towards that shape. For a brief moment in time he had the sensation of flying, where time itself seemed to stand still, where he was suspended, free. Then his outstretched hands struck, and then his face, his chest, crumpling into Anderson's back, the forward velocity of over one hundred kilos dropping Anderson like a stone. Brody wrapped his arms around the smudged shape and hung on tight as they both crashed to the ground, Anderson taking the impact, Brody along for the ride. He was grateful that Anderson lay completely still. Brody waited, not relaxing his grip. But Anderson remained motionless. Brody relaxed a little. Mistake. Anderson bucked back violently, throwing Brody off him, jumped to his feet and was off again. Brody's arm shot out, and he caught him just before he passed out of reach, wrapping his hand around his ankle in a vice-like grip and yanking backward with all his strength to send Anderson tumbling for a second time. Anderson kicked back with his free foot. Brody tried to angle his head away, but the heel caught him on the corner of his forehead. And the foot came back a second time, catching him above the eye. He felt that hot liquid again, but this time it was coming from his forehead and down his face, into his eye. Yet Brody held on. Even as the smudged shape began to fade, he held on. Even as the world went black, he held on.

He held on with a grim determination. He would not let go. He must not let go.

51

On Monday morning, Considine and Sheahan sat in an interview room at Pearse Street Garda station; across from them was Robert Anderson, sitting straight backed and defiant. In a small, adjoining room, the brass watched the video link on a wall-mounted fifty-six-inch TV screen. They included Assistant Commissioner Kelly, a Pearse Street superintendent and two inspectors, a chief superintendent from HQ, a Pearse Street sergeant and a couple of uniforms. No one liked to have one of their own end up in hospital. This was personal. The Pearse Street superintendent had suggested to the chief super from HQ that he bring in a specialist interviewer from Dublin Castle. The chief super had told him to fuck off.

'Mr Anderson, we have your phone,' Considine said.

'How do I know it's my phone?' He looked at his nails, gave a defiant smirk. 'That could be anyone's phone. Where's my solicitor?' Then folded his arms.

'You didn't ask for a solicitor.' It was Sheahan.

'I'm asking for one now.'

'Fine. We'll terminate this interview, at thirteen twenty-three hours, pending the arrival of Mr Aidan Kennedy.'

'How do you know he's my solicitor?'

'Well, he is, isn't he?'

Anderson was impassive, nodded slowly once.

'We already spoke with him. We know all about Margaret's will, your mother.'

'You do?'

'Of course.'

Anderson didn't look so defiant all of a sudden.

Aidan Kennedy wasn't used to being called out to Garda stations in the middle of the day, or any other time for that matter. The old solicitor hadn't been involved in a criminal case in years. But still, fifteen minutes with his client was enough to have a very different Robert Anderson brought up from the cells for a second interview. The fire had gone out, nothing left but the ashes, the writing on the wall painted in bright yellow phosphorescent paint beneath flashing neon lights.

Considine let him stew in his own juices for a little while. For a time no one spoke. Then she asked a simple question.

'Did you kill your brothers, William and Thomas Anderson?'

He did not answer.

'Did you?' she asked again.

And he gave a simple answer, very simple, 'Yes.'

'Because you wanted to be the sole benefactor of your mother's will, is that the reason?'

Another simple answer, very simple, 'Yes.'

'These were your brothers, Mr Anderson.'

'So?'

'OK. Would you tell me where you killed William, the location?'

'No. What difference does it make?'

'We'd like to know.'

Anderson's face softened, not from any sense of regret or guilt, but because he had something that they wanted.

'I'm...' he began, 'not going to tell you.'

The audience, both in the interview room and the one next door, took in this news.

'And Thomas? You drugged him, didn't you?'

Anderson shifted in his seat, those slouched shoulders of his with the head slightly bowed, like he was permanently gazing into a display cabinet. But he looked unusually proud of himself.

'I did a lot of things, but you'll never know.'

'And you ripped his laryngeal prominence out. What was that like?'

'What's it called again, lary... can you repeat, please?'

Considine discreetly clenched her fist, out of sight of the video camera, and straightened the middle finger towards Anderson. He saw it and smiled.

'You put Detective Sergeant Brody in the hospital, you know that?'

'Did I? Little ol' me? Isn't he supposed to be a champion boxer? I did that? Wow.'

'Yes, with a piece of wood that you suckered him with from behind. Very brave.'

'You know what they say? A win's a win... And Chief Superintendent Tom Maguire, or the Old Man as you call him. Isn't he dead too? They're dropping like flies in your unit, aren't they?' He smirked.

'Fuck you,' Considine said.

'Officer' – old Cosgrove wagged a long bony finger at her, and Considine bit her lip – 'your use of profanity. Take this as a warning.'

Anderson leaned into Kennedy and whispered something into his ear. The old solicitor nodded.

'My client has nothing further to add. There is nothing more he will say. This interview is over, ladies and gentlemen.'

52

They called him the Jewellery Killer. The media loved the story – for a time, that is. Because it had everything: sex, money, greed, a client list of the rich and famous, even if the client list was one of mere speculation, because no one would admit to being a patron of Robert Anderson's. Yet even speculation sold newspapers, and lots of them too, and bumped up TV ratings. Before it all calmed again, as it always does, but not before the story had taken on a new twist, which was that Robert Anderson was reported to be loving his life on the inside. He'd made friends behind the big old walls of the 'joy, was giving jewellery making classes, and had been taken under the wing of someone called JJ Harris, a small-time criminal who'd introduced him to the other lags and was helping him settle in. It was actually reported that Anderson had told someone he was the happiest he'd been in a long time. And then, after a month or so, the interest faded and would stay that way, as was usual with these things, until the trial came around, when it would explode back into the public's consciousness once more. There, it would live briefly for as long as the trial lasted, until it finally faded away again, and this time forever consigned to be just another shocking crime in the annals of shocking crimes. But humans are programmed like that, to absorb and forget. The trial was not due for months. And Anderson would be pleading guilty, he had no other choice, and the minimum sentence he could expect was a life sentence. The inheritance he'd gone to so much bloody efforts to secure had gone to probate, and with no other natural heirs, it was likely everything would fall to young Rihanna. It seemed that Anderson's story of a pregnant girlfriend was a lie. Who knew why he'd said it? Because he knew it would hurt like few others? Possibly. In any case, Majella showed no signs of pregnancy. And she certainly didn't have any baby. Robert should have kept his mouth shut about that. Had he done so, his fate might have been very different. Betty was delighted with this news. She and her only child had a close relationship after all, and Betty was already planning on moving her salon to bigger premises. She and Rick were no longer together. Their relationship had finished just before it became apparent that Rihanna was to inherit her grandmother's fortune. Bad timing. He'd been ringing every day since, professing his endless love for her, pleading with her to take him back. Young Rick had no shame. But Betty had moved on. Her new beau, Seamus was his name, was a couple of years older than she was. Which suited Betty just fine. She no longer had to pretend, no longer had to prove anything. To tell the truth, dating Rick had been hard work, and she hoped now her lips would settle down to a normal size again after all those Botox injections. She knew some didn't, so she'd just have to keep her fingers crossed and wait.

But in everything, there was hardly any mention of the two victims, William and Thomas. It was like they'd never existed, were mere flotsam simply cast adrift and forgotten about. But Tamara lived on. She lived on as she would always live on, as an illusion, a memory in the minds of all those people whose lives she had touched, and for some, of course, who had no idea that she wasn't real, she wasn't Tamara.

Now, ironically, it was the one who did *not* exist who actually *did* exist, and the one who really *did* exist who *didn't*. If you follow.

Tamara would have loved that.

53

For a time, Brody looked worse than he actually felt. But thankfully, his injuries were merely superficial. After one night in the hospital, for nothing more than observation, he was released. His experience had emphasised that it didn't matter who you were, Mike Tyson or Jack Brody, if you get clobbered hard enough from behind like he was with a lump of wood, you were going down. He took the experience as a timely reminder of the intrinsic frailty of the human form. Especially now that the Old Man had gone.

The Old Man had gone. He thought about that. But Brody didn't dwell on it. It wouldn't bring the Old Man back.

And now, looking across the table at Ashling Nolan, he also thought of the intrinsic beauty of the human form too.

Ashling lifted her wine glass and took a sip of white wine. She held the glass to her lips and coyly stared at Brody over the rim with those doe eyes of hers. She maintained this pose for a time before lowering the glass again.

'Thank you,' she said.

'For what?'

'For bringing me here. For asking me out. I just want to... thank you, that's all. I didn't think I was ever going to hear from you again. I'm glad I did.'

'I'm glad too.'

'I don't play games, Jack, just so you know. I like you.'

She waited for him to say something, and he was just about to when the man stopped at their table. A man in a light grey pinstripe suit, a dazzling white shirt, canary yellow tie and a canary yellow pocket hanky. His grey hair was swept back, and his skin was tanned, very tanned. Brody couldn't decide if it was a natural tan or a sunbed job.

'Sorry to intrude. I hope you don't mind.' He spoke in the standard south-side timbre of the urban professional.

Brody didn't mind him intruding. The Raftery Room restaurant was that kind of place, where urban professionals routinely did business. It was accepted. But it also had the best steaks in town, which was why Brody had brought Ashling here. She was wearing a revealing crop top and tight jeans. The man glanced briefly at her, his eyes lingering a little longer than they needed to, before he smiled and averted his gaze to Brody.

'I won't keep you, Sergeant Brody. My name's Declan Synott, Borderline Productions; have you ever heard of us?'

'Can't say I have,' Brody said.

'Well, we're quite well known. Check us out. We've been commissioned to make an hour-long documentary on your recent case. Tamara was her name, yes?'

Brody nodded.

'Thing is, we know nothing about who she really was other than what's in the media. Would you talk to us about it sometime? I was speaking with Paul Quinn, he worked the case with you. He's a friend of a friend sort of thing.'

'How is Paul doing, by the way?'

'Sitting the inspector's exam next month. A very sharp guy, yes?'

Brody nodded. 'Oh yes, a very sharp guy. I'm sorry, Mr Synott, I'm actually' – he nodded towards Ashling – 'with someone, as you can see. You can ring the Press Office. They'll tell you anything you need to know.'

He smiled again. 'Oh, you don't understand. We'd like to hire you in an advisory role. Perhaps we could make an arrangement to meet and talk about it?'

The waiter arrived at that moment, placed their plates of food onto the table, topped up their glasses with wine and withdrew again.

'I'm not interested, My Synott, thank you. Now, if you don't mind...'

'You're not interested.' His voice rose a couple of octaves in surprise. 'Why? Really? I don't think you understand. This is an international production; we're talking Netflix and multiple media platforms here. It could be very lucrative for you.'

Jack picked up his knife. The rump steak was fat and juicy.

'And for you too, of course, Mr... Synott, is it?'

'Yes, that's right.'

'Still not interested.'

'We'll talk about it. OK. Here's my card. Don't say anything just yet. Just keep this. We'll talk about it.' Declan Synott placed a gold-embossed business card onto the table. 'We'll talk again. Yes we will. We won't talk now. We'll talk again. Goodbye, Sergeant Brody. If I don't hear from you, I'll ring.'

'Really,' Ashling said when he'd gone, 'you wouldn't be interested?'

He shook his head as he cut into his steak.

'All I'm interested in right now is you.'

'What about that lump of flesh on your plate? You seem awfully interested in that.'

'Not you as well?'

'What's that supposed to mean? "Not you as well"?'

'I have a colleague, recently turned vegetarian, let's just say her attitudes are hardening.'

Ashling spiked a mushroom and cheese vol-au-vent with her fork.

'You vegetarian?' he asked.

She smiled. 'Of course.'

Brody sliced off a chunk of steak.

'I just thought,' he said, raising his eyebrows mischievously, and the fork to his mouth, 'that I might need all my energy... for later, I mean. You can't beat a good steak.'

He felt something soft against his leg, and it stayed there. It was Ashling's foot, warm and sensuous.

They smiled at each other, acknowledging this private moment beneath the table where no one could see. Brody felt like a giddy, horny teenager.

Ashling pointed to that steak with her knife.

'Eat it up, cowboy.'

ABOUT THE AUTHOR

I hail from Mayo in the west of Ireland, although I spent much of my life away, in the US, UK, Europe, Jersey in the Channel Islands and various parts of Ireland.

In my younger years I was incredibly restless. I left home and school at 16 and spread my wings. I've had over forty jobs, everything from barman, labourer, staff newspaper reporter, soldier in the Irish army, station foreman with London Underground, mason, and many more besides. I returned to education as a mature student in the early noughties and hold a BA in history and sociology from the National University of Ireland at Maynooth, and an M.Phil from Trinity College Dublin.

Since 2005 I've been a civilian employee of the Irish police, An Garda Síochána. However, I've been on extended sick leave since 2015 following a mystery illness which struck while travelling in Spain. It almost killed me. The doctors never got to the bottom of it and they call me the Mystery Man. But every cloud has a silver lining. It has given me the time to write. Although I've been writing all my life, most of my output languishes in the bottom of drawers.

Under my real name, Michael Scanlon, I was initially published for the first time in 2019 by Bookouture with the first of three crime novels. Working with Inkubator is another great opportunity for me. This time I'm using a pseudonym, as the style of J.M. O'Rourke books are so different, and also, I really like the name!

I hope readers like them.

ALSO BY J.M. O'ROURKE

The Detective Jack Brody Series

The Devil's House

Time of Death

Printed in Great Britain
by Amazon